About the Author

James is a first-time author who lives in Market Harborough, Leicestershire. His love of travelling and books resulted in inventing his own stories. This book was created during the COVID-19 pandemic, a time when loved ones and families struggled together to get by, but as long as they had each other, that was all that mattered – doing whatever it took to keep everyone safe. He hopes this book reflects that dedication to family and shows how important they are to us all, and he hopes it will give pleasure to anyone who reads it.

The Storm

James Mee

The Storm

Olympia Publishers
London

www.olympiapublishers.com
OLYMPIA PAPERBACK EDITION

Copyright © James Mee 2024

The right of James Mee to be identified as the author of this work has been asserted in accordance with sections 77 and 78 of the Copyright, Designs and Patents Act 1988.

All Rights Reserved

No reproduction, copy or transmission of this publication may be made without written permission. No paragraph of this publication may be reproduced, copied or transmitted save with the written permission of the publisher, or in accordance with the provisions of the Copyright Act 1956 (as amended).

Any person who commits any unauthorised act in relation to this publication may be liable for criminal prosecution and civil claims for damage.

A CIP catalogue record for this title is available from the British Library.

ISBN: 978-1-80439-823-4

This is a work of fiction. Names, characters, places and incidents originate from the writer's imagination. Any resemblance to actual persons, living or dead, is purely coincidental.

First Published in 2024

Olympia Publishers
Tallis House
2 Tallis Street
London
EC4Y 0AB

Printed in Great Britain

Dedication

To Mum and Dad. Thanks for everything you have done and continue do for me. For always believing in me, for being there when I need you, always supporting me and making me who I am today.

Acknowledgements

Thanks to my mum for reading every chapter and being my unofficial editor.

Prologue

The storm chased us through the fields, gaining ground every second, getting closer and outrunning. It was proving difficult. Especially with a severely injured leg, I was already running like a lame horse. The tornado touched down and started to rip through the ground, everything in its path evaporating as it ate it all up like a hungry dog. The pressure was intense as it chased us. With every step, we got closer to safety. Mum and Dad further ahead of me, but still not safe enough for my liking. The door to the shelter stood open, waiting for us to enter. I felt the wind threaten to lift me off the ground and into the air with the rest of the debris.

Just as I got a glimmer of hope, I fell to the ground. My leg gave way as my head took the hit. From what I couldn't say, the pain would suggest something heavy and sharp. Unable to move or even think straight. I watched as the house disappeared brick by brick, layer by layer, deconstructing in the same way it had been built, only in reverse.

Chapter One
So It Begins – *Rob*

The day started like any other. Being a man of routine, I awoke minutes before my alarm sounded. Standing up, I headed for the kitchen, grabbing a coffee pod on my way past. I placed it in the machine. Fetched a mug and pressed start instantly the machine gurgled to life. Spewing a stream of hot coffee into the mug. Coffee in hand, I headed to make some toast. Still only half awake, I applied a thin layer of butter and made my way to the breakfast bar.

A fruit bowl that I kept full was sitting beside me, ready and waiting. Besides that, there was Alexa, my home assistant. "Alexa, open the blinds," I called.

Sunlight started to fill the room as the blinds rose, exposing the large sliding glass doors that stretched the length of the house. The doors led to the back garden, which was great for parties and summer BBQs. After years of renting, I finally got on the property ladder and bought this house eight months ago. It consisted of three bedrooms, a large open-plan kitchen, two bathrooms and a large living area. It even had a garage for my beloved Tesla.

"Alexa, flash briefing."

I liked to keep tabs on the news and found breakfast the ideal time to catch the day's headlines. The entrance music for the *BBC* newsroom started up.

Welcome to the six a.m. BBC News broadcast, it said. *In*

news today, a man has been charged with armed robbery and sentenced to fifteen years imprisonment. Mark McCall held staff at gunpoint in a casino using an imitation firearm. It is reported that he used a 3D printer to make the gun, even though it wasn't capable of firing live ammunition. The judge said that such an act was still severely frowned upon and hoped that the sentence would work as a deterrent to anyone else thinking of trying such a scheme. Stating that anyone caught threatening people with any type of weapon would face the same charges, imitation or not.

In over news.

A scientist from New Zealand has reported further damage to the ozone layer today, saying more needs to be done to slow the amount of gas being emitted into the earth's atmosphere. It comes after a new weather report show of a storm heading across the country today, hitting in the early hours in the early hours of the evening.

Finally, the Prince and Princess of Wales are expected to be opening a new green energy power plant in London today. They hope their presence will show how seriously the government is taking the threat that global warming and the effects it is causing to life as we know it.

That's all major news stories; now for the weather in your area—

The weather in Leicester is expected to stay dry with some clouds for the majority of the day, feeling cooler than yesterday with a high of 27°C and a low of 17°C. Heavy winds are expected throughout the day, making it feel more like ten. A red weather alert is in place in the early hours of tonight, with a storm expected to hit, causing major disruption.
That's all from your flash briefing. Please check back later.

"Another storm," I said, finishing my toast and grabbing an apple from the basket. The debate on global warming and the destruction of the planet was still considered a myth by half the population. Fake news was intended to distract the public and bring down the oil companies. Despite clear sighs that it wasn't. A few years ago, in January, you would have expected high temperatures of 9-10°C. Now only two weeks since the New Year the year now being 2032. We were recording a high of 27°C and that was cooler than any temperature this last week. It was reported that global warming would cause the destruction of seventy per cent of the natural world in just thirty years. With a growing population, it was already getting harder to find space. Ice caps had melted, and entire species had been wiped out. And all because of humanity and it's selfishness.

My dad had spent his whole life working as an ecologist, preaching about the effects of global warming and finding ways in which to reverse the damage and stop us from being the next species to be made extinct. The Mars colony was still expected to take at least another thirty to forty years, if not longer, with no guarantee of success. Even then, it remained to be seen if the project would be sustainable. He finally retired three years ago and moved to Wales, where Mum and Dad would live out their retirement. In an old farmhouse that consisted of five bedrooms and three bathrooms, along with a large kitchen dinner, dining room and two sitting rooms. Mum an ex-school assistant working with disabled kids as well as those suffering from learning difficulties. Had insisted it had five rooms to accommodate the whole family on visits. In all, there were three kids and two grandkids. Adam, the youngest, had moved with them. There was very little to keep him in Leicester, and for the best, he had a fresh start away from the crowd he used to hang around with, who seemed to do nothing but get him into trouble. It had worked; he was now working as a support worker in a care home for the elderly. A job that none of us would have thought he was capable of but had taken to like a duck to water.

That left me and my sister, Sue, in Leicester. Sue was the middle child, but it didn't show she had been the first to move out of the family home and marry her childhood sweetheart, Jay. Jay worked in construction and was responsible for getting me a hefty discount on the house, him being CEO of the construction company that built it. He had done well for himself, proving cable of bringing not only enough for Sue to stop work and become a housewife but to build the biggest and nicest house in the area. It had been her choice to stop work, saying it would be better for the boys, her being home more. She had previously been a manager at the local store, but the hours were long and she didn't need the money. She called it a day a little over four years ago. Not one to sit around, she helped Jay in the office when needed and volunteered at the local charity shop two times a week.

Finishing my coffee and looking at the time twenty past eight, I didn't start work till ten a.m. and it took half an hour to get there. I considered putting in an hour at the gym before deciding it was too much of a rush. I put the dirty pots in the dishwasher, and headed for the bedroom. I entered the on-suite bathroom and jumped in the shower, telling Alexa to put the radio on as I did. The news bulletin was on, and the prime minister, speaking from 10 Downing Street, had just announced that he was calling for a general election to take place in March. Also announced that he would be stepping out of the race as leader of the Labour Party; instead, they will be deciding on a new candidate to take his place. He has been under pressure to resign recently after failing to act quickly enough during the economic crisis last year, with half his party voting against him, and many of his cabinet resigning in protest.

That was followed by the traffic update. Announcing long queues and delays throughout Leicester.

Stepping out of the shower and drying off, I got dressed and made the bed. Having heard the traffic update, I decided to make an early start not wanting to be late. Grabbing my gym bag that I always kept packed and ready by the door. it would Save coming back for it after work. I headed for the door.

Chapter Two
The End Is Nigh – *Rob*

I headed out the door and used the fingerprint scanner on the door to lock it. Heading for the garage and entering the code. Inside was the closest thing I had to a child my beloved Tesla. I upgraded it just last year; it was a thing of beauty. It had upgraded the wheels and I had paid extra for a limited edition metallic black finish. When it hit the light at a certain angle, it reflected star-type shapes all over the bodywork. Getting in, I put the gym bag on the passenger seat and started the engine. The battery level was at fifty per cent enough for roughly 200 miles. They had taken a massive leap forward with electric cars, and the production of gas-powered cars where now banned in the UK. Anyone who owned one also incurred higher taxes and increased insurance premiums. All in an attempt to discourage people from owning them while also offering a high discount and zero tax on all high-end electric vehicles. Even insurance companies were offering as much as a twenty-five per cent discount for new and existing customers with electric vehicles under the age of two years old. I was one of the first to jump ship and buy electricity; this would be my third.

    I put it into gear and felt the car pull forward, making no sound. You wouldn't even know the engine was running unlike most gas cars. Even at full power, this car only made twenty per cent of the noise expelled from a gas engine; even then, all it created was a whirling noise.

I took a left at the end of the street and followed it to the first junction. I lived just on the outskirts of Leicester, so getting out wasn't as much of a problem, but even on the outskirts, you could be delayed by some considerable traffic. I took a shortcut through the new housing estate. Jay was running the site with the company logo advertising JRC (Jay Roberts Construction) at the entrance.

Having completed the first phase, they had gotten planning permission for the adjacent field and were now expanding it. Turning before I reached the workers; I took the first right and was soon signalling to join the main road. The shortcut had taken half the road away, bringing me nearer the exit. An Audi TTE flashed and let me out. Pulling out, I thanked him and drove like a snail along with the rest of the traffic up to the roundabout. Most of the traffic was heading towards town, with the rest being split between four other junctions: one to the motorway, which was nearly as busy as the one for the town, the next went into a housing estate, the third through an industrial estate; and then into countryside. The final heading was back the way I had come and into the town from the other end.

It wasn't long till I was on the island and taking the third exit; trucks and lorries were the only other vehicles taking the exit with me. I headed straight through, past all the warehouses and manufacturing plants, and out into a vast openness of fields. There was little traffic on the country roads, and it wasn't long before I was taking a small country lane that would bring me out to where the pub stood. Pulling into the car park, I parked in the same spot as usual, reserved for the head chef, it had been printed on the ground in large white letters. But that didn't always stop people from using it. Switching off the engine, I stepped out to see cows in the field beyond. I walked through the double gate and up to the kitchen door. It had a digital lock requiring a code, everyone had their own code, so you could track who opened the door and when. The pub itself was old and in need of repairs. Some of which were underway. Although I was still early, I used the retinal scanner and clocked in before heading for the lockers where my chef whites were kept.

As soon as I was dressed, I approached the handwash basin before entering the main hub of the kitchen. It was a large, rectangular kitchen with every appliance you could need. The owners were generous with equipment, never skimping out on a purchase that was needed. Looking in the diary, there was a note asking about a buffet this weekend for a fiftieth birthday party. It was for a regular who spent more time here than any of the staff. Underneath was the prep list. With it being January and everyone having overindulged over Christmas, we had very little to do. All the list compiled was soup of the day, veg prep, and a note informing me we required a special. Grabbing some leeks and potatoes I started to the soup. Then I turned my attention to setting up the salad section and turning everything on to ready for service. Leaving the soup to boil, I went a made a cup of tea. There were two chefs a shift; the second was due to arrive at twelve when we opened. I knew he made a good cheese souffle and decided to delegate the special to him. As twelve approached, Sam appeared, I was blending the soup before pouring it into the soup kettle.

"Afternoon," he said, clocking in at the same time. "Want a drink?" he asked, switching the kettle back on.

"I'm good, thanks. So, what's on the job list today?"

"Not much; I'm afraid you're going to be on cleaning duty most of the day."

"My favourite."

Having got changed, he finished making his drink and walked towards me, mug in hand. Looking at the book.

"You weren't kidding?"

"Do you want me just to go home? It looks like you don't need me?"

"Nice try, but I have plenty of paperwork to do, orders to place, and a buffet to organise, so I will be in there if you need me," I said, pointing to a small office just to the side of the kitchen. "But don't worry, I need you to finish the prep for carvery, and I want your cheese souffle on as a special so plenty to keep you busy."

"Don't forget we finish at six today," I said as I headed to the office.

The other two chefs would be taking over from us. As we had covered them a few weeks ago, and now it was time to return the favour.

"I've not," he said thinking of hitting the gym after if you fancy it.

"Already got my bag," I replied before walking into the office.

The next few hours flew by, I checked on Sam a couple of times, making sure he wasn't trying to be the hero of the kitchen and trying to manage all by himself; he was never any good at asking for help. I needn't have worried, we had two tables of four all lunch with bar snacks it made a total of ten orders; most of them being elderly had soup. It was five by the time I switched the computer off all orders were complete and the paperwork was all up to date. Sam came through with a mug in each hand.

"Here, thought you could use a drink."

"Thanks, take a seat." I pointed to the spare chair at the side of me.

"Two seconds," he said, walking back out and leaving his mug behind.

"Two minutes late." He appeared again, this time holding two perfectly risen souffles.

"Well, we have to taste them, don't we?" A smile spread across his face.

"You're the master of souffles," I declared as I finished. "They better all be like that or you're in trouble. We were still sitting in the office when Harry and Colin arrived, ready to relieve us."

"Working hard, I see," Harry said.

"More than you ever do," Sam shouted back.

Standing up, we walked over and got ready to hand over the kitchen. With very little to report, we filled the time with idle chat before calling it a day and waving goodbye as we headed out the door. It wasn't until we left that we realised how much the wind had picked up.

"How did you get here?"

"My sister gave me a lift; I knew you were on so I could get a ride back."

"Well, jump in." I moved my bag from the seat and put it on the back seat; Sam did the same with his. We headed out of the car park and saw a few customers arrive. "Looks like we beat the rush," I joked. Sam was playing a game on the central control. Although he didn't drive, he loved my Tesla about as much as I did, always finding any excuse to go in it. The traffic report came on, informing us of more delays on the ring road. I changed my route and headed away from the house and towards the motorway, turning before I took the dual carriage past the town and coming in the opposite end, entering the city centre from the opposite direction.

Everyone was now trying to get out of town and not in, which meant we were soon pulling into the gym car park. And heading for the doors. The receptionist recognised us as we walked in and automatically buzzed us through the electric double doors. Sam stopped to give her a wave, and as usual, her cheeks blushed bright red as he did.

"Still not made your move yet," I said as we stopped in front of the lockers and put our bags down.

"No, I'm not sure it's the right time."

"Well, don't leave it too late. Just ask her out what's the worst that could happen."

"She could say, no."

"She won't, and if she did, at least you would know where you stood."

"Who made you the king of relationships? I can't help but notice you're still single."

"That's my choice," I said, stuffing my bag into the locker and putting the key in my shorts. Sam having done the same. We walked into the gym and headed for the treadmills, a normal workout?" which consisted of mainly cardio.

"Sure," Sam said, filling his water bottle at the tap.

After half an hour on the treadmill, fifteen minutes on the rower, and ten minutes with some weights, we finished off on the cross trainer.

"So, what are you going to do about the receptionist? Are you going to ask her out or not?"

"I don't know; I don't even know her name."

"It's Hailey; it's on her name badge; I don't suppose you ever looked at that."

"Too busy looking at her."

We finished and headed to the lockers. I grabbed my bag

from the locker and headed to the shower cubicles meet you back here. I was first back at the locker lockers, Sam not far behind me.

"Do you want dropping off at home?"

"No, it's all right; I will get the tube."

The council had installed an underground tube network like in London in the hope of cutting down the number of cars on the roads, but it hadn't worked. As we entered reception, I saw Hailey sitting at the desk working on the computer.

"Go on then," I said.

"No, I can't."

"Without hesitation, I pulled him by the arm and walked him towards the desk."

"Excuse me, my mate here wanted to know what personal training course you did."

Sam looked at me with a death stare. She blushed again, most likely guessing what I was up to. She looked straight at Sam before fishing out a booklet detailing all the available sessions. Look at the time; I better be going see you tomorrow, heading straight out the door and not looking back, leaving Hailey to go through the booklet on training sessions with Sam.

I was halfway home when the phone rang, as I expected, it was Sam.

"I'm going to kill you."

"Don't know what you mean," I said, holding back a laugh. "I just thought, you might want to up the ante and improve your fitness."

"Yes, well, we're going out Friday night." He hung up before I could say anything.

Back home, I backed the car into the garage and grabbed my bag out the back. I went to the side and attached the charging

23

cable. Battling the wind as I made my way to the front door and slammed it shut behind me. There were a few letters and leaflets on the welcome mat in front of the door. I flicked through them as I walked into the kitchen, one about double glazing, a catalogue on home improvement and an application form for a credit card. Opening the bin, I dropped them in, feeling hungry after the work I decided to do dinner.

Half an hour later, I was in the living room a bowl of steaming pasta on the coffee table while I turned on the TV. My love of comedy box sets, especially old ones, was notorious, after flicking though my to watch list I settled on last of the summer Wine, an old comedy that would always be one of my favourites.

Chapter Three
In the Eye of the Storm – *Rob*

I was woken up by the ever-growing noise of the storm; it was causing havoc outside. Just the thought of road closures it would cause by morning, not to mention the time and stress I would have to set my alarm earlier than usual, looking at the clock approaching ten p.m., I must have fallen asleep watching TV. Too many long days were taking their toll, not to worry, one more shift, and I was off for two weeks. I had the garden to do and the housework to catch up on. Then I would be on the road to Wales for a week to see my parents. It had only been a few weeks since we had seen each other, but six months since I had been over to see them.

Lightning cracked through the sky, and the thunder was so loud it vibrated the ground so hard the house shook. The lightning lit the sky like a fireworks display, making it look like the whole world was about to have an electrical shortage. Car and house alarms could be heard in the distance. My phone started ringing, and Alexa answered it was connected via Bluetooth to the built-in home system that Alexa also controlled.

"Rob, its Mum, I could hear the warning siren over the phone. Were on the way to the shelter."

Storm shelters were something else that had made an appearance in homes around the UK, including mine and all new builds, they hadn't been used since the war but were now recommissioned as the threat of deadly storms became more likely. I just wanted to check you were all okay."

"Yes, we are fine no sirens yet."

"Ann, come on! Let's go."

"You get in the shelter; I will ring you later."

"Okay, take care will you ring your sister for me?"

"Yes," I said as the line cut off.

Looking up the news report on TV, a Breaking News update tells people to stay indoors and not go out, asks all shops and restaurants still open to close, and everyone to be prepared to seek safety in their shelters.

The news this morning was correct with their forecast for once, this storm was nothing like anything we had had recently. It sounded so fierce and angry. Mother Nature is reeking her revenge, no doubt. It had been a year since they had closed shops and restaurants due to a storm, and two since anywhere in the UK had even heard the sirens apart from the monthly practice drill.

I went into the bedroom and got some clothes just in case the siren should go off. I kept a small emergency supply in the shelter as well as food as advised, all tinned and dried foods along with bottled water. All as a precaution should you ever get trapped in there and the water supply is affected.

The thunder was getting louder and nearer all the time; it was definitely heading this way, the News was now saying that tornadoes could appear across the UK and Wales. Also, a threat that they could cause an earthquake effect if the pressure kept building.

Thirty minutes later, it came. The siren! Warning everyone to get to safety and away from the storm. Grabbing the pre packed bag I went down to the basement and to the shelter door. It was like a vault door, the type you would find in a bank, but with two-way handles so you could open and lock it from inside and out.

The government took to having them built into the foundation of the houses now, as opposed to outside like many had. It was deemed to be safer with it being deeper underground and less exposed.

The shelter itself was built like a doomsday bunker, said to withhold a three hundred thousand miles per hour wind. The walls were nine feet thick, with solar options to keep it powered if needed. With it being airtight, it had its own air supply that activated upon entry and had to be turned off manually at the wall. It also boasted its own water supply, using two tanks to recycle water. It wasn't the biggest shelter; it was made for a small family and furnished for three adults. It featured three rooms.

The vault door opened into a small hallway with a reinforced door, should it be needed. That door led into a living/sleeping area with two sofas that turned into beds. A TV and bookcase holding several books and a stack of movie sticks (like USB sticks that contained films) and DVDs sat near the door; it also contained some board games. The room also hosted a DVD player that I had installed in case I was ever stuck here (not that I expected to need it this time). It was home also to a coffee table and computer station, this whole unit had voice activation using LED screens to show a view of the outside to make it feel like being in your own living room upstairs. This was useful, as you could check on your surroundings before leaving.

There were two more doors in this room, one straight ahead and one on either side. The one straight ahead featured a simple storage cupboard. The one to the right led to a small but well-equipped kitchen with a small fridge, four cupboards, an oven, a microwave, a kettle, a toaster, and a coffee machine. It also had a small freezer for freeze-dried supplies. The one on the left led to the bathroom, small and simple, with a toilet, sink and shower squeezed in comfortably.

I went to the door and placed my finger on the scanner. The door was equipped with three locking security methods, all controlled from a front panel, it could be opened by fingerprint, iris recognition, or a six-digit code that only I knew but was registered with the S.H.E.L.T (SHELTER, HEALTH, EMERGENCY, LEGALITY, TREATY). In case of emergency, authorities can contact S.H.E.L.T. and gain the access code to the unit using four-digit shelter number (this was like a house number only for the shelters).

With a split second, the door began to open, and you could hear the mechanism inside the door turn as it started to unlock. It sounded like a cell door, metal against metal, as the complex system of gears and electronics worked together to allow me entry. A few seconds later, the door was open and welcoming me in. I entered the unit, bringing with me the few items I had brought with me. A sudden silence fell over the place as I sealed out all sounds of the storm and sirens coming from the outside. All I could hear was the slight hiss of the air supply and the hum of the generator, neither of which would bother me in the slightest.

It occurred to me that this was the first time I had cause to use this shelter for actual refuge; the only other time it had been used was as a spare room for Christmas when all the family were over. I checked the air levels, making sure they were full and stable. The red light above the door told me the door was locked and the airlock was in place. With no faults coming up on the control panel. It was alerting me that the siren was still active and not to leave (not that I would any time soon); it would also notify me when that changed.

Picking up the bag I headed to the kitchen unit, I put the food on the counter, not bothering to put it anyway; it would all blow over soon anyway, I had brought it down purely as a precaution. Upon re-entering the living space, I picked up the remote and turned on the TV, which was mounted on the wall. It was a 50-inch ultra-10k HD, with a virtual reality projector built in. The news flash came straight on, feeding information on the storm and telling me where and what damage it was causing as it raged on.

I walked over to the computer to look up the weather report for the next few days, it said the storm would last till at least seven a.m. tomorrow. It was going to be windy and dry, with a high of 22 Celsius.

I thought to myself if I was going to have to spend the night down here then I might as well make myself comfortable. Heading back to the control panel I upped the heating, (there were several extractor fans placed around the shelter this was to prevent it from becoming a hotbox) Then headed to the kitchen and got the Gin, good job I brought this down with me, I was going to need it. I told Alexa to set an alarm for six a.m. she would inform me if anything changed outside. In the meantime, I Settled in on the sofa grabbed a tablet off the side and looked for something to stream on the TV.

Chapter Four
Sheltered Existence – *Rob*

My alarm roused me at six as requested. With everything going on outside, I wasn't expecting to have slept much, but being in the shelter was oddly peaceful. The quiet made it easy to forget about the world outside the shelter. This alone made for a good night of uninterrupted sleep. I could see from the wall that the shelter was still locked. I picked up the tablet on the side and opened the shelter app. I was instantly informed that the emergency code hadn't been revoked yet and that we were still locked down. I also checked the shelter's air supply had not gone down, and everything was normal.

Begrudgingly, I got out of bed and made for the remote, turning on the TV, and the news came on. *(The storm is expected to last till late evening, and the weather for the day is forecasted heavier winds, more thunder and lightning with heavy damage expected.)* The shelter warning showed no expected time to be removed.

It looked like work would be off today—an early start to my holiday. There was no chance of getting there, and even if I could just have to shelter with them, not to worry about it, being a government regulation, I would still get paid. I made my way to the kitchen and boiled the kettle. I got some bread off the counter where I left it yesterday and put it in the toaster. As I was waiting for the toaster, a breaking news report came through: "Tornado hits South Wales." Lucky Mum, Dad and Adam were in the

North. Just hope that it didn't travel that far over. Their house was old and had a specially built outdoor shelter; it was well within government regulation but not the safest or most secure you could get, either way, it would do its job. Maybe after this we could look into something more robust.

After my usual breakfast, minus the fruit, I had neglected to bring with me. I decided a shower would wake me up and give me something to do as well. I kept the news running so I could hear any developments whilst I showered. It wasn't till I stepped into the shower that I realised how small of a cubicle it was—it barely big enough to move in it was never made to be used apart from in emergencies, but it did its job just as well as any other shower, so I couldn't complain too much.

After a shower and change of clothes, I folded the bed and placed the bedding back in the cupboard. I shouldn't be needing it again, the alert couldn't stay on for much longer; it was already eight a.m. It should have originally been lifted an hour ago. Picking up the remote, I changed the source on the TV to DVD setting the news to break in if any big developments came through.

Looking through the bookcase, I found the complete Ronnie Barker collection. "Selecting Open All Hours" his hit comedy show, featuring him as Arkwright, the money-grabbing miser, with his corner shop tricking everyone into buying stuff they didn't need.

Just what I needed—some light-hearted comedy—something I could just sit back and watch while I waited for it all to blow over. I was halfway through the first episode when I received a message from Mum asking me to ring them. Mobile reception was weak in the shelters, but they had their own phones using satellites, which used the same connection to power the

Wi-Fi. I rang Mum straight away, worried about what had happened, thinking the worst and trying to predict what she wanted. At first, the phone wouldn't ring, telling me the line couldn't be reached at the moment and to try again later. By the third try, I was really panicking, so I went to the computer, trying to stay calm. Maybe she was on the phone to Sue, assuming she had sent the same message to her. She could have beat me to it.

I loaded Skytel, the video calling service used in all shelters to help keep connected, found Mum's account, and pressed call. I waited for a response, willing them to answer, but then it timed out due to no response.

I sat for a minute trying to think what to do next I had limited phone signal on the mobile with only enough to receive text messages or Wi-Fi platform messages. I grabbed the phone and sent them a message maybe their phone was just playing up, sending messages to Mum, Dad and Adam surly one should get the message. The next thing I did was to ring Sue who was no doubt in their own shelter which was better equipped than my own despite mine being newer. She answered straightaway sure enough, she had received the same message I had and was having as much luck as me in gaining contact. I opened the message and went to information, it told me three things where the message was sent from, when it was sent and finally when I had received it. Looking at the location it told me that it was sent from their address in Wales, and it was sent at eight-fifteen a.m. being received by me at eight-thirty a.m.

A fifteen-minute delay in what could have happened in that time, I loaded the North Wales web page, hoping it would shed some insight. The storm tracker for the area showed no sign of tornadoes or earth tremors. Winds were at 90mph, with thunderstorms still ravaging the area. The same red alert was in place, telling people to get to safety and stay in their shelters until told otherwise. Checking my phone for a reply and not seeing one, I tried to reassure myself it could take a while. It had taken fifteen minutes to receive theirs; it was barely two since I had sent off mine.

Talking into the shelter phone, I told Sue about the text difference in time. Like me, she was trying to stay calm and figure out what had happened or ways to contact them. I considered going out of the shelter to try and get a better signal, but Sue said that it would be useless. The damage to the area was already being reported, and the telephone masts that covered this area had already been blown down. The whole area was now relying on satellite data to keep them going. Even if I left, I would be lucky to get one bar, not enough to cast to the next door, never mind all the way to North Wales.

Speaking to Sue on the phone, we arranged a plan; she would try and contact them over Skytel. I would try the shelter phone. And report back in twenty minutes or sooner if we hear anything. Ending the call, I redialled the number, still getting no answer, checked my phone again, and refreshed it manually. Trying to speed up any response coming through. I checked online, but they were all offline, not that they used the internet much as it was in normal circumstances.

Fifteen minutes went by, and I kept trying their phone, but to no avail. Something was wrong; I could feel it. I knew I shouldn't have let them move so far away, but even if they hadn't, there was nothing I could do.

Five minutes till Sue should ring back, I could only hope that she had managed to find something out but I didn't hold much hope, after all, she hadn't rung to inform me yet, and I had tried to keep the phone free in between calls to allow her to get though, it looked like she was having as much luck as me.

Loading up Google, I went to *www.shelterlive.com* the live tracker for all shelters across Britain it could be used to track servicing, maintenance and in general everything that you could get from the control panel. Loading the web page, I was asked for the unit number and password confirmation. The password wasn't the problem Dad used the same password for everything and had done so for years never changing it once, I knew that because I had to register the shelter for him. Unit number would be the issue I once had it all written down but hadn't seen it since the move, it had to be in here somewhere as everything from my previous shelter was simply boxed up and the boxes moved directly into this one. It was in a little black notebook that contained all the unit numbers and passwords for all our shelters. It used to live in the desk drawer but had found a new home in this small unit, the question was where. I was halfway through searching the bookcase; the only other logical place to keep it, when the phone suddenly went, and I ran to answer it in the hope it was them. But not to my surprise it was Sue ringing for an update. Having found nothing there was very little to add, and she had less in return. I asked if she knew or had the unit number for the bunker but of course, she didn't, she used to mock me for keeping it, saying it was a waste of time and that I would never need it. Well, now we did, and I could not find it I put the phone through the speakers and went back to searching the bookcase. I tried to restrain myself from telling her again that she should have had a copy of the information as well as me, which I had told her plenty of times before.

Having exhausted the bookcase, I moved to the cupboard the only other place I could think it would be after all where else would it be, it was packed with everything else. I looked through the clothes, spare bedding, and storage boxes which only contained a few essentials like spare bulbs, a first aid kit and a sewing kit something Mum had bought us both. I even checked the mop bucket to see if it had fallen in.

Having no luck there the only other place I could think was the kitchen. I headed for the door all the time; Sue was in the background advising places I had already checked like a backseat driver. If it wasn't in here, I would have to try and get the unit number from the site admin, but that could take a while, and it wouldn't be their main priority even if they would release the information which was unlikely as it wasn't meant to be shared.

After emptying the kitchen cupboards and turning every pot and pan upside down, tipping out the cutlery tray and even emptying the freezer I gave up and sat on the sofa. Trying to think, Sue was moaning at me now asking how I could have lost it. Then I remembered there was a safe built behind one of the photos on the wall, it was a new feature to me. I ran to the picture and pulled it open; it swung open like a door hinged to the wall. I thought to myself as I brought the house, why you would need a safe in a vaulted shelter if people could break into the shelter, then they would have no problem cracking the safe. I looked at the safe and noticed it was already open not having bothered to lock it proving the point of how pointless I found it.

I opened the safe, my heart now pounding with worry, I could feel myself losing my calm and about to fall to pieces. There it was under a copy of my Birth Certificate Driving License, Identity Card and Passport. I remember Dad insisting I put it in there for safekeeping, he was worried because of the sensitive information it contained. That was the problem with putting something in a safe place you can never find it when you need it.

"I have it," I said to Sue. While I ran to the computer, taking my time to avoid the mess, I had left from my search. I went to the computer and entered the unit number and waited while it loaded the page. Just then a news bulletin came on the screen, and a tornado was expected to touch down around North Wales in the next fifteen minutes. The webpage had given me access to the shelter, but was still collecting data. I sat there willing to hurry. Sue had gone quiet as I had while we waited for the page to load, both holding our breath, not knowing what it would say. Then it came up (SHELTER NOT IN USE).

Chapter Five
That's What Friends Are for – *Rob*

I sat there looking at the screen, not knowing what to say in disbelief, surely there must be some mistake I checked I had entered the right code, but it said—

Name: Mr and Mrs Wolf.
Unit: NW6435.
Location: Snowdonia National Park, North Wales.
Coordinates-53.0685°N, 4.0763°W
Shelter status: Not in use.

There was no doubt it was the right shelter. I heard Sue calling my name. It woke me from some form of the trance, and she wanted to know what it said. How could I tell her that the shelter that was supposed to be keeping our parents and brother safe wasn't being used and that we now had no way of knowing where they were or if they were all right?

I just said it outright; it says it's not in use; they're not there. Silence from both of us as we tried to take it in; now we know why we couldn't get through. I looked at the page, accessing the enter log detailing every time the door was opened.

Going to the last entry.

The door opened – at 8.14 a.m.
12/01/32
Door-locked – 10.14 p.m.
11/01/32
Door opened – 10.12 p.m.

11/01/12

What would make them open the door? I opened the shelter properties.

Air supply – active
Status: green
Usage: 0.01 per cent
Satellite connection – Connected to Skytel satellite 2
Water:
Tank 1– 99.9 per cent
Tank 2 – N/A
Errors: c26: door open
Heating: 21celcius
Alerts: red: please remain in the shelter.

I read this all out as I went informing Sue, so she knew neither of us could think of what would have happened. Why did they open the door to the shelter in the middle of an alert? There were no errors or issues with the shelter or supply—well none—that were showing on the system. I checked my phone again, still no reply. I went back to the tab with the storm tracking for their area; it showed no sign of a tornado yet in North Wales but had high levels of pressure, making it likely there could be.

Outside the winds had built up to 90 mph along with a thunderstorm in the area, the strength of which was dangerous, to say the least. Where were they? I was out of options, I could only hope that wherever they were, they had found safety.

Before Sue rang off, we both agreed that there was not much either of us could do now but sit and wait. I promised to tell her if I heard anything and her the same. I sat there going through the webpage again, trying to find anything I missed but found, nothing of importance.

I was no use, sitting there doing nothing and still taking in the shock of what I had just read. I sent new messages asking them to get in contact ASAP. Looking around at the mess I started to clean, it couldn't stay like this and it wasn't like I could do anything else. It would be a distraction something to keep myself busy, I was halfway through sorting the bookcase when the Skytel call came through. I ran to the computer, hopefully it was them, but it was Sam I pressed answer, it took a few seconds for it to connect and both cameras to activate.

"How's your unexpected day off?"

"Always like Sam trying to make light of any situation, can see you keeping busy having a sort out?"

"Probably the first time he had seen any part of my house in a mess. I was always so tidy and organised it must have come as a shock."

"You're still talking to me," I said, laughing it off and the sort out wasn't planned. "He could tell something was wrong and not just frustration from being stuck in the shelter, even though he knew I get restless with limited freedom and lack of mental stimulation."

"What is it? What's wrong?"

"My parents' shelter isn't being used, the door is open, and we can't get in contact and to make matters worse there is a tornado expected in the area."

Silence for a moment before he asked, "What happened?" An inevitable question one of which I wish I could answer.

"I don't know, I received a text from Mum asking to ring her, and when we tried no answer."

"How long ago?" he questioned with concern.

Looking at the clock, I saw that it was almost two hours since the door had been opened. Part of me started to worry and part gave me reassurance that the tornado had not yet touched down and if it did there was no saying it would affect them. They had a good two hours in which they could have found safety from the storm.

"About two hours ago." The next question was one that I had expected sooner. "What happened to the shelter?"

Looking at the screen and the preview screen showing my camera, I could see myself all the stuff from the cupboard on the floor, the door wide open, as well as the photo and the safe.

I was looking for the login info for my parents' shelter, but my dad, in his infinite wisdom, moved it from the desk to the safe for safekeeping. He knew my thoughts of the safe he thought the same.

Now he was laughing. The thought of me running around like a headless chicken trying to find something always made him laugh; he knew from work it was the most stressful I got.

"I take it the safe was the last place you looked," he said.

"Of course, it was, I didn't bother to keep looking after I found, I did it?"

Even now with the jokes, I was the main culprit for untimely Dad jokes at our workplace.

Always time for some light-hearted humour, I was used to handling stress you had to be in my job. "Do you want me to give my dad a call?"

He lived a few streets away from mine in Wales; it was something else we had in common. "I'm not sure what good it would do, but I suppose it's worth a try."

"I will try the next-door neighbours, and see if they have seen anything, with any luck they're with them."

We ended the call so he could ring his parents, and I could find the shelter number for my parents' neighbours. I had their mobile and house numbers and then mine, but both would be useless now it was the shelter number I needed, going back onto Skytel I loaded the directory, and clicked the search bar all shelters had their number registered all I needed was the name and location;

Names – Mr and Mrs Dunlop
Address – 18 Snowden Road
North Wales,
Snowdonia.
Number – 0124842

Grabbing the shelter phone, I dialled the number and waited for it to connect. I rang three times before being answered.

"Hello?"

They sounded confused, I do not think they were expecting a call it was a small family, but they all lived together so no one really would be calling. They had become good friends with my parents in the last few years, they had taken time to look in on them and often went out together, and invited each other to dinner. Dad and Scott had even become golfing partners, leaving Mum and June as the golfing widows as they called themselves.

"Hey, Scott, it is Rob Wolf."

"Well, this is a pleasant surprise, how are you?"

"I'm good, I hope you are all okay."

"We're fine, thanks. To what do I owe the pleasure? I hope everything is okay. I take it is not just a courtesy call."

"Unfortunately, not. I had a message from my parents asking me to call them, but when I did, I couldn't get through I've accessed the shelter records online and it says the shelter is unused. I know it is a long shot, but I wondered if you had seen or heard anything."

"Regrettably not, hold on, I will just check the cameras."

I heard voices from the other end asking what was going on, and Scott telling the youngest to get off the computer much to his displeasure. We sat in silence while he loaded the cameras.

Nothing came up as abnormal, apart from the debris from the storm.

"Okay, thanks anyway," I said.

"Not a problem I hope, they're all right."

"I'm sure I'm worrying about nothing."

"Well, I've got the Rover I use for monitoring the backfield. I will send it over there if it can make it. See what I can see."

If you could, that would be brilliant. I left my number with him to get back to me if he found anything. And rang off.

Chapter Six
As Safe as Houses – *Adam*

Even being locked in the shelter, we could hear the storm beating away at the walls. Yes, the shelter was up to regulation standards with everything you should need to survive any storm, but it was old. At the last maintenance inspection, they said that it was showing signs of aging. Most houses around here had already upgraded there's and it was on the cards soon for us to do the same. The appointment was booked for next week. We were going to have the whole thing redone, I was just hoping it wasn't too late.

It had been a long night; the shelter was originally made for two. But we upgraded it to three with the use of an old camp bed. Dad was folding away the old sofa bed. And I was putting away the bedding in the storage boxes we had installed. When we had moved in three years ago, the shelter was bare just an empty space with a small, rundown kitchen and a toilet the size of a small cupboard. The only way to use it was to walk in sideways and sit down. We had a maintenance inspection straight away, and the report was reassuring more cosmetics that structural only a few panels on the outside needed replacing; the rest was just a matter of decorating and revamping.

I wished we had been in Leicester with Rob or even better, Sue. At least their shelters were secure, built into the foundations of the house, and with much better protection. Dad had told Rob that the shelter was made to withstand winds of up to 2000 mph when it only withstood fifteen-hundred, but it was a white lie. It was only just over the standard of thirteen-hundred if he knew he would have had it ripped out and a new one put in. Before we moved, but Mum insisted, we moved in as soon as possible and didn't want a delay, saying it could always be fixed up after and so it should have been, but like many other things, there was always a reason to put it off something more important to do. Leaving it now susceptible to severe damage and us at the risk of insufficient protection.

"What do you want for breakfast," Mum called from the kitchen which was mainly a gas stove on a worktop with a small sink and two cupboards.

"I will just have toast and some cereal. I wasn't that hungry."

We sat down at the small potable picnic table Mum insisted we had, as Mum brought through a pot of tea and the milk along with the individual cereal boxes and the toast rack.

Pouring myself a cup of tea and buttering some toast I looked at the selection of cereal available. The news was on in the background, heavy winds and reports of the damage a tornado had caused in Tenby, South Wales.

Tenby was all but destroyed it had taken a few hits over the years, but it looked like it had finally succumbed. It used to be a nice seaside town in its day, but global warming has destroyed it with more beaches than the ocean now. I selected cornflakes and poured them into the bowl adding milk.

We should get in contact with Rob and Sue. Mum said carrying two bacon cobs and handed one to Dad.

After breakfast, I said they will be all right their shelters are under a house not exposed like ours the news said that the alert would likely last all day. Dad said apparently the storm seems to be circling the area and not passing through.

Looking at the time seven-thirty, I was due at work for nine but under the circumstances, it wouldn't matter they would all be in the shelter under the home and no staff would be coming or going. The rest of breakfast was eaten in relative quiet all of us watching the news.

I needed a shower I had only just got back in from work yesterday before having to come down here, but unlike most shelters nowadays this was one of the few that didn't feature one. It was on the plans for the new shelter.

Having finished eating and the pot being empty I stood up volunteering to do the washing up to give me something to do.

I told Mum and Dad to go sit down, they didn't sleep well either for two reasons the first being the storm you could still hear even though faintly. The other is the old mattress and springs on the sofa bed being only just slightly more comfortable than the old camping bed that dipped in the middle.

I went to the kitchen and filled the sink trying to find the washing-up liquid and a sponge. Finding them in the bottom cupboard I started washing the pots and placing them on the side to dry off. I could hear Mum getting flustered in the living room and Dad being moaned at.

"Adam?"

Leaving the pots and drying my hands I entered the living room. Mum was staring at the shelter phone getting more flustered by the second.

"Can you get this to work? It won't let me call out."

I took the phone and placed it to my ear. I didn't hear a dialling tone. Going to the base to check it was all connected, I found all the wires where they should be. But the base wasn't transmitting a signal to the phone; just showing a red light. Typical of this bunker being made of wrought iron and not having the benefit of having the modern communication features built in, it was hard to get a good signal once the door was shut. I checked the mobiles, and the same issue no data whatsoever.

"It's not getting a signal," I said we will have to try the laptop. Going to the laptop we kept in here I turned it on, but it came up with a no battery sign.

"As anyone seen the charger for the laptop? I think it got moved to the house when our one broke," Mum announced.

"Well, that's it," then I said no signal and now no computer to access Skytel. When this is over the first thing, I'm doing is getting this whole thing pulled out and a new one put in.

"Then how can we contact them?"

"We can't," I said as I was trying to coax some life into the laptop.

Having no joy, I went back to the phone, I was playing with the wires when the signal came on.

"Got it," I said as the sound of thunder broke though it sounded louder as if I was outside. And it was getting colder in here as well I could feel a breeze. "A BREEZE," I turned round to see the door open no one in the shelter. Dropping the phone, I ran to the door to see Dad running towards the house. Half the roof was missing, and a few windows were broken already. What was he doing, Mum was out the door a well on her phone trying to make a phone call.

"What are you both doing," I shouted.

The storm was loud the wind hitting me full force and pushing me back. Dad was too far away to hear me; Mum was on her phone not paying much attention.

"What are you doing," I said as I got nearer.

"Trying to get through to Rob, thought, I would get a signal out here. I sent a message, but he hasn't replied."

"He won't, shelters have limited signal. Now get inside while I go and get Dad what's he even doing going indoors for?"

"I was shouting to be heard this storm was covering any noise making conversation impossible," he said about going to get the charger for the laptop.

I was speechless, why did they think it was a good idea to leave the shelter, never mind go inside a building that was probably suffering from structural damage by now? Dad was just going through the door when what was left of the roof fell off. I saw it in slow motion as roof beams tiles and the contents of the attic fell into the house. Get back in the shelter and shut the door, I will go get Dad. NOW! I said as I ran towards the house.

The wind stopped pushing me back as I ran towards the house. I stopped as I reached the door and couldn't see a sign of Dad. The wind was blowing a swirl of dust and grit around, it looked like we were in the middle of a sandstorm the force of the wind had turned up the ground leaving no grass or remains of the garden intact. I yelled as loud as I could, "DAD! DAD!" Nothing I could barely hear myself, so little to no chance he could. Realising there was nothing for it, I went into the house.

The hallway had a clear path heading to the stairs. Already I could see dust and pieces of roof tile scattered around them. The top floors must have suffered some serious damage. I couldn't believe this was happening. Looking around I saw no sign of Dad anywhere which meant one thing he was upstairs. He was probably heading to the office to get a laptop charger. I could see the office door but no movement coming from the room, the house lit up blue followed by the crack of thunder.

Chapter Seven
How to Outrun a Storm – *Adam*

I ran up the stairs in seconds, taking them two by two until I reached the top. The floor was covered in roof tile and pieces of ceiling mums Christmas tree lay on the landing; we had put it in the attic last week. I looked up to see massive craters above looking straight up to the sky. It was dark, it was hard to see where I was going. I was trying to find my way to the office, stepping carefully on the debris as I went. As I walked into the office, I could see there was no roof left and on the floor was a mound of plaster, wood and broken tile. I just stood there I could see no sign of Dad maybe he hadn't made it upstairs after all. The desk had broken in two everything was now spread all over the floor. There was no sign of the laptop or charger, or had he already got it? I turned around to leave and tripped over falling on my front. As I did, I saw a light shining up the stairs. It took me a few seconds to gather myself the fall had taken the wind out of me; I lay there trying to catch my breath I could just about make out my mum's voice calling up the stairs. "Adam! Peter! Are you okay?" I tried to shout back down, telling her to get back to the shelter, but it only came out as a whisper.

It wasn't till I was trying to stand I realised my ankle hurt it felt swollen. Using what was left of the desk to help myself up I only succeeded in tipping it over and adding what was left onto the floor I fell back down again the desk crashing beside me. The light was getting closer Mum was clearly making her way up the stairs.

"Go back down," I yelled as best I could. I tried moving my ankle if I was lucky, it would only be sprained not broken, she came into the room and shone the torch into my eye.

"Adam," she said in alarm. "Are you all right?"

"Yes, I held my hand up shielding my eyes from the beam of light coming from the torch."

"What did you do?" she said, walking over a falling piece of ceiling missing her head by inches and landing by her feet.

"I just tripped. And twisted my ankle."

She knelt down to where I was grabbing my ankle and had a look moving it about and looking for puncture wounds.

"Can you move it?"

"Yes, slightly." Let me help you up it just looks like a bad sprain. More of the roof fell on the landing bringing with it more plaster dust that was sent spiralling back into the wind.

Holding on to Mum I stood up, placed my foot flat on the ground and felt a twinge but as long as I was careful it should be all right.

"Did you find your father?"

"No, I was looking for him when I fell, it does not look like he was in here! He might still be downstairs."

"Well, I'm going to look in the bedroom, he sometimes takes the laptop in there you stay here."

"No, I will go, I can walk a little, and I want you to go back down to the shelter. I will find Dad and meet you there."

"I'm not going anywhere without either of you."

"Fine, well at least go check downstairs and leave the upstairs to me at least that way she would be safer from any remaining roof or brick that could fall."

"Take the torch," she said, pulling another out of her pocket, she kept two on the console table in the hallway, she must have grabbed them as she entered. Using the torch to navigate my way through the rubble I could see it piled up outside the bathroom well he wouldn't be in there anyway. There were only four rooms up here the office that doubled up as an extra bedroom, it was clear he wasn't there. The bathroom which it looked unlikely he would have got in there before it all fell. That left both bedrooms across the landing. One being mine, I placed my bets on him not being in there. I hobbled over to the last room using the banister of the stairs to help support me trying to avoid another fall or injury from anything above not that there was much left to fall.

I reached the bedroom as the lighting struck through the sky. Lighting up the sky and room in one the thunder soon followed, shaking the house with its ferocity. I crouched down waiting for more of the house to fall around me. A box came crashing onto the landing spilling tinsel and baubles. Looking up you could see where it had been teetering on the edge. Closing my eyes and taking a deep breath, I dragged myself up and across the rest of the landing.

Once in the bedroom, I shined the torch around. Dad was in the corner laptop and charger clutched to his chest. Half a wardrobe having fallen on him and chucks of ceiling on top of that. Ignoring the pain in my ankle I ran over as fast as I could. He was still conscious.

"Are you all right?"

"What are doing here? You should be in the shelter with your mother. He hadn't lost his sense of duty."

"And you shouldn't have opened the shelter all for a laptop charger," I bit back.

"Your mum wanted to check on the others you know how she worries," he ashamedly said.

He always would do anything to make my mum happy it was what made their love so special and I admired him for it I only hoped one day I would be the same.

"Are you hurt?"

"No," he replied, just can't lift this dam thing off! Attempting to lift the wardrobe again to prove he was trapped. As more of the ceiling fell.

"He was covered in dust and cuts from the chucks of plaster."

"But nothing that looked life-threatening; I only hoped there was no damage further down. I gave Dad the torch."

"Shine it over the wardrobe," I said as I started to clear some of the rubble off the top of the wardrobe in the hope it would make it lighter and easier to lift. A sudden flash of blue light lit the room again. Once again, I prepared to take the impact from the thunder, but nothing came down this time. It was only the timbers left above us now, but they didn't look stable.

"Having cleared most of what was covering the wardrobe, I prepared to lift."

"Okay, lift in three… two… one… and push. Damn this thing was heavy; we had only succeeded in moving the matter of an inch or more."

"What's in this?"

"It is your mums; you know what she is like never throw any of her clothes away. That's why we have so many in here."

"It was true there were four wardrobes around only one was Dad's and even that had some of Mum in."

"Let's try again."

I grabbed a chunk of wood to try and prop it up against if we could just lift it enough.

Three… two… one… push the sudden pain in my ankle

from the force of lifting was excruciating taking my breath with it making me drop it back down again. I stopped and tried to catch my breath.

"You, all right?"

"Yeah, I'm fine. Just give me a second, then we will try again." I heard a voice again, turning my head and seeing a torchlight coming towards us.

"What are you doing back up here," I had to yell to be heard over the wind. You were supposed to be downstairs.

She walked into the room, and stopped when she saw us. "What happened?" She was quickly by his side and wiping dust off his forehead.

"Here's that charger, my love."

"You're a silly man," she said with a smile, briefly replacing the expression of panic and worry. She leaned over and kissed him.

"That's it," I interrupted. Stop that you can do that when we get out of this mess.

Mum took the charger, and put it to one side.

"Right, let's move this thing and get out of here."

Taking one end of the wardrobe I took the other and prepared the wooden prop to hold it up.

"Right, Dad, this is the plan; once we've lifted it, I'm going to prop this under I'm not sure how long it will hold it. So as soon as it under roll out as fast as you can, you got that."

"Yes, let's just get this over with." Taking a deep breath getting ready to take the pain again as I applied pressure to my ankle, I said in three… two… one… and pushed.

I screamed out in pain as I pushed putting the full force of the wardrobe on my ankle.

But with Dad pushing from underneath, me and Mum lifting

each corner I was able to elevate it enough to place the wood under.

"GO!" I shouted.

We all let go it hit the wood as Dad rolled to the left and I fell to the floor, the next bout of thunder hitting the skies just as the wardrobe crashed onto the floor breaking the wood in two.

I sat clutching my ankle tears in my eyes from the pain. Mum and Dad are also breathless from exertion.

"Are we all right?" I asked not daring to look.

Dad was getting to his feet and brushing himself off.

"I think so," he said apart from you. I was still clutching onto my ankle. The pain not having dulled yet.

"I will be fine, just need to rest."

Dad helped Mum up, and they hugged. Even in these circumstances, I could not help feeling a warm glow of warmth and pride looking at my parents hugging, just happy to be together each taking comfort in the embrace, you could not buy that kind of love.

Chapter Eight
One Shelter Is as Good as Another
– Adam

We stayed where for a few minutes. All just trying to get our breath back. Mum grabbed a scarf that was lying on the floor and bent down, pulling off my trainer. She tied it around my ankle to support it. She also got a sturdy pair of walking boats from Dad's wardrobe which was still upright. Luckily, me and Dad took the same size shoe, she laced it tight.

"If you had stayed in the shelter like you were supposed to, this wouldn't have happened," Dad said pacing the room and looking at the danger you both put yourself in.

"If you had stayed in the shelter, you would have probably died in the house; you should thank him for coming to your aid," Mum bit back.

I blame myself; if I hadn't made such a fuss about the charger, you wouldn't have come here, we would all be in the shelter and Adam wouldn't have near enough broken his foot.

As in most marriages no matter how much love they shared. The kids are always what they argue over the most. In my case, Mum was protective, always there to listen but still firm enough to keep us in line. Dad was on the more practical side, saying we should get ourselves out of our own issues but still proving he was the man around the house. That's what he was doing now trying to save his pride and show that he was back in control, but

I didn't think that either of us was in control. The only thing I knew for sure was we needed to get back to the shelter and now.

"This is getting us nowhere. I'm sorry, Dad, I didn't mean to endanger Mum, I did tell her to stay in the shelter. He knew what Mum was like and that she never listened, which is where we should all be now interrupted Mum let me help you, coming over I gave my arm. Dad the other side they pulled me up till I was on my feet. The adrenalin had gone now leaving me feeling tired and weak. But I had to make sure we all made it back If Rob found out about this, he would go mad the last thing he said to me was to look after Mum and Dad. I doubted if we would remain here after this, especially from the looks of the house, he would insist on us moving back where he could keep an eye on us. I draped my hand over Mum's shoulder she was on my right with Dad on my left. We started to walk out of the room."

"Hold on," Dad said, letting go and going back picking up the laptop and charger. We went through all this to get them; I am not leaving them here now.

"We made it onto the landing; there wasn't enough room for all of us with all the rubble lying around, so Mum went ahead lighting the way."

The sky was solid black now; if I took a guess at the time, I would say it was late into the night, but although I couldn't tell you exactly, I could only be touching mid-day. The wind was getting stronger, it was a battle just to walk in it with two good feet, never mind a sprained ankle, it seemed to be coming from every angle. It was like being attacked by four different winds, all forming into one and hitting us in every direction.

We took the stairs one-by-one, the stairs were covered and slippery, and we didn't want to have any more accidents. We made it downstairs, and Mum veered to the right. We looked at each other. The door was straight ahead. Where was she going?

"Ann, what are you doing," Dad shouted.

"Go ahead; I'm just getting the first aid kit and some ice; we might need it."

"Forget that," we both said. "Aren't we in enough trouble?"

"She came back though with the first aid kit in one hand. And started heading to the freezer; forget the ice and get to the shelter," Dad demanded.

"Okay," she said, heading to the door and muttering something we can only assume about trying to help us thinking, we knew best. We looked at each other in disbelief before taking the next step towards the door.

Without the protection from the house, the wind was stronger as we battled our way towards the shelter. Mum was just standing there, staring. "What are you doing?" we both shouted, and then we saw it a tree had fallen in front of the door, completely blocking entry. The door was bent out of shape, so even if we could move the tree and gain access, we wouldn't be able to shut or secure the door, leaving us vulnerable. Dad left me and went to the shelter to see what could be done, but we had a worse problem.

The winds must be higher than forecast because the steel sheet around the shelter were lifting off. Some have already flown away.

"What do we do now?" he said as I stumbled over to look at myself.

"The tree had been upturned, and even with the three of us all fit, we wouldn't stand a chance of moving it."

"What about the panels it's ripping the shelter to pieces."

"There's nothing we can do about that now," he said.

"But we stand more of a chance down there than we do out

here," he said pointing to the shelter door.

"But how are we going to get in?" shouted Mum. We can't move the tree. "We don't want to," I said. The doors were broken, so we wouldn't be able to shut it; even if we could, it wouldn't lock and it would just blow open again. The tree will work as a barricade and offer us more protection.

"But we can't get in behind the barricade," yelled Dad.

Looking over at the shed, it lay in pieces. It had fallen into five pieces, all four walls, and the roof lay on top. "Go see if the shovels are under that lot," I said.

Leaning against the tree, I felt helpless, unable to help the way I should.

"Why do we need shovels?" asked mum.

Dad was already making his way towards the shed; he knew what I was planning and was probably pinching himself for not thinking of it first.

"There's a gap under the tree," I said, if we dig it out, we can crawl under into the shelter. That way, the tree is still blocking the door. It's the only hope we have.

"Dad was rummaging through the remains of what used to be the shed, he pulled out a shovel and what looked like a snowplough; these will have to do," he said turning around and trying to make his way back and being repelled by the wind. Finally, he made it and started digging.

"Pass the snow plough."

"You can't dig with your ankle the way it is."

"Sod the ankle; it will be the least of my problems if we don't get back in there soon."

Mum stood holding the first aid kit, laptop and charger close, afraid they would blow away, standing back not knowing what she could do to help, realistically, there was not anything. Trying to shelter as best we could from the wind, we dug from below the tree, the wind blowing the soil back at us and into the air as we shovelled it behind us. Thunder roared behind us, lighting still filling the sky and the ground shaking from the vibrations.

After what felt like five minutes but could be two, we had lost track of time ages ago. We stopped and surveyed the progress between us. We had excavated enough to comfortably fit an arm though. Taking a few seconds to grab our breath, we started again this time with more vigour. I could feel the wind rising trying to lift everything off the ground including us. Mum appeared at my side sliding the laptop under the tree and into the doorway followed by the charger and first aid kit. She had found a trowel from somewhere.

"Where did you find that?" I asked.

"I left in the flower bed yesterday when I did the garden."

Looking over at what used to be the flower bed, now just a pile of soil. How it had remained there when all the flowers and the planted sides had gone, I don't know. All three of us were digging away at the bottom of the tree when we saw some light appear getting closer and closer, at first, I thought, *It was lighting until it shone straight.* I turned round to see Scott Dunlop's rover approaching what was it doing all the way out here.

He used it to maintain his backfield in bad weather. It used tank-like chains for wheels, making it capable of navigating more tenuous terrain. It ran three large car batters and weighed a tone all spread out evenly to stop it tipping over. It was one of his most prized possessions as it got closer, I could hear a sound it sounded like someone was talking. Look at this, I said Mum and Dad turned around.

"Dad smiled as he saw it good old Scott," he said. It slowly approached until it was only a few inches away. It was Scott's voice coming out of the speakers.

"What do you think, you're doing?"

"Having a picnic came Dad's response."

"Stop with the jokes Peter now's not the time."

"We had a slight issue," I said, "we're trying to get back in the shelter, but the trees blocked the door. We thought, we could dig under it."

"Why are you even out of it in the first place?"

Dad started to explain it's a long story before, I interrupted saying, "I would explain another time". Dad looked annoyed that I had cut him off, but we didn't have the time he was never much for conversation but recently he and Scott could talk more than the average housewife.

"You've not got time for that, he said a tornado is heading this way expected any minute. Turning around I could already see the clouds trying to form into whirlpools."

"Get to my shelter if you can, I will let you in but hurry."

"Dropping the tools, we started making our way towards Scott's; do you know where his shelter is," Mum asked.

"Yes," he said, "let's just get there. We were halfway through our garden when Mum remembered the laptop and stopped."

"Why are you stopping I forgot the laptop we need to go back."

"No, you're not," said Dad, "leave it's caused enough trouble for one day."

Reluctantly, she started again I looked behind me and saw the tornado touch down.

"Quickly," I said. "We could see the Dunlop house ahead you two go, don't hold back for me."

"We're not leaving you."

"Yes, you are," I insisted. I will be fine. Now, go I will meet you there.

Dad forced Mum to go ahead with him promising to come back once Mum was safe, running was becoming more like dragging and stumbling this was impossible, the pain in my ankle becoming pure agony. *This is it*, I thought this was how it would end; the only comfort was that Mum and Dad would be safe I knew Rob would see them right. I looked behind me the tornado was still quite a way behind me. It was yet to reach our house, and we were two fields past. But the crosswinds were already blowing stuff around. The sky illuminated blue as lightening flashed, the thunder roared and cracked so loud the ground shook sounding like the earth was about to break in half. I could see Mum and Dad they were nearly in the Dunlop's Garden now. I was a few metres behind them adrenaline the only thing keeping me going. I could see the shelter door open and Mum getting in Scott was trying to force Dad in as well, but I could see him fighting it.

"GET IN!" I yelled. "GET IN!" But he couldn't hear me, "GET IN! GET IN!"

I was nearly there just a few more feet and I would be safe, my ankle sent a wave of unbearable pain up my leg with every step but I was soon distracted as something hit me on the back of my head, I hit the ground. Withering in pain unable to think or stand, my vision was blurred but one thing I saw clear as day was our house being sucked up, I lay there mesmerised watching it crumble every brick disappearing one by one as if being deconstructed one at a time vanishing into thin air. Suddenly, I felt something pulling me dragging me across the ground by each shoulder. I looked up and saw two blurred faces, I could hear the muffled sound of a dog barking and voices shouting as I felt the ground change underneath me slithering though the grass until it was cold and hard, I couldn't see the tornado any more my head hurt it felt like it had been cracked open. Nothing, was making sense all I felt was pain. The last thing I remember was seeing a dog run towards me followed by the sight of a door shutting before I blacked out.

Chapter Nine
A Tight Family Unit –
Sue

I was watching the news in the kitchen while I loaded the dishwasher and saw the weather warning. *Better pack the shelter,* I thought after all there were four of us to look after me, Jay, Tyler and Declan. Jay was my husband, he worked in construction all his life going from the bottom up, and he was now CEO of his own company. He liked to be hands-on and muck in with men as much as he could, you were more likely to find him on-site than in his office. Relying more on his laptop than his computer. His secretary saw him as less than the head foreman.

Having someone in the building trade had its benefits. We had bought a run-down five bedroom house giving us plenty of room to raise the kids. At the time I thought, *It was a bit big as I was only expecting our first Tyler now eleven.* By the time, we had signed the papers and got the keys we only three months till he was due, and the house was near derelict. But having an army of builders at his disposal turning down work and employing them all for a month to work on the house it wasn't long before it looked fit for a royalty with every mod con installed and decorated to a higher standard than would be seen for miles. It even featured a secure perimeter with big double electric gates. It all ran on green energy, using a power mill from a stream in the back as well as solar panels on the roof and a wind turbine as well. We soon found that we were powering enough energy to not only our house, but two more on the street sighing an agreement with the government to sell them the power, we soon found that we were paying nothing towards the keep, in fact, we were gaining money.

We soon brought a field behind the house using the stream again, we turned it into a power plant. My dad used his contacts to get permission and a grant from the government. They took hundred per cent of the power generated to power homes in the area that struggled to gain green energy. We owned the land and equipment, but they took care of the upkeep in exchange for fifty per cent of the power for no cost leaving us a fifty per cent cut of the profits. This along with his job allowed me to leave work and become a stay-at-home Mum; Tyler was six months old when I fell pregnant again nine months, later Declan 9 now completed the family.

The family had also benefited from our connections when Mum and Dad moved to Wales. Rob sent Jay over with his men, giving him the task of doing up the house before they moved, always the cautious one. There was always one person in the family who seemed to command control; in our case, it was Rob. Although Dad would have liked to think it was him, and until recently, it was. But Rob had assumed power, making it his job to oversee any major problems in the family. Dad had trouble handing over power, but Mum had convinced him over wise (saying, you're retiring. Let someone else take the strain now it's time you took a step back; you're always saying they need to look after themselves now they're old enough to do it).

Adam my other brother was all too happy to take the side lines like myself, Adam was very much Jack the lad of the family.

His string of relationships was never-ending opposed to mine who settled down with my childhood sweetheart, and Rob who had never found the right person and looked as if he would remain single indefinitely, he was always the level headed of us three, and the clear candidate to take the reins from Dad. Adam had calmed down and now went to Wales to keep an eye on Mum and Dad an arrangement that worked for all. Mum had at least one of her kids around, Dad could still have some control, and Rob and I had some security that someone was there to keep an eye on them, Rob, more than I had found some comfort in that, as well as worry of what trouble he could cause. Adam got to start a new life away from his past, where he was proving to finally be growing up.

Jay was even able to get Rob a discount on his home being the show home equipped with all the best fixtures and fittings, Jays' firm had built the whole complex not five minutes from our own home and added a few extras to Rob as he went.

Jay had come home early tonight the wind was causing issues and hindering production, better to give in and start again tomorrow he had said especially given the forecast for tonight. Getting a coffee out of the pot, I was just about to head out to do the school run.

I'm off to get the kids you want to come. The boys always preferred their dad picking them up over me I never took it personally they were both proud of their dad and it wasn't often he managed to get away in time to fetch them, so it made a bit of a rare treat.

"Give me a second to get changed," he said, drowning his coffee and burning his tongue at the same time.

"Careful it will be hot."

"You don't say."

"I will meet you in the car," I shouted heading out the door.

I opened the door to the garage it housed our Land Rover e+ edition their latest model; he insisted we got a new car a few months ago saying the range and durability of this model by far exceeded our current model despite it only being two years old. I went to the back and disconnected the charger. Seeing it was green it told me it was fully charged; a full charge should last the best part of a week. Opening the passenger door, I climbed in Jay always liked to drive it gave him pride to drive his family.

I was checking my phone and looking at the time, we would be late if he did not hurry up, leaning over I pressed the horn it sounded just as he appeared in the doorway. Walking over to the driving side he climbed in.

I'm here, he had changed into a pair of jeans and a navy jumper, changed his work boots for his trainers, I could smell his scent I had brought him last Christmas.

He started the car and pulled out, the garage door shutting automatically behind us and the main gate opened on cue to match. The school was only a five-minute drive away and we managed to avoid the worst of the school traffic, even managing to find a space in the car park and avoid having to park on the street. Walking towards both classrooms, they were separated by one another so standing in between the two we could be seen by both.

"Have you got anything special planned for dinner?"

"Was just going to chuck something from the deep freeze."

"What about treating the lads to a meal out, he always did like to spoil them."

"Suppose we can. I'm not in the mood to cook anyway."

The school bell rang, and the doors opened one by one, the kid's names were called out as the teachers saw the parents/grandparents that were there to collect them. I heard Tyler's name first, shortly followed by Declan's, they both appeared to see me first and started to walk but turned into a run when they saw their dad standing there as well, both reaching him at the same time they ran into either side of him embracing him in a hug.

"Well, nice to see you too," I said, glowing with pride in my family.

"Sorry, Mum," they said, leaving their dad and coming over to embrace me. It only lasted a second before going back to Jay we headed back to the car Jay holding either one of his hands as I led the way both bombarding him with questions of why he was there.

Back in the car, I returned to the passenger seat, leaving Jay to drive the boys in the back in their booster seats.

"Who fancy's Quacks for dinner?"

"Me!" they both shouted."

I looked over to Jay, a smile on my face looking back at me we could not hide the amusement on our faces.

"You spoil them you know."

"There is plenty of time for them to get over it."

Quacks was a family restaurant that featured slides, ball pits and a kid show to keep them entertained, while the parents had a full all-you-can-eat buffet and bar should they wish to escape. As we walked in, we were greeted by a host wearing fairy wings.

"Welcome to, Quacks. Have you been before?"

"Yes."

"Do you want to sit in the family area or the quiet room?"

"The family area will be fine," Jay replied.

"Please follow me. She showed us to our table."

"What are your names," she asked the boys.

"Tyler."

"Declan."

She wrote them down on an armband and added the table number.

"Here you go," she said handing them over.

"Can we go play?"

Five minutes then be back here for dinner otherwise you will miss the show.

They had a show once an hour, and one was just due to start. They ran off to the kid's area and were stopped at the gate while they had the armbands checked before being allowed in. A waitress walked over to this one wearing Mickey Mouse ears.

"Would you like a buffet or a regular menu, in all the years I have come here, I can't recall ever seeing anyone use the menu options."

"Two adult buffets and two kids, please."

"And to drink?"

"Coke for me, please; two fruit quack, Jack's orange, please." He looked over at me.

"A raspberry gin with lemon tonic, please."

"Will get them now."

We sat there looking at the kids playing in the ball pit. Tyler had found one of his school friends Josh; he had come to the house a few times for play dates. I suddenly felt a hand on my shoulder.

"Susan, how are you?" Looking over, I saw Beth taking a seat at the side of me. Beth was Josh's mum; we had seen each other at a few parties and school events, we even shared the same hairdresser not to mention collecting and dropping each other's kids off for numerous play dates.

"Hey, Beth, how are you not seen you for a while."

"It has been too long, you must be, Jay," she said passing her arm over towards Jay. It only just occurred to me they had never met."

"Nice to meet you." Shaking her hand.

"Beth is Josh's mum," I said filling him in with all he needed to know.

"Good kid."

"Thanks," said Beth. It has not been easy since his dad left, but I tried my best.

"He's a credit to you," I said, trying to save Jay any more awkwardness; he never was any good with the other kid's parents. Preferred to be on-site than at a school gathering, not that he would ever miss seeing any of his kid's plays or parents' evenings.

We will have to arrange a play date sometime soon, and it's Josh's birthday next month I hope both your lads can come I am sending invites out next week there at the printers now.

"I'm sure it can be arranged," I said as the waitress appeared again a tray balancing on one hand.

"One gin," she said, already handing it over.

"Thanks."

She placed the coke down in front of Jay, along with the tickets for the buffet and both quack jacks in the two spaces one taken by Beth and the other empty.

"Well, I better get Josh out and fed she stood up."

"Josh out now, she bellowed time to get food."

I saw Tyler and Declan laughing.

"And you two as well," I said in a way of scolding them.

They all looked at each other as they fought their way out of the ball pit and the gate where they were let out. Joining us at the table.

"Well, catch you later."
"Yes, bye, Beth."
"So that's Beth."
"She's all right; you just have to get to know her."
"Thought, she was the stuck-up one."
"She is."

Chapter Ten
Home Time – *Sue*

The lads had a quick drink before we stood Jay, gave me two tickets, one adult and one kid. Taking one each so we could keep an eye on what and how much they were having. we Approached the line and handed the tickets to the server, given the mundane task of collecting the tickets. After handing them over we received a stamp on the back of our right hand in case we wanted to go back again. Starting at the front where I was given two plates one small and one large, Jay was in front, already placing food on Tyler's plate, complaining he didn't like corn and why couldn't he have more chips. I was glad Jay took Tyler recently; his eating habits were getting picky unless he was around his Uncle Rob, who would make sure picky wasn't an option. Funny how they were more worried about their Uncle Rob more than their own parent; little did they know how much of a pushover he was when it came to them, the last time we were there I had to tell him what they would and wouldn't eat. After going down the line making sure he had a variety of food, some wholesome, some with no nutritional value, whatever, but it was a buffet, not a home meal as long as there was some form of veg on the plate, I wasn't too fused. Reaching the end, we got to the desserts. Not now, I said we will come back for them if you finish all this, I had not filled his plate so I knew he would.

We went back to the table where Jay and Tyler were already eating their food.

"How was school today?"

"Boring," replied Declan. "The teacher wants us to read a book."

"What book?"

"Can't remember."

"What about you, Tyler?"

"Had science. We're doing space, what is the ozone layer?"

We had made sure they knew about the changes global warming had made to the world and what we as a nation were doing to tackle it, but never went into too much detail.

"Well," Jay said the ozone layer is a layer of gas that encircles the earth's stratosphere it's made up of three types of oxygen.

"But what does it do?"

"It protects the earth and everything living in it."

"That's right," said Jay. "It protects us all from the UV rays emitted by the sun."

"But why can't I see it?"

"Gas is invisible, you can't see it you can only see it from out of space."

"Can we go to space?"

"No."

"Why?"

"Because we can't only astronauts can. Besides it damages the earth every time, something protrudes its surface and it is already damaged, so we need to stop causing any more trauma before we lose the ozone completely."

"I could tell that all this was going way other Declan's head and Tyler himself was struggling to keep track. But what will happen if we lose the ozone layer?"

"Well," I said. It will majorly change how we live our lives on this planet. Looking over to Jay trying to convey that we were to say no more than that.

"But how?" Tyler asked, now getting interested.

"Well, that's what they will teach you at school; we can't have you going in being a no-it-all now, can we?"

"I was just asking."

"How about we go and get some of that dessert?" They had nearly finished, and I knew it would distract them. It worked the previous convocation was forgotten, as they ate dessert with very little sound than those of enjoyment they had just finished when Josh ran up to the table.

"The show started are you coming to watch it."

"They turned around looking desperately at us."

"Off you go, but came straight back after so we could head home. it was a school night."

"They ran off all desperate to be the first there and get the best seats."

The show lasted for around fifteen to twenty minutes giving all of us parents a well-earned break.

We will have to have a sit down with Tyler without Declan and explain things a bit more in detail Declan's too young to know of such dangers yet he is still scared of monsters under his bed and if they're going to be teaching it in school then I don't want Tyler to worry him.

I will have a word later, but you are right it is a good thing they are teaching it, but it could cause some worry at such a young age.

The waitress appeared asking, "If we had finished."

"Yes," I said. "Thank you, it was lovely."

"You're welcome, can I get you anything else?"

I looked at Jay.

"Yes, actually can I get a bottle of your best chardonnay and two glasses, please?" he said

"I will bring it right over." She walked away taking the plates with her.

I put my head on Jay's shoulder. "What is the wine for, you are driving remember?"

"I know, but I felt like we could use it, besides, I'm allowed one glass and we can take what's left home, I fancy a nice night in just the two of us."

Sounds like heaven. "Looks like we're about to get some company," he said, looking behind him. I turned my head in time to see Beth walking back over.

"Mind if I take a seat," she said, sitting down as she spoke.

"Of course not, we lied feel free." The waitress appeared with the wine.

"Looks like someone's celebrating."

"No, not all just thought we deserved a treat will you join us?"

"If you offering."

"Sorry, can we get another glass?"

Jay poured the wine handing one glass to me and the other to Beth. I sipped slowly while Beth drank half in one gulp. The waitress having brought the extra glass for Jay to pour his wine.

"I take it you have been getting questions on the ozone as well why do they have to teach them such things at this age?"

"Eleven isn't that young, and it's better to install it now as opposed to later," said Jay, "but I do agree they could have done it more subtlety."

"Well, I might have a word with the teacher tomorrow to see what they think they're doing. I told him, it's nothing to worry about and that the school will tell him all he needs to know what did you say."

"We just explained what it is and that it needs to be looked after before we destroy it beyond repair," I said quickly before Jay could get in. "I could tell he wasn't warming towards Beth probably even going off her more by the second."

"Well, aren't you worried that you would scare them," she said, angrily?

"No! Jay beat me to it we think they should know what dangers it holds he lied yes; we did have reservations, but not on Tyler's part he was old enough not that we would tell her that."

She was about to argue when her phone started to ring.

"I will have to take this if you will excuse me." She downed what was remaining of the wine before heading to the door.

"Thank gods, she was gone," I said before picking up my wine glass and resuming my position on his shoulder; we watched the kids in silence just happy to be close seeing them happy was what made it all worthwhile.

We watched as the show came to an end and the kids returned, Josh behind them. We got up ready to leave and looked around for Beth, but she was nowhere to be seen.

"She went outside to take that call," Jay said.

"I will go, have a look."

"I'm coming to mummy came a chirpy voice from Declan he never wanted to be left behind when he thought, he might miss out."

"Okay." Taking his hand off we go. We headed for the door and heard shouting from outside. Stepping foot out into the reception area we saw Beth having an argument over the phone. She went quiet when she saw us.

"We will deal with this later," she said before hanging up the phone.

"Is everything all right?" Even though it was clear it wasn't.

"Yes, she tried to lie why wouldn't it be?"

I looked at Declan. "I want you to go inside. Go to your dad and get Josh to collect their belongings."

"Have you already settled the bill?"

"Yes, it's all taken care of."

"Having sent Declan on his way, I kept a lookout until I saw him reach Jay."

"Come on, let's get some air." Heading to the main door we went to the patio furniture and took a seat. The wind was strong, half the furniture had tipped over a few chairs had blown across the play area. I pulled my coat tighter over me; this wind was chilling, I would have brought a thicker coat, had I known I would be staying out this long. It was dark out, but the outside and car park were well lit up. What's the matter, and don't tell me everything's fine."

"It's Josh's dad, he's refusing to take any responsibility for him and saying that I have no right to claim the house in the divorce as it's in his name, and I haven't put a penny into it."

"That's terrible. What does he expect you to do with Josh if you don't have a house."

He said, "He doesn't care; he wants a DNA test to prove he's even the farther accusing me of having an affair with someone else and claiming Josh was his, all because he has black hair and both ours are brown, I keep telling him mine was black when I was a kid, and it will change as he grows up, but he won't listen."

"You need to speak to a lawyer."

"I have them trying to sort it out now, but he's refusing to speak to them."

Just then Jay walked out surrounded by three kids holding them close from fear of blowing away. "Is everything all right?"

Seeing us sitting down Beth took a deep breath. Before turning around Josh came running up to her for and embracing her in a hug.

"Hello, my dear," she said, hiding her emotions for a second. I admired her strength; she always held things and appeared to be in control and seemed so well put together but scratched the surface and it was a different story altogether.

"Let me see you to your car." Josh looked at her, not knowing what to say.

"We don't have one; I sold it." That's why I've been avoiding being seen at school. I spoke to the teacher, and she kept Josh in the class till last, and I hid around the corner what would people say if they knew? She looked ashamed. Well, how did you get here?" The way I get everywhere, the bus looking over at the bus stop at the same time. "Well, you are not waiting for a bus in this weather. Looking over at Jay," I said. "Jay, can you set the spare seat up from the boot, please?" The car was kited for five, but with seats that folded into to boot floor to expand it to seven. He went ahead with the kids.

"You go help them, please," Beth said to Josh. "We will be right behind you."

Josh ran off to catch up shouting at them to wait as he did. "I don't know how to thank you. I thought, you would be happy to see me fall so low."

"It hurt that she thought it was true." I never had much time for her and always felt a bit of annoyance when she approached, and it was true that a few others would relish in the demise of this proud woman whom they all envied because they knew they didn't have an ounce of her strength.

"Well, I'm not, and don't think that for a moment. Let's get you home safe and sound, shall we?"

We approached the car; Jay was strapping in the kids. "We don't have another booster seat," he said.

"Can we place Josh in the middle seat, so he is sandwiched between the two," I asked.

"I suppose," he said not sounding too sure it won't be ideal. "But it's the best we can do." Jay had lifted the seat in the boot.

"Do you want to go up front?"

"No," she insisted this would be fine the front is where you belong.

I settled Beth in the back and shut the boot as Jay tightened the seatbelt around Josh, making sure he was as secure as he could. He had even removed the neck rests off the front seats using them as cushions for him to sit on shutting the door. He headed for the driving seat as I got in the passenger side.

"Already," he said, a resounding yes came from behind, Josh seemed to be enjoying himself in the back getting joy from all the excitement as the kids showed off the gadgets in the back and the tablets built into the back of the headrests. I hoped Beth wouldn't feel we were being insensitive trying to rub it in her face.

"That's enough back there; I'm sure he doesn't want to see everything it can do."

"Do you know where she lives?" Jay asked.

"Yes, abode street."

It was only a few blocks from us not far out our way. Looking at the sky it was black, a storm was defiantly on its way. We drove in silence most of the way the kids now too tired to do much just sat there staring out the window Beth was in a mind of her own I touched Jays' hand.

"I love you," I said.

"I love you too."

Chapter Eleven
Into the Shelter, We Go – *Sue*

We approached Beth's house. "Which one is it?"

"The last on the right."

Beth lived in a two-bed detached house, not the most desirable, but nothing to be ashamed of. It had a well-kept front garden with some garden ornaments that had been blown over and spread over the crazy patching. Jay parked outside the house where their car once took pride of place. The wind blasted me, instantly nearly knocking me over as I got out. I had to open the door and release the child lock. I forced the boot open to allow Beth to climb out. Jay opened the other passenger door and released the buckle, securing Josh.

"Here we are."

Fishing a card, I had made with all my contact information on, I handed one to her. "Call me anytime." Jay was getting back in the car. "Are you free tomorrow?"

"Yes, why?"

"Well, I drop the kids off at eight, I will swing by and get Josh to save you from getting the bus have you still got his booster seat?"

"Yes, but you don't have to I've already caused you enough hassle."

"Don't be daft, we can tell people your cares in the garage. Then we will go get a coffee and have a chat to see what I can do to help."

"Thank you." She was wiping a tear from her eye.

"You got in, I headed to the car and fought the wind to open the door.

"You are a good person," Jay said as I got in and shut the door.

"I can't leave her like that, she needs help." I put the seat belt on as Jay checked the mirrors indicated and pulled out onto the road again, I looked behind to see Beth and Josh waving before heading for the door.

"Still you didn't have to offer help, especially after how she's treated you and others you could have just rubbed it in her face, it takes a big person to offer the hand of friendship. That's why I love you."

"We all need help at times, and she didn't do anything wrong just needed to be humbled. She's not a bad person."

We turned into our street and saw Jay press the button on the remote clipped to the sun-visor to open the gates onto the drive and garage so we could drive straight in. Here we are announced Jay while turning the car off and shutting the gates and garage to keep out the wind. We got out of the car and released the boys who had already taken off the belts to their booster seats.

"Right, you two upstairs showered and bed it went seven and well past your bedtime."

"Okay, Mum."

"You have ten minutes. I will be up soon to tuck you in said Jay any longer and no chocolate in tomorrow's lunch."

We entered the house Tyler and Duncan darted for the stairs in fear of losing their lunchtime treat.

"You shouldn't tease them like that," I said, trying to hold back a smile as I headed for the door to the house.

"They know I'm only kidding." Jay retrieved the wine from

the storage compartment.

"Let's not forget this." He locked up and followed me into the house shutting the door.

"I hope the kids didn't have any homework to do, we might have to write them a note and catch up tomorrow."

"You worry too much," he said, flashing me that cheeky smile as we walked into the kitchen. "I missed loads of homework at school, it will just make them more popular."

"Well, someone, as I said flashed him one back and now Mrs Worry is going to get the shelter ready, I don't like the look of this storm, looking out the window at the sky above it had gone dark with no sign of the moon or stars. He walked to the fridge and placed the wine in it then walked over to me."

"That's not worry that's called being responsible." He kissed me on the cheek and then shouted ready or not here I came and left the room heading for the stairs.

I looked out the window for a bit, I couldn't help but feel sorry for Beth. It wasn't her fault, her husband left; he was the one having an affair with his secretary well that was the rumour going around any way, I'm sure I will find out what actually happened tomorrow. A lightning bolt flashed through the skies and I grabbed some bags from the cupboard and started to fill them with essentials milk, bread, and meat. Leaving the kitchen, I headed for the cellar door and down to the shelter when we brought the house the shelter was outside. Now the outdoor shelter was used for storage it acted as our shed and stored all the kid's summer garden toys. They had the cellar floor excavated during the renovations and had a state-of-the-art one put in. It was the one thing he had employed someone to do it being a specialist skill that required a close adherence to the government speciation's.

Using my fingerprint, the door automatically opened. The shelter ran the length of the house it had four bedrooms one kitchen dinner a large living area complete with a games table and a fully functional bathroom including a shower, bath toilet and a double sink on the wall facing mirrored cupboards containing emergency supply's the main bedroom had a large wardrobe and on suite with its own shower and toilet. Entering the shelter each room ran off the corridor. The kitchen was the first door in the hallway that was the best place for ventilation. I Placed the food in the fridge and I checked the supplies making sure everything was still on and working correctly the freezer was stocked and on temp. Moving to the bathroom, I made sure we had enough toiletries to last. Jay came up behind me placing his arm on my shoulder and made me jump.

"So, Mrs Worry, is it all okay?"

"Yes," I replied, having taken a second to let my heart stop racing. "I checked that everything was okay and ready just in case."

"You know, I can think of worse places to be stuck," he said, pulling me in close to him. It was by far the best shelter money could buy bigger than most houses.

"Agreed," I said, turning to face him and letting him snuggle into his chest for a hug.

"Are the kids, okay?"

"All cleaned and tucked up in bed although, I may have promised them extra chocolate tomorrow, if they don't bother us for the rest of the night. I didn't even have to read them a story. That's the best thing about Quacks, leaves them so tired they practically sleep as soon as their head hits the pillow. Now, Shal, we go upstairs, light the fire, and finish that wine."

Turning us both around, we led me out of the shelter. Jay

shut the door behind us and sealed it shut in the process.

"Why did you lock it," asked jokingly. "Were not in there and were not going anywhere. I don't know, force of habit, maybe come on," he said as we climbed the stairs up to the house and out of the cellar.

We walked into the living room. It was a large room with three large reclining sofas placed in the shape of a square the empty side facing the TV. That was mounted on the breast of a hanging fireplace. Hung from the ceiling.

A tablet controlled everything in the room like a remote, from the TV to the blinds. I turned the lights down to ten per cent and turned the fire on. Flames instantly flung to life it was electric after they put a ban on burning real wood to stop imitations and deforestation. But you couldn't tell the difference between real flames, especially as they used heat jets to make it feel more real and produce authentic smoke, and even had sound effects to add the crackling sound of the logs. I sat down Jay walked in with the bottle of wine and opened up the drink cabinet on the wall out two crystal glasses he brought the glasses and the wind and placed them on the coffee table before, pouring wine into both of them and handing one to me. He sat down next to me, and instantly I cuddled up to him. "What should we watch?" I said looking through the tablet. We selected the new Batman movie we had yet to watch and it had been out for a year now. The TV looked like a mirror until you turned it on then its high graphics appeared Christal clear well to us. Rob would say otherwise; Jay even took him with him to choose it only six months ago, but it was now out of date.

I sat there; only part watching the movie sipping my wine slowly, I was looking at the TV not paying attention. My mind was wandering over the events of today. "Sue! Sue!" I looked up and saw the credits rolling how I missed the whole movie.

"What did you think?" Jay asked pouring more wine into my glass.

"Erm, it was; I liked it."

"You didn't watch it, did you?"

"No, I am sorry, I was daydreaming."

"I know, I could tell."

The whole room suddenly flashed blue followed by a loud rumble. Sounds like the storms getting up some force.

"Sounds nasty," I replied, taking a sip of my wine. I looked at the clock; nine-thirty p.m. nearly time for bed. I said, "You've got to be up at seven and I promised to take Beth to breakfast."

"Let's not call it a night just yet."

"What else we got." He picked the tablet up.

"What about family, guy." Something light-hearted as he sat back down and poured the last of the wine into his glass. As we finished one episode, we agreed on one more. "It hadn't long started when the siren came, we looked at each other."

"You go get the kids," I said, slamming my glass down on the table almost spilling it everywhere. "I will go open the shelter. I ran to the cellar door to meet Tyler on the way I heard the siren." He yawned.

"Good boy," I said, pulling him close. "What about your brother?"

"I think he's still asleep."

"I will go get him," Jay said. "You head down."

I opened the cellar door and sent Tyler down first, following him down. He had already opened the cellar door using his hand Rob had insisted we were all on the system in case the boys were alone or with a babysitter for the evening.

"Straight inside, straight to your room," I said.

As stood in the doorway, waiting for Jay to arrive with Declan. I saw him appear at the top of the stairs carrying Declan down a smile on his face. "Someone didn't want to get up," he said, carrying him into the shelter. I kissed his forehead before. "Tyler's gone straight to bed," I said. Better put him in bed as well. He's practically asleep anyway. Jay took him to the bedroom while I shut the cellar door and then sealed the shelter door looking up. I saw the light turn red and heard the hiss of the air supply kick in.

Jay appeared shutting the bedroom door behind him. "There we go; he is all safe. I'm going to make us both a cup of tea," I said, walking into the kitchen.

"Shame. We didn't bring the wine," Jay shouted back as he headed for the living area.

I could hear the *BBC* newsroom starting as I boiled the kettle and got two mugs out, adding a tea bag to each and two sugars to the other, years on the job had left Jay only drinking builder's tea. I walked into the living room tea spoon still in hand and sat on the arm of the sofa and listened as the news readers read the broadcast – the whole of the East midlands has been put on red alert, everyone is advised to make their way to shelters and find safety where they can, the alert is expected to last throughout the night and predicted to be lifted around seven a.m. tomorrow. A government spokesman said that everyone must follow the drill from the monthly practice sessions. And not leave it this alert is lifted for people's safety they must stay in their shelters and not try and get to loved ones outside of their homes. We will be providing a live weather stream throughout the night tracking progress on the storm.

"Looks as if you're going to be late for work," I said, jabbing Jay in the ribs with a teaspoon.

"Owe," he said, acting the part.

"Where's this tea?" I heard the kettle click as he said it, "Coming up now, sir." I bowed as I walked out. In the kitchen, I added hot water and to both milk to Jay's, I always drank mine black unless Jay was left in charge of making it then it was builders tea all-round. Taking the biscuits, I placed them both on the tray and carried it into the living room placing it on the coffee table tea is served," I said.

"Shut up and sit down, he said."

"No thanks, I'm going to get into bed It's way past my bedtime and I don't fancy sitting here waiting to be released." I took my tea and a few biscuits and headed into the bedroom where I set an alarm for seven am, before getting into the bed.

Chapter Twelve
Lost Family – *Sue*

I was woken up by Declan poking my shoulder. I'm never any good in the morning, and it took me a few minutes to realise what was happening.

"Mummy, can I have a glass of water?"

I glanced over with one eye open at the travel clock we kept in the shelter, it read six am, one hour till the alarm was due. Somehow, they always managed to beat the alarm. Of course, I yawned while reluctantly pushing aside the bed sheets and getting out of bed. You stay here, and I will go get it. Getting out of bed was one thing, but walking out of the room still not fully aware of my surroundings was another, and I managed to walk into the door frame on my way out getting a laugh as I did.

Still rubbing my eyes, I made my way into the kitchen and started searching the cupboard for cups it had been a while since we had used the shelter and, in my daze, I was struggling to adapt. Finding a mug, not a cup, I filled it with water and turned back to take it back to the bedroom.

When I got there, I found he had roused Jay, and they were both sitting up in bed having a morning cuddle. "No coffee," Jay said with a smile as I handed the water to Declan. Just making it now, I lied, half turning to head back to the kitchen.

"No, you're not the laughed, you get back into bed. I will make the coffee." Chucking the sheets to one side, he bounced out of bed, kissed me on the cheek and headed for the kitchen.

Working in construction he had become something of a morning person while I still suffered with them.

I got back into my side of the bed and struggled to wake up. Declan, having finished his water, cuddled up close and handed me the mug. I was falling back, sleep when he woke me up again. "Mummy, how long do we have to stay down here?"

"Don't know, darling, until they say otherwise; I shouldn't imagine it will be too long now."

"Will I still have to go to school after?"

"I don't know it depends on what time they lift the alert and if the schools are open."

"So, I can have the day off?" he said, excitedly.

"I'm not sure, possibly."

He jumped off the bed and ran to the door. "I'm going to tell Tyler." Jay was walking through the door with the coffee in each hand. He saw him just in time and moved out of the way allowing him to pass. "What's all that about?"

He's excited that he might have the day off school because of the storm.

"Oh, to be young again," he said, laughing.

He handed me the coffee, no milk, just how you like it. He took the coffee from him nearly burning my fingers as I did. "I don't know how you drink it like that," I said. Jay always had his coffee with more milk than water and sugar and two spoons of coffee. "Far too rich and far to sweat."

"The way it's supposed to be."

I had just started placing my head on Jay's chest when Declan's head reappeared from behind the door frame. Mummy, one more thing, we both looked over.

"Yes, Declan, what is it?"

"Will this affect the ozone layer?"

We looked at each other in shock. "What makes you think that?" Jay asked. He had walked back into the room now and was sitting at the end of the bed.

"Well, yesterday you said it was damaged and if it breaks it will change the way have to live."

"Well, yes, it would."

"Does that mean we would have to stay down here forever?"

"Well, possibly," we said, all the excitement from moments ago when he thought, he would get a day off school had now been replaced by anguish and despair.

"But I don't want to change the way we live," he said, now close to tears.

I put the coffee down on the bedside table. And pulled him close, "Listen, here, do not you worry about it; it is going to be fine."

"Do you promise?"

"Yes, I promise now to go and get your brother up, and I will make us some Pop-Tarts for breakfast." This put him in a better mood, and once again he bounced out of the room, yelling, "Tyler! Tyler! We're having Pop-Tarts for breakfast."

We sat there looking at each other, bewildered. "Well where did that come from? I know we spoke about it last night, but what made him think of such a thing?"

"He's a bright boy," Jay said. "He's smarter than we think."

"Well, looks like we had better get up. We are not going to get any sleep now."

Throwing the covers aside, we both got up. I put on a dressing gown that was hanging on the back of the door and tied it around me, then grabbed my coffee and walked out of the bedroom. I could see Declan straight ahead in Tyler's room, shaking him like it was Christmas day. We are having pop tarts, he was shouting. Although only eleven Tyler had become hard to awaken recently, I dreaded to think what it would be like in a few years. Stop bothering your brother, I heard Jay say from the bathroom and Tyler got up. Jay met me in the kitchen as I was getting the pop-tart boxes out of the cupboard. Why do we even have pop-tarts down here anyway? While he was searching the cupboard for bowls.

"For occasions like this, I said I must keep them happy; also, I may have hidden them down here so they didn't find them, cereal and bowls are in the bottom cupboard."

"I know that," he said, shutting the top one and opening the bottom instead.

"I am sure you did," I jibbed back, and cups are in the far right in case you did not know.

"Cutlery?"

"Third drawdown."

Having finished my coffee, I had woken up enough to remember where everything was, but I still put another pod in the machine and listened to it whirl into life. As Jay got some individual boxes of cereal out to place on the table, he had just finished as the boys walked in. "Morning," said Tyler, sheepishly walking over to give me a hug.

"Morning, sweetheart, sleep well?" All I got was a nod in the form of a response. "Good," I said, getting the orange juice out of the fridge. I handed it to him. "Could you take this to the table, please?" He walked to the table orange juice in hand and gave it to Jay. Both boys loved their dad, but Tyler was a mummy's boy at heart.

"Right, who wants chocolate and who wants strawberry?" I asked, three shouts for chocolate, always the same answer every time one day they would say strawberry, then I would have a problem as we didn't have any.

I dropped the first pack in the toaster and retrieved my coffee from the machine. It was only a two-slice toaster, so it would take some time to get them all done behind me. I heard the rustling of cereal packets followed by the splashing of milk. I stood there cradling my coffee, and once again my mind suddenly drifted to thoughts of Beth and Josh, *What would they be doing right now in their little shelter, just the two of them?*

I was snapped out of it by the sound of the toaster popping up. Followed by the arguing over who got the first batch, Tyler thought he should because he was the oldest and Declan because he was the youngest. Always the same, and I always had the answer you get one each, I said, "Like always, and they second when they were ready." Handing one plate to each and putting the next two in the toaster; we finally got an end to the argument. Jay came up to the side of go sit down, he said, "I will finish these." He had already eaten his cereal, and now he would take over the cooking. It was a system that worked well. I sat down at the table and poured myself some cereal. It didn't take them long before they had eaten, and I demanded to know how long till the others were ready. "Here they are," Jay said taking back the plates and handing them back with a new one each.

By the time he had cooked the last pack and sat back down not only had the boys eaten theirs but gotten restless with no prospect of more food to keep them there. "Can we go now?" Tyler asked.

"Yes, you may leave the table," I said. Go get changed and make your beds. "I will be checking later," I said as they ran out the door.

I looked at Jay the second coffee only just kicking in.

"We are awake yet," I replied, by giving him a jibe in his

ribs he soon backed down. "Okay, okay," he said calm down cranky. We picked at what was left of the breakfast in silence listening to the boys in the other room fighting over some toy. "Who's turn," I asked Jay.

"Neither let them work it out for themselves," he said. "If they don't stop in a few minutes, I will go in."

"Any news ?"

"Not checked yet."

I stood up and started collecting the breakfast pots off the table it was covered in crumbs and half-eaten cereal. "What mess you boys make?" I said.

Jay took that as his cue to leave. "I will go and make our bed," he said, setting an example for the boys.

"Brown nose," I shouted back after him.

I cleared what was left of the pots and wiped the side down. Before heading for the living room checking the boy's rooms as I did.

I was surprised to see the beds had been made the same as ours, I wonder what Jay bribed them with. As I entered the living room I could tell. They were both sitting on the sofa watching the kids' channel. Jay was at the computer looking at the news for updates. "You shouldn't bribe them, you know," I said, trying not to show my amusement.

"Do not know what you are talking about," he replied. "Well, it looks like we're going to be here all day according to this not lifting the alert till late this evening, and the storms are set to get worse."

"No school today, boys," he shouted over to the boys. "Cheers came from the sofa. Well, you just made two ppl very happy," I said.

As the phone went off. "That will be Mum," I said. I am

surprised we have not heard sooner. I picked up my phone and saw the message from Mum, "Call us."

"Pass me the shelter phone," I said, taking it with me to the bedroom. I went into the phone book and selected Mum and dialled it rang but no answer hanging up, I tried again maybe she was on the phone to Rob. Someone else, I was surprised hadn't called yet.

I walked back into the living room and went over to Jay. Any luck, he asked no response. Maybe they could be on the phone with Rob. Could be he agreed you saw this, he said showing the latest article on the storm. Severe damage across the East midlands with trees telegraph poles and cell towers being blown over. "I think, I will try them again," I said, just in case.

I walked back to the bedroom, where I had left the phone and dialled again but once again got nothing. I had this horrible feeling come over and settle in the pit of my stomach. Something wasn't right, I picked the phone up about to call Rob when the screen lit up, *Talk of the devil,* I thought.

"Hey, Rob, I was just about to call you. Is everything okay?"

"Yes, I'm fine. Listen have you heard from Mum or Dad?"

"No," I said, "that's why I was about to ring you. I had a message to ring but couldn't get through on the phone. Thought maybe you were on the phone."

"No such luck." I was hoping the same about you; I can't even get through on Skytel and no mobile signal in these things. "I have the same problem here," I said. Skytel would have been my next option, but like usual, Rob had beat me to it.

"What are they playing at?" he said. "I have messaged them back, but nothing yet. He went quiet for a few seconds before coming back on the line. They sent the message at eight-fifteen, I received it at eight-thirty; it gives them fifteen minutes from sending the message to when we received at eight-forty-five, so it's been half an hour."

I picked up my phone and checked my signal; one bar I fired off a text to Adam, Mum and Dad. I've just texted them; if it's anything like this, it could take up to fifteen minutes to get through and probably another fifteen for the reply. Maybe I should go out of the shelter and message them to try and speed things up. No, it won't make any difference; the news is reporting the damage and the phone towers are down, so is a satellite, you wouldn't get a better signal than you already have. "Good point, we will have to wait. I'm going to try again to call you in twenty minutes, sooner if you hear anything."

"Will do," I said before ringing off.

I sat in the room, not knowing what to do. I tried ringing again but got no answer. Eventually, I went to the living room, where Jay had joined the kids on the sofa. He was in the middle his arm around them both, "Any joy?"

"Not exactly," I spoke to rob; he can't get through either. We promised to ring back in twenty minutes and give each other an update.

"I'm sure they're fine," he said. "And if Rob is involved, you can guarantee he will find out what's going on."

We sat huddled together on the sofa; I kept an eye on the clock. Constantly checked the phone to make sure it hadn't died on me. Fifteen minutes had passed and nothing from Rob or anyone. "What was taking so long? Why hadn't they replied?" It reached twenty minutes and I grabbed the phone once again and excused myself. Leaving the room, I gave one more try before I called Rob but there was still no answer.

I dialled Rob's number. It rang twice before he came on the line.

"Hey, any news?"

"No, sorry, you?"

"Nope, you don't happen to have the shelter number, do you?"

"No, you have them all."

"Did is a better way of describing it," he said. I heard the phone switch from handset to handsfree he sounded flustered which wasn't normal; he was never panicked with being a chef came the ability to handle pressure and think fast.

"Well, what happened to them?"

"I don't know, I've not seen them since I moved; everything went into boxes and into this room; they must be here somewhere. I could hear things falling and hitting the ground as he searched frantically, I had never heard him so flustered it came as a shock."

"Have you tried the bookcase?"

"Yes, the cupboard?"

"Yes! the desk."

"YES!"

I could hear it in his voice. With every yes came the sound of annoyance. Well, where else could it be? He was in the kitchen now and could hear the sound of plates, crockery falling, pots and pans banged together as they were moved. Eventually, it stopped, and all I could hear was silence. I matched it not knowing what to say the number of times; I ridiculed him for keeping such codes, deeming them unnecessary despite the number of times. He had told me, I should have them two, I would never hear of this now.

Finally, I heard him shout, "THE SAFE!"

I had held my breath afraid to breathe praying they were there.

I've got them they were in the safe. We sat in silence as he entered the code and password. Waiting for the page to load it seemed to take forever although it must have been seconds. Then I heard the sound of the welcome tune from the page what's it say, I asked in desperation no answer, "Rob, what's it say!" He cleared his throat before answering this wasn't going to be good, I could tell it, said the shelter was not in use.

I could hear it in his voice the sound of all hope gone. After that, we went through a few of the shelter settings and features checking their status, but nothing was wrong no reason for the shelter to be opened that we knew of, all we knew was what the entry log said they had used it. But they also had manually opened it at 8.14 but what it didn't tell us was why. Jay came in just as we were ending the call promising to let the other know if they heard anything. But we both agreed we could only sit and wait now.

Jay walked into the bedroom and saw me sitting on the bed bewildered and numb trying to take it all in; I was in shock. "What's happened? He asked.

"They're not there," I said. The shelter was opened and none's there we don't know why or where they are.

He put his arm around me and said, "I don't want to worry you any more, but a tornado is expected to touch down in North Wales. That was the last straw I burst into tears; I was never going to see them again."

Chapter Thirteen
The Call – *Scott*

I awoke from a restless night; I had never liked shelters and could never get over being locked in them, no matter what I did. Something about being locked in somewhere just filled me with dread. I even had this one built last year to make it feel less of an ordeal, but it hadn't worked.

It looked like any other outdoor shelter, but I had it expanded. And it now ran under the house. It featured everything: four bedrooms, a large kitchen, a separate dining room, bathroom with bath and shower, a living room, even a cinema/games room to keep the kids entertained. But even after all the improvements, I still couldn't get used to the fact that the door was shut with me inside it.

It had just gone eight and I could already hear June in the kitchen, I doubted the lads would be up, yet Jacob fourteen and Jake sixteen both fit and strong from helping me with the farm but also full of adolescence and attitude. I lay there looking at the ceiling, the alert was due to be lifted in the early hours as the storm passed over. Why was it still active sitting up? I retrieved the remote from the bedside table and loaded the news channel. A red alert was expected till late afternoon or mid-evening.

A day stuck underground, June walked in with a cup of coffee and a bacon sandwich. "You're awake," she said. "Sleep well?"

"Not really, you know, I hate these things."

"I don't get why you should feel more secure down here." Taking the bacon sandwich and coffee from her, I replied, "It is not a matter of security, it is about being underground. I am telling you now when I am gone, I am not to be buried."

She laughed, giving me a kiss on the cheek before shouting, "JAKE! JACOB! Get up; I'm not telling you again if you're not up in the next five minutes; I'm getting the water." Now it was my turn to laugh; it wouldn't be the first she had poured a cup of water over them when they refused to get up.

"Why came the calls of complaint? It is not like we have anything to do," said Jacob.

"Or anywhere to go," Jake chimed in, "they're a team now," I said with a smile.

"Well, they can't work together without killing each other, and now they're a team. It won't last."

"I don't care; now get up before I give your breakfast to the dog," June replied to Jacob Rex, our red cross border collie. "Supposed to be man's best friend, well, this one wall all about the women. I originally got him with the intention of a working dog, but soon discovered the only thing he worked at was sitting around the house with June, and it wouldn't be the first or last time he had devoured the kid's breakfast either."

"Why do we have to get up and get it when Dad gets in bed?" they complained.

"Because I said so. We had long since given up making excuses."

They walked off into the kitchen grumbling as they went, "You coming?"

"With the mood, the two are in no thanks; I think I will stay here."

I was halfway through the news when I heard Jacob shouting

my name. "What's the password for the computer, Dad?"

"Shelter!" I shouted back.

"What a stupid password," said Jake as he walked past the room.

"I kept it simple for a reason," I replied. Why did it even need a password? It was only the shelter computer. I finished watching the news before heading to the kitchen with my plate and cup. "As I walked in, I saw Rex in his bed happy and content any more coffee," I asked, pointing to the coffee machine in the corner; it was spewing and gurgling as it filtered the coffee. "I thought, we could use a pot," June said. "After all we're going to be down here all day."

"I helped clean the kitchen before heading to the bathroom, anyone needed the toilet before I have a bath?" I asked and waited for a response, only June replied with a definite no.

"Does anyone need the toilet before? I go to have a bath!" I repeated louder this time, so there was no way they could of not have heard it. Two grumbles came from the living room that only just made sense, making what sounded like the word "no" from both.

I grabbed some clean clothes out of the bedroom; we had brought them down with us last night. I didn't like keeping many down here, just the bare minimum, as I intended to spend as little time down here as possible.

I entered the bathroom and started to fill up the bath. I was usually a shower kind of guy, quick and simple in and out, but baths were supposed to be soothing, and it would do me good under the circumstances. As soon as my body hit the water, I felt some tension leave my body, it wasn't long till. It came back, though, when the sound of arguing came from living room, probably over the computer. June could sort it; she always did. I had learnt even from them being young, they would never argue with their mother, saving all the ammunition for me.

Sitting back in the water again, I must have drifted off in the bath because the next thing I knew was the sound of someone knocking on the door. "You okay in there?" June's voice said. "You've been a while."

"Yes," I lied, "just finishing up."

The water was lukewarm now, so I grabbed the soap and did a quick wash before pulling the plug and getting out. Grabbing a town of the racking, I quickly dried myself off before chucking on my clothes. Having hung the towel back up, I unlocked the door and entered the hallway; June was walking up with two cups of coffee in her hand. "Have a good sleep in there," she asked, handing me a coffee cup.

"How did you know?" I asked, shocked.

"I know because you forgot to do your hair," she said, ruffling it up for good measure.

"And you were snoring came two voices from the living room."

Having been caught out, I took June's hand and walked into the living area, where the dog had now taken pride of place on the sofa. Jacob was on the computer, and Jake was on the game console, the news report at the side forecasting a tornado in the next fifteen minutes. Both boys were complaining, Jacob that it wasn't a proper gaming computer and the internet wasn't fast enough. Jake said that the game console was old and had no up-to-date games.

Pushing the dog off the sofa, I sat down just as the phone went off. Who's that? no one had this number and the only people who would want to contact us were already in the shelter? I took the phone out of the cradle and answered it. "Hello?" I said, cautiously.

"Hey, Scott, it's Rob Wolf."

"This is a pleasant surprise, how are you?"

"I'm good; I hope you all are. I could hear it in his voice, trying to keep calm but not hiding the sound of desperation." Clearly wanting to get the pleasantries out the way and to the point of his call.

"We're fine, thanks. What do I owe the pleasure of the call, I hope everything's okay. I take it's not just a courtesy call."

"Unfortunately, not," he replied. I had a message from my parents asking me to call them; when I did, I couldn't get through, I've accessed the shelter records online, and it says the shelter is unused. I no its a long shot, but I wondered if you had seen or heard anything.

"Unfortunately, not," I replied. But I can check the cameras.

Getting up, I walked over to the computer. Rex took his place instantly. "Hey, you off there for a minute; I need to use the computer."

"But, Dad, I am halfway through this game."

"I don't care."

"Come on, Jacob, let your dad use it; you can have it back after she knew something was up, and it must be important if I was going to use a computer. I put the phone down while I loaded the camera feed from the cameras around the house, I could see the mess the storm was making outside but did not get a clear view of the wolf's house. Nothing came up as abnormal apart from the debris from the storm."

"I can't see anything. It's too dark."

"Okay, thanks; anyway, not a problem." I could hear it in his voice how disheartened the news made him.

"I hope they're all right," I said. It wasn't like Rob; I had met him a few times now, and he was a very responsible and well-put-together person. I knew he was at the centre of the family, the apple of his mother's eye, and the one Peter was the proudest of, not that this devalued their love for Sue or Adam.

"I'm sure; I'm worried about nothing."

"Well, I've got the rover I use for monitoring the backfield. I will send it over there, if it can make it see if I can see anything."

"If you could, that would be brilliant. The news adds some form of hope to his despair."

"Okay, I will get on it now. I will ring you back once I know anything. What's your number?" Getting some paper and a pen, I wrote it down, and said our goodbyes.

Chapter Fourteen
The Rescue Party – *Scott*

I put the phone down as June came up behind me. "What's wrong?"

"That was Rob Wolf."

"Peter and Ann's son? What did he want?"

"He had a message asking him to call them, but he can't get through, so he's accessed the shelter records."

"How the hell did he do that?" she asked. I thought, *Only S.H.E.L.T had them.*

"Well, he's done it." And it says, "The shelters are not active."

"You mean there, not in there," she said, sounding alarmed.

"Exactly, I have looked at the camera from the house but can't see anything."

"Can I have the computer back now?"

"No, you can't go and get changed, June snapped at both of you."

They both stood and walked out of the room, "You can make your beds while you're in there," she shouted after them.

"Calm down; it's not their fault."

"I know," she said. But was time they got changed anyway? Now what is this about the rover? Clearly She had listened to as much as she could. I'm going to try and send it over to Peters to see if we can see what's going on.

"Well, get on with it," she said.

"Yes, nurse," I said, turning around to the computer. She worked as head nurse at the local hospital, and at times like this, I could see why everyone, including the patients, was scared of her.

I had to end Jacobs's game, which he wouldn't be happy about, but he would live. I loaded the webpage that gave me control of the rover I logged in. Waited for it to load, and once loaded, it had three options. Scarecrow mode, in which it stayed in one place and released ultrasound frequency over the field inaudible to a human ear but clear to various pests. The second was perimeter roaming where it would roam the field protecting it and scanning for threats. The last was manual override, which gave me full control over its movement. Visually and soundly the computer worked as a wireless control. It took a few seconds for it to connect and change the rover to manual. I sat there, hoping the storm wouldn't affect any signal.

The screen went green as the signal confirmed, and the screen changed to show the controls, with a window in the middle showing you a visual of what it was looking at. Right now, it showed the field that was destroyed; all the perimeter fencing had blown down.

"How is this thing still standing?" exclaimed June.

"Told you this would come in handy," I said. She had long since given up asking why I had bought it; we had a normal scarecrow for years and did daily inspections of the field come rain or shine. Well, now in bad weather, I could avoid it and get the rover to do it for me.

"How is this thing still standing?" June repeated.

"I added weights last winter to stop it blowing over; obviously, it's worked," I proudly remarked. I started by turning the rover around so it was facing the right way before moving it forward. The progress was slow as it battled the wind and rode over fence, roof tiles and whatever else was around. The boys walked back now, having changed. "We made the beds as well," Jake said before they could be accused of disobeying an order.

They walked over to the computer. "What are you doing?" Jake asked. "Is that the rover?" They had been interested in the rover since I had bought always wanting to play with it I, but I had always refused this was the first time they had seen it in action from this end.

"Wow," said Jacob. "That's so cool."

"Not now," June said.

"Your dad is busy."

"What is he doing?" they asked. "I'm checking on the neighbours."

"Isn't that an invasion of privacy?" Jacob asked in a teenage know-it-all voice.

"Either be quiet or go elsewhere," June barked.

After that, I worked in silence with three faces watching from behind. I took the rover out the field and down the side of the house, I could see the roof was damaged, but the building still looked sturdy enough. Turning right, I drove it across the garden. Squashing what was June's flower bed not that I caused more damage than the storm had. Coming to the end of our garden, we passed onto the wolf's where a picket fence with a gate had once stood to mark the boundaries. In the distance, I could see the shelter door with what looked like the big apple tree pressed against it sure enough the door was open the storm was making the visual hard so it wasn't until I got closer that I could see three figures all on their knees digging at the tree. In the background, I could see the house the roof completely caved in or blown off either if not both. I pressed on the rover was a few yards away when I activated the microphone. Turning the volume up full, I shouted into the computer, "Peter, Peter!"

I saw Adam turn around first the look on his face told me he couldn't hear me, moving the rover closer, I asked, "What do you think you're doing?"

"Having a picnic," Peter replied. "Really, I thought jokes at a time like this."

"We had an issue," Adam said. "We're trying to get back in the shelter but the trees blocking the door, talk about stating the obvious."

"Why are you even out of it in the first place?"

"Well," started Peter before Adam cut him off.

"It's a long story, I will explain another time turning back to get the shovel."

"I admired his bravery and quick thinking, but I could see from the camera the state of the shelter and from the looks at the clouds behind the tornado was less than a minute away even if they could get in, they didn't stand a chance. You haven't got time for that," I said, telling them about the tornado. "Get to my shelter if you can," I said but hurry. They dropped the tools and started running. "I could tell from the way." Adam stood and moved that he was hurt and in pain.

I moved the rover to the base of the tree and squeezed it into the corner as tight as I could. Hopefully it would be safe there if not, it was no more danger than before.

I switched the screen to the house cameras so we could see them as they approached. Leaving the computer with June I hurried to the door and unlocked it ready to be opened. "What did they think they were doing?" I said. "Have they gone mad in weather like this?" A red alert they decided to go for a walk.

"We don't know that," said June. "That's just you assuming that's what they did. Well, I tell you one person who won't be happy to hear about this. Just wait till rob find out.

Chapter Fifteen
A Family Crisis – *Scott*

We stood in silence waiting for a sign of them. "Come on, where were they, what was taking so long?"

"The tornadoes down," said June. "I can see it."

"What about them? Can you see them?"

"Not yet," she said, flipping through the screens.

"Just there," said Jake in the background.

"That's only two," said June.

"Just as the third appeared from behind looks like he is struggling," said Jake.

"That will be Adam, he didn't look too steady."

"They are nearly here," said June.

"They better have a good excuse for this," she said, joining me at the door.

Opening the door, the change of atmosphere hit me full force in the face the sound of the wind battering the side of the shelter the sound of thunder causing the ground to shake around us lightning light the sky illuminating every inch of the ground. I could see the tornado behind them gaining ground; I could feel the pressure from the wind and hear it as it whistled past the open door threatening to pull it off its hinges.

"HURRY UP! Quickly get in here." Peter was now forcing Ann on ahead, Adam falling behind clearly struggling, June, Jacob and Josh were behind me all of us watching the whole scene with amazement and fear. Ann and Peter were approaching, now only a few inches away grabbing Ann as she came closer. I pulled her in and saw Peter go to turn around as if to head back. "Don't be daft GET IN HERE!" I YELLED.

"I can't just leave him," said Peter.

"GET IN! NOW," I insisted.

Just then we watched Adam fall as some flying roof tile hit him on the head from the crosswind. "ADAM!" yelled Ann, starting to run back out, June holding her back.

Peter had turned back and heading straight for Adam, suddenly Jake and Jacob came running out from behind us, followed closely by Rex barking at the storm. "STOP!" This time was June's turn to try to get out. I used myself as a barricade, trying to stop anyone else from leaving. Peter had reached Adam and was trying to pull him towards the shelter. Jake and Jacob were battling against the wind, getting there as fast as they could, flying debris skimming past their heads. June stood at the behind me, panic-stricken watching them as they went, Rex running after them. They were only a few yards away, but as I watched the scene, it appeared to be in slow motion, everything going slow but the tornado. Risking the lives of four people I held dear to me and our beloved family dog.

We watched helplessly hearts beating in our chests as they reached him, Jake and Jacob grabbing one of his arms each and dragging him towards the shelter Peter following behind, Rex among them as if guiding them to safety, four years we had him and this was the first time he showed any sign of being a sheepdog. As Adam wasn't moving, or trying to fight we could only assume he had been rendered unconscious. We stepped back as they approached the shelter, and watched as the tornado sucked up what was remaining of the Wolf house. "QUICKLY!" SHOUTED June as they approached the door and dragged him in leaving him just past the door shortly followed by Peter, June and Ann ran straight to Adam, "REX! Here, boy, COME ON!" he came bounding over and into the shelter just as me and peter forced the door shut and sealed it tight cutting off all sound and leaving the storm behind. We turned around just in time to see Adams's eyes shut.

"Is he all right?" we asked, leaning against the door. Exhausted Jake and Jacob hovered behind Adam, looking as worried as the rest of us as June was feeling for a pulse now in full work mode. We all stood, holding our breath, as we waited for her verdict.

"He's fine; he's just passed out," she said as she stood up. "Scott, go and get me my first aid bag." As I ran into the kitchen to get her bag, I could hear her having a go at the boys, and as for you two.

"What did you think you were doing going out there like that? What came over you? Don't you ever, ever do that again?"

You hear me, hitting them with every word, them walking backwards to avoid the latest blow. I entered the hallway just as they hugged. "Sorry, Mum, but he needed help; we couldn't leave him out there," said Jake.

"I don't know how to thank you," Ann said. "You saved his life, I'm forever grateful."

"Me too," said Peter, who was now kneeling near Adam.

"I have your bag," I said, handing it over.

After one last squeeze of the boys, she went back into work mode. Being a nurse, the first aid bag had a full-size doctor kit inside, she opened it and joined Peter and Ann on the floor. "Is there anything I can do," I asked.

"Yes, get some hot water from the kitchen, Jake go get me some towels and Jacob strip the covers off the spare bed."

We all dispersed as fast as we could to get on with the tasks given. Jacob was the first to appear, having thrown the covers off the bed, leaving them in a pile on the floor. "Okay, we need to try and lift him carefully," said June. "We do not know what injuries he has or how serious and probably won't until we get him to a hospital."

Jake returned with the towels, placing a large beach-style towel on the floor. They carefully lifted him onto the towel and Peter and June took one shoulder each, Jake and Jacob lifted from the feet. After they all grabbed a corner of the towel, carefully lifting Adam using the towel as a stretcher. They carried him down the steps and into the bedroom and placing him carefully on the bed, I was right behind them with the hot water. "I didn't think you should move people," I said, putting the bowl of water on the bedside table. Well, they dragged him into the shelter; any damage would already have been caused, so it wouldn't make much difference.

We all stood there as June opened her bag and started rummaging, grabbing instruments, swabs, medications and dressings. Feeling his pulse again, she then lifted one eyelid she shone the light from her ophthalmoscope without saying much. She grabbed her blood pressure monitor she pulled the cuff on his arm before tightening it. We heard the hum of the machine and could see the cuff tighten before the hiss of air being realised and the cuff loosening. The whole time, she was looking at the clock while feeling his pulse. "Is everything all right?" Ann asked.

"Yes," she said, just checking his vitals; they seem stable. After writing them down along with various other information. She turned on the lamp and put it on its side, so the light at the top pointed towards the head wound. She then stood for a minute, examining.

After she lifted his top, she examined his chest and worked her way down before she examined every joint and muscle for injuries. "He's pretty cut up from the storm," she said, but nothing too bad. "It's the laceration on the side of his head that worries me most," she said. "He seems to have pre-existing injury to his right ankle," she said, looking up at Ann.

"Yes." He tripped in the house we tried to strap it up as best we could. She was nearly close to tears now with worry you did the right thing, said June.

Turning to the boys, she said, "Why don't you go take Ann and Peter and make them both a cup of tea? Get yourselves cleaned up as well." She said, "I will see to Adam the best I can, then come see to you both." Although still standing and feeling fine, they had taken and beaten from the storm and suffered some cuts and bruises that were already beginning to show, not to mention shock. Reluctantly, the boys walked past Peter, followed reluctantly by Ann, who didn't want to leave his side, but Peter persuaded her insuring her, he was in good hands. As they left shutting the door behind them, it left just me and June in the room.

"They got themselves into a right mess," she said, going back to the head wound.

"Looks deep." Blood was dripping onto the towel underneath; something white was visible inside.

"Looks worse than it is. I think she grabbed some antibiotic fluid and mixed it in the water. He will need it scanned at a hospital after this to make sure there is no internal damage, though."

"And if there is?" I asked, sounding worried.

"Then we must hope it is not serious and nothing happens

before we can get him there."

Using cotton buds and swabs, she carefully cleaned the wound, removing bits of sand, debris and soil that had embedded itself, pulling the light closer, she made one final check before attaching some butterfly stitches. I had to admit the wound looked better just being cleaned, and with the stitches now holding it together, she placed a pad over it before she secured it with a bandage wrapped around his forehead. We heard a knock at the door, it was Jake. "I brought you both a cup of tea as well," he said, bringing both into the room.

"Thank you," I said. "It must have been the first time he had ever brought me a hot drink without a prompt, with the exception of Father's Day, when he used to try and surprise me with breakfast in bed, although it had been years since they had outgrown it, and he had never succeeded having made to much noise or setting the fire alarm off."

Getting ready to leave again, he stopped, "Mum, he is going to be all right, isn't he?" Adam had become something of a big brother to Jake, recently helping him with his homework on several occasions, especially mathematics, which Jake had trouble with and Adam excelled. They had even been known to go to a movie now and again. There were not many people around North Wales of his age apart from school, and most lived in different villages. Although Adam was five years older and entering his early twenties, he had taken a shine to him.

Looking over to him, she replied, "I can't say, dear, his wounds look superficial, but until I get him to a hospital with a proper doctor, I can't say for sure." Jake looked worried but not a word to Ann or Peter. "Let me talk to them when I'm done okay?"

"Yes, Mum," he said, and he started to walk out the door

before turning to us both again.

"Mum, Dad, I love you." With that, we walked out and shut the door.

I could see June on the edge of tears. "This really shocked him," I said.

"Well, it's the first time they have experienced anything like it," she said, their first insight into the hidden dangers of the world. I sipped my tea while June carried on working, cleaning a few other wounds, only one of which needed stitching. Then she moved onto his ankle; she had already taken off his boot in her initial examination, but what looked like a scarf was still tied around it. She cut the scarf and sock off with scissors; it was heavily swollen, and red. His ankle and foot seemed to have meshed into one. Carefully feeling about it, she then started to slowly move it around. "I don't think it was broken," she said. "But I would say he's snapped his tendon, it will need x-raying and most likely plastering for six to eight weeks, maybe even surgery." She positioned the foot and inserted some wooden splints to keep it straight before bandaging.

She then checked his eyes, pulse and blood pressure again before jotting them down. "We're done here for now," she said.

Getting ready to leave and collect all her equipment, she picked up the bowl of water, now red with bits of cotton wool floating in it, and headed to the door. "I will come back in five minutes to check him again; should we be worried that he's not regained consciousness?" I asked.

"Yes and no," came the reply. "It's common with people who have experienced trauma," she said, "on the other hand, it could be a sign of an underlined issue."

Chapter Sixteen
An Explanation – *Scott*

I picked up both cups of tea and followed her out of the room and into the hallway. "We could see Ann and the lads in the living area. Ann had the blanket from the cupboard over her, she was shivering shock," said June. Completely unfazed, while entering the kitchen, I could hear Peter in the bathroom and the water running in the sink. June poured what was left of the water down the drain, washing it out.

She then refilled it with fresh water, digging in her bag for more antibiotic fluid. I handed her the tea. "Here, have this first," I said, "they can wait a bit."

"Thank you," she said, putting the water to one side.

"You know," I continued, "you truly are a remarkable woman. I know I've joked all these years, but I've never seen you in your medical capacity fully before now, and I don't know how you do it."

"Thank you," she said with a smile on her face.

"It's nice to be appreciated, does this mean that's an end to all these nurse jokes?"

you wish?" I replied.

Sighing, she asked. "How did they even get into this mess, and why didn't they just stay in the shelter."

"Probably good they didn't," I said, putting my empty mug down on the counter from the looks of it on the camera. "It wouldn't have survived the tornado."

Well, one thing is for sure, they are telling us what happened, and now she downed what was left of her tea, grabbed her bag, and walked out of the room, bellowing at me to bring the water with me, I followed as she made her way to the living area. Peter was walking out of the bathroom after having had a quick wash. "Is he all right?" he asked as he saw us.

"As best as can be hoped," she said. "He's still unconscious, and I think he may have caused some serious damage to his ankle, I would say a bad sprain and a snapped tendon. He has a bad laceration on his head, but I've temporarily stitched it for now and bandaged it. I will check on him every five minutes to make sure he stays stable." As she was saying all this, she was looking at a cut just above Peter's eye. "This looks like it might need some stitches any other cuts," she asked.

"No," he said. "Please don't fuss, it's Adam that needs you. Well, there's not much more I can do for him, but wait now, so go in there, sit down, and let me sort that cut." This was said in way of order, with no hint of it being a question. We headed to the living room. Peter in front, so he couldn't get away.

"walking behind. I could feel her glare without having to see it.

Go get some fresh water we can't use that,

Yes nurse.

Watch it, mister, or I will stitch something else shut.

Ann and the lads were sitting on the sofa. June having Grabbed the chair from the computer, and instructed peter to sit in it. Both the lads were trying to comfort Ann, who was a shivering mess. She saw June enter and started to stand. "Stay where you are," June said with so much authority. "You wouldn't dare do otherwise." Jake moved off the sofa, leaving space for June as she approached. Sitting by her side, she relayed what she had said to Peter in the hall.

"Will he be all right?" she asked. "Well, I cannot say hundred per cent. We do need to get him to a hospital where he can have some scans, but unless he deteriorates, everything looks like he should make a full recovery."

"Thank you," she said.

"I can't thank either of you enough; that's what friends are for," said June. "Now you're suffering from shock, so go and have a wash. Scott will go and keep an eye on you, and one of the boys will go make another cup of tea with plenty of sugar."

"I will," they echoed before both running out towards the kitchen, arguing over who made it.

"Back to normal," I said, leading Ann to the bathroom.

"Right then, Peter, let us get you sorted, shall we?"

I led Ann to the bathroom and started running the taps on the sink, pulling the laundry hamper over. I placed it in front of the sink here sat on this. "Are you hurt anywhere?" I asked as I waited for the sink to fill.

"No, I'm fine; it's just well, and I can't believe that."

She was sobbing as she spoke, turning down the sink, I kneeled beside her and listened. "He is a strong lad; he will pull through; he has Wolf blood in him." She gave a slight laugh.

Right," I said, standing to turn off the tap. "Let us get you cleaned up, shall we?"

Having helped Ann scrub off the sand and dirt from the storm, I handed her the towel. The water had helped the shock, and she wasn't shaking so much. Wrapping the blankets back around her we headed back to the living room, where June was just finishing applying the stitches to Peter's cut. "You're all done now," she said, pointing to Ann. "Come on, take a seat. Let us get you checked. I am fine, honestly," she protested.

"Well, I will be the judge of that," she said, pointing to the seat.

"Peter had just vacated; better do what she says," I said, thinking twice before making another nurse joke.

The boys walked in with a pot of tea the cafeteria a plate of biscuits as well as a milk jug and sugar bowl. Well look at this said June now becoming more herself and less of a nurse. "Who would have thought you boys knew how to make tea and coffee at the same time, I'm impressed," she said.

"Me too," I replied, reaching over to grab a biscuit. One criticism I said, "You seem to have forgotten the cups." They looked at each other before running off back to the kitchen.

"Bless them," said Peter. "They really are trying their hardest it can't be easy for them."

June having finished checking both of them over, Ann had joined Peter on the sofa who took her hand in his and kissed it. "Well, I'm going to check on Adam and when I get back, I think you both have some explanation to do." They looked at each other and bowed their head in shame. The boys entered with cups and two spoons that they had realised they had also forgotten, feeling proud of themselves they served the drinks as June went to check on Adam.

A few minutes had gone by, before June returned everyone was now drinking tea or coffee and Jake passed a tea to June as she sat down. "He all right," I asked.

"No change," she said. "But no news is good news."

She looked at the boys. "Do you two want to go in the games room, while we have a chat?" she said.

They looked at each other. "You could see they both wanted to know as much as we did what had happened out there."

"It's all right," Peter said, putting his cup down. "I think after what they did, they deserve an explanation as much as the next man. They looked relieved, happy, to not be left out."

"Okay then," said June. "So, what happened?"

"It was all my fault," said Ann, almost breaking down and bursting into tears again.

"No," said Peter. "It was mine; I opened the door, but you only opened it because of me," she said.

"Yes, well either way I take the blame," he said, cuddling up close to her and giving her a hug.

"Buy why," said June.

"I had decided to let June do the questioning knowing full well she would get to the truth."

"It seems so stupid now," said Peter. "We had left the laptop charger in the house and none of the phones would work there's no signal down there and the battery had gone flat."

"You opened it for a laptop charger," June said, her mouth falling open from the shock of pure idiocy. "All because I couldn't get in contact with the kids sobbed Ann and now, I nearly killed one."

"Calm down," Peter said, "he will be fine. Anyway," Peter continued, "Adam was trying to get the phones working when I opened the door Ann must have followed me out, I wanted to get a phone signal, she interrupted. Peter tightened his grip on the hand."

"I ran to the house," said Peter and headed for the stairs half the roof had collapsed in already. "Anyway, I made it to the bedroom and went to the laptop, I had the charger still in the wall so I bent down to unplug it when the thunder sounded and the house shook. I do not know if it was the wind or the vibration but suddenly the wardrobe fell with me under it, I was trapped I could not move it due to the weight."

"You are lucky, your alive," said June. Getting angrier by every word I looked over trying to give her a signal to stay calm it was over now and couldn't be changed no point getting mad about it.

"And Adam," she said.

"Well, he came running out after me," he said. "Not that I knew it, he had followed me into the house and up the stairs."

"He went into the study," Ann said. Having recovered some composure again, he went in the study assuming that's where Peter would be, but the roof fell in on him you see I waited for a few minutes outside the shelter, but when no one came back so I went in after them I couldn't leave them in there alone. I went to the bottom of the stairs and shouted up. I could see that the roof and attic floor had gone leaving a clear view to the sky so when no one answered, I went to table in the hall I always kept some torches in there I got them and headed up myself. I found Adam in the study trying to stand but struggling. I went over and helped him up but more of the roof kept falling after a while he managed to find his feet and we agreed to split up he insisted that seeing as I wouldn't go back to the shelter, I should go and check downstairs where I would be safer and he would take the top floors.

"That is when he found me," said Peter. By this time chunks of ceiling had fallen but I was lucky, and none hit me the wardrobe took the impact in many ways it saved me. He came over and between us we tried to lift it, but it was too heavy we tried again when Adam fell in pain. "That would have been when he tore the tendons," said June. "You can't lift heavy loads with a sprained ankle without risking causing more damage."

Well after that Ann appeared, she must have come back up she came over to the two of us and we all lifted together even then it was too heavy so once we got high enough for Adam to put wood from a broken beam in the roof underneath to prop it up and rolled out from under, it just before the wood broke and crashed down.

"Oh my god," June said, turning away. I am surprised any of you even made it out of the house what were you thinking you know how much worse this could have been. What happened after that asked Jake enthralled in the story. Well, we made our way out of the house and down the stairs. Ann led the way and we followed that's when we saw the tree. It was Adams's idea to dig under it he thought seeing as the door wouldn't shut it would add some protection. "Not a bad idea," I said it makes sense. June glared over in disapproval she didn't want anyone to agree to any part of this or agree any part of it was logical to her it was sheer stupidity.

"That's when you come in," said Peter, "the rest you know."

Chapter Seventeen
A Telling-off a Deep Secret and an Awakening – *Scott*

June stood up and started pacing the room, angry now. You could have been killed, she said, "All of you, and all for the laptop charger. I do not know what you were thinking. Well, you weren't thinking were you that's clear enough to anyone. It was sheer stupidity sheer, sheer stupidity. I would say you deserve everything you got exposing yourself to such danger, but that poor lad in there has nearly been killed, and the best part is it was all for nothing."

"Where is the laptop now, hey?"

It was a rhetorical question that wasn't supposed to be answered, but Ann did. "We did get it we pushed it under the tree once we made enough space," Junes stared directly at Ann in belief. "I wanted to go back for it but Peter wouldn't let me," she carried in before bursting into tears and folded into Peter.

"For god's sake," she exclaimed. "Did you lot not learn anything," she said as she walked out the room slamming the door shut behind her.

Standing up, I walked out of the room I could see her going through the kitchen door. I followed as she was leaning against the countertop. She was crying now the sheer force of her anger and frustration finally coming out. "Come here," I said pulling her close. "I do not know what they were thinking," she said. "Do they realise what they were doing and how dangerous this was? "I'm sure they do," I said". Not only could I have lost my friend, but I could have lost my sons in the process. I can't help thinking of Katie all those years ago."

Katie was June's twin sister, she had died when they were kids, but she had never been able to tell me what had happened. What happened, June, you never told me. "I suppose you should know," she said, pulling a locket from around her neck. "I had never seen what was inside." She clutched as she spoke. "We were thirteen and the school made a trip to America funded by the government in an exchange scheme so a student from there came over here for a month and us there. Well, we got picked to go Mum and Dad thought, it would be an exciting experience and agreed to house two fellow students in exchange for us to go. We had been there two days when a storm hit there was no warning and we ran to the shelter we could see the storm behind us as we ran. I made It to the shelter in time, but Katie did not the storm lifted her up and into the vortex. I never saw her again, I will always remember seeing her face as she flew into the air how scared she looked, how desperate she was for help. I tried to run after her, but they pulled me into the shelter and slammed the door, the next day my parents arrived and took me home."

"I'm so sorry," I said, looking her in the eyes.

"Why didn't you tell me sooner," I said.

"I don't know, I've always felt it was my fault, why didn't I do more to try and help her. My heart went in my mouth earlier when the boys ran out there its why I scolded them so much the thought of what could have happened scares me to death. All I could see was Katie all over again."

We saw a movement behind us we both jolted around just in time to see Ann walking out ANN! June shouted running after her. "Catching her in the hallway. I'm so sorry," Ann said. "I came to apologise and couldn't help but overhear I had no idea you even had a sister never mind such a tragic story once this is over, I will understand if you want nothing to do with me," she said, turning around to walk away.

"Don't worry," she called back. "I won't tell anyone."

"Ann," said June her voice softened now. "I don't want to do such thing, it's true that I don't agree with what's happened you're still my best friend and Peter is Scott's only friend so don't even think about going anywhere you hear me." They both embraced in a hug. "And as for keeping it a secret I don't want it to be, I realise now all these years I've been hiding my true feelings not allowing anyone to know when all along I should have been celebrating Katie's life keeping her spirit alive through our family. Letting her live through me. All I ask is you give me time to tell the boys they don't even know; I had a sister I kept it from them all these years thinking it was the best way to avoid answering the awkward questions."

She opened the locket she had been clutching the whole time she spoke. "It was my mother's," she said. "I kept it after she died it's the last photo ever taken. It contained two photos both looked identical this is Katie," she said. We all stood there and hugged all three of us their friendship rekindled the only secret she ever kept from me in the open. Turning to me she took my hand. "Can we tell the boys together," she asked.

"Of course," I replied. "However, you want."

We re-entered the living room,. "Everything was all right?" the boys asked. It was clear June had been crying.

"I looked at June not just now," she said later.

"I have one question," Peter asked while we all resumed our places. "You know, why we were out there but what made you drive the rover over there?"

"Rob," I shouted, "I forgot to tell him." I looked at the clock it had been two hours since he called, and he was expecting an update.

"What about Rob," asked Ann.

"He called me," he said. "He could not get hold of you; apparently, you texted him, asking for him to call."

"Yes," she said, just before I left the shelter.

"Well, he tried and once he knew the shelter was open, he called asking if I had seen anything. I was at the desk now where's the pad gone with the number on," I asked.

"I put it in the draw," said Jacob. We tidied up, so it was not a mess.

"Good boys," said June. "I am immensely proud of both of you today and once this is over, I think it's about time we renewed the phone contracts for you both."

"Really you mean it," they shouted.

"Yes, I do."

"Well, how did Rob know the shelter was open," Peter asked.

"He accessed the record online don't ask me, how he must be some computer whiz," I said, finally pulling out the pad. Picking up the phone ready to dial, I could see from the only remaining camera working a blue sky coming over us. "It has been two hours," I said as I dialled, and I promised to ring back as soon as I knew anything.

Peter laughed. "Good, old Rob," he said, "I knew he would be behind this somehow."

"How did he access the records," June asked.

"He keeps a record of all our shelter numbers in case of well in case of times like these," he said. "I forgot he kept them."

I pressed call as a sound was heard from the bedroom a cry of pain. "June shot to her feet, sounds like someone's woke up," she said as she ran out the room closely followed by Ann. Just as the phone was answered.

Chapter Eighteen
A Severe Scolding – *Rob*

Having ended the call, I sat at the computer staring at the screen. I changed tabs going back to the shelter's info page hoping that it would say shelters in use, but no changes were shown. The pressure was getting to me now I could feel myself losing control I stood up and paced the room. Walking helped me think and the living room was the only space available it wasn't like I could leave the shelter and go get some fresh air.

I was looking at the clock the whole time willing the phone to ring. Anyone to ring with some news; I hated the feeling of not knowing what to do the feeling of uselessness. Going back to the desk I picked up the phone again, I should probably tell Sue what had happened since our call I hoped she had some news as well. Dialling the number, I waited while it rang it was taking them a while every ring made me nervous. Eventually, it was answered by Jay. "Thank god," I said. "What took so long?" I realised, I was holding my breath that whole time and calmed down to regain my composure. I was someone who never wanted to show weakness in situations I should be in control besides this wasn't about me it was about Mum, Dad and Adam.

"Sorry," he said. "I didn't mean to worry you, Sue, left the phone in the bedroom and we were in the living room. How are you holding up?"

"I'm fine," I lied. "How's Sue?"

"She had a bit of a breakdown after you hung up, but she's

come around a bit now, don't you worry, I'm looking after, don't worry you have enough to worry about."

"Make her some hot chocolate," I said.

"It always calmed her down as a kid," we said in unison.

"You've told me before. I liked Jay. He was a good choice for Sue, they reminded me of my mum and dad he would do anything for her, and you could see how much love they had. I had worried. When she married young, and she had recently admitted introducing Jay to me was the most worrying of all the introductions."

"Anyway," he asked. "What can we do for you? He knew I would have had a reason to call. Have you heard anything from them?"

"Sadly not, I was hoping you would have."

"No, not yet; we would have rang you straight away."

"I know, well I thought, I would give you a bit of an update on what's happened so we all know what happening."

"Want me to get Sue," he said. "Or should I pass on the message?"

Pass on the message, it is not worth upsetting her again. Anyway, I have spoken to Sam, he's ringing his parents, his dad has connections that might be able to shine some light, but more importantly I have contacted Scott Dunlop. Mum and Dad's neighbour, before you get too excited, he's not seen anything, and he's looked at his cameras around the house and can't see anything out of the ordinary. But he has a Robot he uses for field maintenance and he thinks he might be able to take it up to the house to see if he can see what's going on so I'm waiting till he gets back to me.

"Could it be a fault on the door?"

"I doubt it, it says, it was opened with the code and no errors have shown up either current or previous apart from the door being open on a red alert."

"I am sure, it will be fine," he said. "Adams there and your dad is resourceful there and more than capable of improvising some kind of protection."

"Jay!" Sue shouted from the living room.

"Sounds like you better go that's all there is for now if I hear anything else, I will ring you straight back."

"Much appreciated," said Jay, "and if anything happens this end rest assured, you're the first to know." We said our goodbyes, Jay promised to go and make that hot chocolate for her and the kids; something they had taken from their mother was her taste for chocolate.

I ended the call and went back to the storm tracker it said a tornado was now active in the area the satellite graph showed it moving right over them as we spoke, and all I could do was sit here doing nothing to help them. Standing up again, I started to pace the room it occurred to me, I was still halfway through cleaning. It would be better than nothing. I stared in the kitchen I stacked all the pans back neatly in the cupboard next to the plates and put the cutlery and tins away before turning my attention back to the living space. I started by putting the books back on the shelf and finding one I hadn't read for years. Putting it to one side to read later, if possible, I started to put everything back in the cupboard and this time made sure the book with the numbers and shelter codes in the desk draw. Having finished packing everything away I swept the room and looked at the clock. It had been one hour since I spoke to Scott, I picked up the phone again and started to dial. Then cleared the number I had bothered him once already and if had found anything he would have rung me looks like another dead end.

As I put the phone down and sat on the sofa, I heard the computer tone and looked over it was Sam again. Changing the sofa for the desk chair again, I pressed accept and waited while it made a connection. "All right," came Sam's voice, shortly followed by the camera. "Cleaned up, I see."

I had to do something; I was going mad just waiting. "Did you find anything out?"

"Yes and no," he said. "My dad made a few calls. Now we don't know where they are or what's happened, but we know where there not."

"Well, eliminating anything at this point is a bonus," I said. "Well, let's hear it; where aren't they?"

"Well." He pulled a few strings with the officials and accessed some records; he shouldn't have one of them being hospital and shelter logs and there are no records on either, so we know they're not hurt or in one of them like. I said, "It's not great news. He got in contact with my uncle, who's in the police and he's promised to either go or get it checked as soon as it's deemed safe for official personnel to be allowed out of shelters. Officials and emergency services would be the first to have to alert lifted giving them time to prepare and evaluate damage giving them the best chance of being able to help. Sorry, it's not better news mate."

"That is fine like you said it just eliminates places even though if they were in either of them, I would know they were safe or what happened."

"I know," he said, sympathetically.

"Well, thanks anyway."

"As soon as this is over, I will come over and see what I can do to help."

"Thanks, you're a good friend."

After ending the call, I walked back over to the sofa. Deciding not to ring Sue there was nothing that wouldn't cause worry all it would do was stress her more and let her have some hope. Sitting down I sat on something hard and pulled it out from under me. It was a pile of photos Mum had given us all when we first moved out and I must have missed them when cleaning up as I started Looking through them, I drifted into my own world as I looked at their faces and went on a trip down memory lane.

I was pulled out of the daze by the sound of the phone ringing it took me a few seconds to comprehend what it was. "Grabbing the phone," I answered, I heard Scott's voice sounding flustered. "Rob, it's Scott, we found them. I'm sorry," he started before I cut him off.

"Are they okay? Where are they? What happened?" I bombarded him with questions.

"There here with us," he said. "Yes and no, I'm sorry, I didn't ring earlier it's just."

"Don't worry about it," I said, "what did you mean yes and no?"

"Well, they're all here, your mum and dad are fine but Adam's not so good; June is looking after him. She feels confident that he will be fine, I will let her explain more in a bit he's just woken up so she will know more then."

"What happened?"

"I will pass you over to your dad," he said, passing the phone over.

"Hello, Rob."

"DAD!" I shouted. "Are you all right?"

"Yes, I am fine, just a cut above my eye."

"What the hell happened to Adam?"

"He's hurt his ankle and got a bad cut to his head from some flying roof tile."

"FLYING ROOF TILE!" I shouted. "Why the hell was he near flying roof tile?"

"It was the tornado."

"YOU WERE OUT IN THE TORNADO!" I was getting angrier by the second.

"Yes, well, we had to run to Scott's shelter for safety."

"You should have been in yours," I asked. "Why was it even open in the first place what was the issue?" It went quiet.

"Dad, why did you open the shelter," I demanded.

"We couldn't get a signal on the phone and the laptop charger was in the house and you know what your mums like she worries." He sounded like a naughty school kid caught skipping class.

"No, you did not," I said, "please tell me you didn't go in the house."

"It was only going to be a quick trip then Adam followed that's when he did his ankle well the first time."

"THE FIRST TIME! What do you mean the first time? I was trying to stay calm, but drastically failing."

"Well, June thinks that is when he sprained it, but it's when he tried to lift the wardrobe that he tore the tendons."

"Just stop," I said angrily, unable to hear any more. "We will go through this later, I have a feeling this is going to be a long conversation that we need to have another time now, where's Mum?"

"She's in the bedroom with June and Adam," he said. "But please don't go mad at her, she's already having trouble beating herself up over this."

"Well, so you both should be," I said. "Put Scott back on."

I heard Scott come back on the line. "Everything all right," he asked.

"No," I said. "But I will sort them out later. I don't know the whole story yet, I'm not sure, I want to but I would like to thank you for getting them and keeping them safe, I don't know how to thank you."

"Don't mention it," he said, "anything to help a friend."

"I don't mean to impose any more," I said. "But would it be possible to set up a Skytel conference using your computer, I think it will be better if Sue hears this herself."

"Not a problem," he said. "Do you want the username?" sduncan02."

"I wrote it down, I thanked him, right," I said. "I'm going to ring Sue and let her know what's happening, I will be in touch if you need anything just ring."

I ended the call and instantly dialled Sue. The phone was answered on the first ring.

"Sue, they are fine."

Chapter Nineteen
Relief All Around – *Sue*

I sat at the end of the bed Peter holding me close. "What are we going to do?" I asked. "We are never going to see them again."

"Yes, you will," he said. "They will be fine besides, I bet Rob's got some trick up his sleeve he will not let this lie. Now how about we go join the boys there's nothing we can do, but wait."

"You go," I said. "I will be along in a minute; I just need to get my head around it."

"Well, don't be long."

"Don't tell the boys," I said as Jay walked out. "They don't need to know anything, until we can tell them exactly what happened."

I sat there staring into space for a while. Jay was right they would have found some way to shelter and Rob had a way of working these things out that I would never have thought of he would think of something, I knew he would.

I stood up and went to the bathroom to wash my face, I didn't want the boys to see I had been crying it did the trick, as looked at myself in the mirror and quickly tided my hair before walking out of the room and into the living room forcing a smile on my face to keep up appearances.

"Everything all right, Mummy," Jacob asked.

"Everything's fine. I lied was just doing so tiding."

"Dad said you were having a lie down," said Jake.

"Well, I did after I turned the room. I looked over to Jay we weren't used to lying to the lads and it showed one pathetic attempt to cover up a short absence. I didn't for a second think they believed us, especially Jake, but to their credit they didn't show it or ask any other questions. So, what we were watching," I asked.

"Reruns of the Simpsons," said Jake.

"Dad said, we should see how it started."

"As we sat as a family in quiet for a while just watching TV; I couldn't help but think of all the years I had sat as a family when we were young, Mum putting out snacks and sandwiches in the form of a dinner we would choose a film and just sit together discussing the events of the week. I would give anything to do that again just one more time and if by some miracle we survived this storm completely as a family wherever it be I would do it again the whole family together. I saw Jay standing up before, I heard the phone ring looking up, he said. "I will get it you stay here." But I started to argue.

"If it was for you, I will bring it straight to you."

I sat in the room staring at the door anxiously. Jake and Jacob had gone quiet now whispering together they knew something was up they also knew not to ask what. I turned my head back and saw them staring at me, Jacob took my arm. "Don't worry, Mum, we will be out of here soon the news said the storms passing by faster than expected and to clear in the next few hours."

"When was this," I asked. "When you were having a lie-down? A news report came up."

"JAY, you okay?" I asked, hoping for him to give me a reason to leave. I was close to breaking down and losing control.

A minute later, Jay appeared. "Who fancies hot chocolate?

he said. I looked at him I could guess who put that into his head and at a time like this there was only one person who could make hot chocolate good enough to help me relax. But the main worry was why did I need one.

"Want to give me a hand," he asked.

"I don't know where you keep, the marshmallows, sure I said be back in a minute boys."

I followed Jay out of the room and into the kitchen. "So, what's he saying? And why didn't you come and get me?"

"How do you know it was Rob?"

"Come on," I said, "you making hot chocolate and only one person thinks that solves everything."

"Well, doesn't it?"

"Yes, but unless he gave the recipe. It won't do the trick half as well."

He laughed. "Well, we all know he will never give that away and I didn't come get you because it wasn't worth it."

"What do you mean?"

"Well, firstly, he was checking how you were and making sure I was looking after you."

"Hence the hot chocolate."

"Correct."

"Secondly, he's spoke to his mate Sam from work his dad has contacts that could help."

"How does he find these people? All my friends wouldn't be any use unless I wanted to get drunk." We both laughed.

"Mine are only good for car repairs and construction," Jay added. "But that's not all," he said while pouring chocolate powder in the milk and whisking. He's managed to get in contact with their neighbour Scott and although he's not heard anything, he's apparently sending a robot over to check it out.

"A what?"

A robot apparently, he uses one to monitor his field. "Pass me four mugs, please."

"So, is that it?"

"Yes," he said, passing over the mugs.

"Are you sure your brother is a chef and not a secret agent for MI5. I don't know how he gets this information and tracks these people down but it's impressive." We watched as the milk boiled and he transferred the contents evenly into the mugs.

Handing me a mug go on then, he said "Try it I sipped it."

"Well?"

"Still not got it right," I said, amusement on my face. "Well," I said, "if in half an hour Robs found out all this. I give him ten more till he knows where the king and queen are and what condition their in." He started walking out of the kitchen with the mugs on a tray. "Oh, marshmallows."

"We don't have any."

We returned to the living room and handed out the hot chocolate. "Where are the marshmallows?" the boys asked.

"There in the house." They both pulled a face of disappointment.

"It's not as good as Uncle Rob," Jake said. After taking one sip.

I laughed out loud sending hot chocolate flying out my mouth. "That's it," he said, "when I get out of here, I'm making him tell me the secret."

We spent the next hour wandering around the shelter watching the Simpsons and talking. Looking at the clock it was approaching twelve p.m. nearly five hours since they left the shelter and still no sign. "When we having lunch," asked Jake.

"When do you want it is everyone hungry now?"

"Yes," came three replies.

"It will have to be sandwiches, I'm afraid didn't bring much more down with me".

I picked up the phone as I left the room. I entered the kitchen Jay following me thought you could use a hand.

"You don't have to follow me," I said. "Just because Rob told you to look after me doesn't mean I can't be left alone."

"Fine, I will go," he said, heading to the door.

"Stop," I said. "I didn't mean I don't want you around just that you don't have to," I said, giving him a kiss. "Now what sandwiches are we doing?"

I had started looking through the fridge for fillings when the phone went; I grabbed it hitting the answer button as I did.

"Hello, Sue, they're fine." I burst into tears the relief instantly exploding out of me in one go.

Jay grabbed the phone and put it on speaker. "What's going on?"

"they're Fine," he said again. "Well, as fine as can be, considering their sheer and utter stupidity. I don't know the whole story yet but what I do know of it there lucky they're alive."

"Where are they?"

At Scott's, he must have managed to get the robot to them and led them to his shelter just in time from the sound of it.

"Are they okay?"

"Yes and no Mum and Dad are apparently fine, but Adams suffered some injuries serious too from the sound of it."

"Well, what happened," Jay asked.

"I don't know exactly like," I said. "I've only got the basic story, but they couldn't get a signal in the shelter and the laptop charger was in the house for some reason. You're not saying this is all over a laptop charger, are you?"

"Yes. It appears to be, and I'm about as happy with them as you are."

"Well, why didn't they just go back in?"

"I don't know," I said. "I stopped him before I lost it completely. Look I need to ring them back and get the full report on Adam, Junes a head nurse at the local hospital, so he is in good hands. I'm looking at setting up a conference call to sort this out between us."

"Okay, we will be waiting just give us time to explain to the boys we didn't tell them until we could explain what happened."

"Okay, I will ring you back soon. Bye."

"See told you they would be okay," he said, holding me tight as the phone cut off.

"We should go tell the boys. Before Rob rings back."

We walked back into the living room all thought of lunch gone. We entered the room Jake and Jacob were sitting on the sofa still. "Where's lunch?"

"It's coming," I lied. But first we need to talk," I said, turning the TV off. "It's about Grandma, grandad and Uncle Adam."

"What about them?"

"They appear to have got into some trouble with the storm."

"Are they okay?"

"We're not sure Grandma and Grandad are fine, but Uncle Adam has suffered some injuries."

"What type?"

"We don't know yet, Uncle Rob is getting to the bottom of it now and arranging a call. We're sorry, we didn't tell you earlier, but we didn't want to worry you."

"What happens now?"

"Well, Uncle Rob is arranging a conference call so we can

find out what happened."

"Can we be in it?"

I looked at Peter. "I don't know it depends on what your Uncle Rob thinks, I don't think it's going to be pretty he's not happy, to say the least."

"Anyway," said Jay. "I'm going to make this lunch."

Chapter Twenty
Planning – *Rob*

As I ended the call, I sat back in the chair allowing myself to breathe for the first time in what seemed like ages. At least now, I knew where they were the rest I we could work out together. I got up and made a cup of tea taking a few more minutes to prepare myself. Before I rang Scott to get the report on Adam.

First, I rang Sam I didn't want to impose on his family any more or take his uncle out of his way when he could be helping someone else, I pressed call and waited for it to connect, having now regained my composure and feeling more in control. "Hey, mate, what can I do you now do you want my famous souffle recipe?"

"No," I said, letting a smile spread across my face. "I rang to tell you, I've found my parents."

"That's great, are they all okay?"

"Well, alive, just my brother suffered badly, I'm not sure how bad he is, but luckily, they are sheltering with their next-door neighbour and she's the head nurse at the local hospital."

"The only hospital I know of is St Lenard's, and the head nurse is or was June Dunlop."

"Still is, you know her?"

"Yes," he said, now sounding excited. "She looked after my dad when he had the heart attack, I knew she lived nearby but could never find out where. I've never been able to thank her properly."

"That will make both of us, I don't know, how I will make up for anything she and Scott have done."

"Well, he couldn't be in better hands. She's the best nurse I've ever met, high praise from Sam who having had health issues himself as well as dealing with his mum and dad's illness for years he had met his share of nurses."

"Anyway, I better go and see what's happening. I've still not found out the full story. Will talk you later and thanks for helping."

"Hold on just one thing," he said as I was about to end the call. "When you go up there and don't say you won't; we both know you will be up there as soon as this alert is over. I want to come with you, I want to check on my dad and if possible, thank June in person."

"Okay," I said. "That's the least I can do after everything, but only if and only if I have time if not, I owe you a trip at a later date."

I hung up and took a deep breath before I rang Scott's number. "Hello."

"Hi, its Rob," he said before I could. "You're the only one that has the number."

"Which one do you want to speak to now?" I heard Mum in the background. "Is that, Rob? Well, I was hoping for June if she's free," I said, "but I suppose it can wait for a bit."

"Rob, are you all right?" Mum said, clearly snatching the phone off Scott.

"ME!" I said instantly, lost my cool before remembering what Dad had said about Mum beating herself up, I quickly softened my tone before carrying on. "I'm fine now, it's you lot, I'm worried, about especially Adam."

"I'm sorry, I didn't mean for any of this to happen."

"I know."

"I just wanted to make sure you and Sue were okay, it's all my fault. I could hear in her voice that she was close to tears."

"I know, I know; we will speak about that later there's nothing we can do about what's happened all, I can do is try and arrange something that can help us get out of this mess."

"Like what?"

"I don't know. All I know is, I have spent the last five hours wishing I could talk to you and now, It's not you I need to speak to its June."

"I will see if she's free." It took a few minutes, before I heard a voice come over the phone. "Hello," came a strong firm voice.

"June?"

"Yes!" She sounded annoyed at what was clearly a blatantly obvious question, before softening her voice how are you.

"You sound different over the phone," I said. "And I'm good thanks just trying to think of a way to get my family out of the stupid mess they seem to have gotten themselves into."

"Oh, trust me, I've told them my opinion, nearly cost me your mum's friendship, but they had to hear it."

"Good on you, sounds like you've done half my job for me and that includes looking after my stupid brother."

"Do not be too hard on him, none of this was his fault, he was trying to save them."

"Really?"

"I take it, you have not heard the full story?"

"Not yet, I made him stop at the highlights, had to before I killed him."

"Well, may I suggest a strong drink to hand," she advised.

"I will bear that in mind."

"I take it the reason you wanted me was to see what

condition your brother is in."

"Yes, sorry if it seems insensitive."

"Don't be daft, it's natural he will be your priority."

"So, what are we dealing with?"

"Well," she said. "He's got a badly sprained ankle with what I expect to be a snapped tendon, I've strapped it with some splints to hold it together, most worrying is the head wound, although it's not as deep as we first thought there is a clear sign of concussion. He is back asleep now I gave him morphine he woke up which is a good sign, but he was in too much pain to get any sense out of him."

"Do you think, he's in danger of deteriorating?"

"Well, he's stable, his vitals are all fine and haven't changed but that is not always how head wounds work he does need to be checked in a hospital, where he can have a scan and x-ray."

"Is there any more, we can do in the meantime while we wait for the alert to be lifted?"

"No more can be done than I've done already, but the big problem is the nearest hospital with the right equipment is Swansea, I know people there and can have them ready for his arrival but it's quite a way out and the roads will be near on impassable for a good few hours, at least."

"That leaves us with a problem, would the air ambulance be able to help?"

"That's the only other option," she said. "But it will run off its feet once the alert is lifted and for critical cases only, and I'm afraid he won't be counted as one unless his condition worsens and if it did it could be too late."

"Can you get me permission to use the Helipad at the hospital?" An idea instantly came to me.

"I could try," she said. "What you got in mind?" she asked,

sounding confused.

"Something and nothing? You will have to leave it with me. Have you told any of this to my parents?"

"No, I didn't want to worry them. They are both suffering from shock your mum especially. But I get the impression you are all facts and no-nonsense."

"I appreciate you being so direct, and please don't go into detail with Mum and Dad. I'm planning a conference call soon, we will explain it all then, thank you for everything I will make it up to you somehow. Pass on my goodbyes to everyone please and I will set up a conference call once I'm ready, and I would like you to be part of it."

"Of course, and if anything changes, I will give you a call back."

"Thank you," I said before ending the call.

I had already opened the Skytel directory and searched for Sean Hensley while on the phone to June. Sean was an old school friend I had kept contact with, when we were younger, we had both fallen in love with the idea of becoming a pilot, and both enrolled on flight courses. Ironically even though we both passed and had been granted our flying licenses neither of us had taken it up as a career, me because they had yet to build a green energy plane and had only just created the hybrid helicopter. Sean had been rejected by various travel companies until he found himself running the Leicester airfield. He also sold planes and helicopters.

I had brought a small kite from him something small a one-seater great for tricks and he had kept a matching one for himself both were stored with him. We would meet once a month and go out in the planes, it was bad for my carbon footprint but once a month didn't cause much damage.

Finding his number, he had two listed one for his home shelter and one for the airfield. Knowing he worked nights on a Tuesday. Pressing the number for the airfield shelter I sat back and waited. It rang three or four times before it was answered and the screens connected, "Rob, my man, what can I do for you?"

"I need your help."

"Anything for you, what can I do?"

"Do you still have that second hand air ambulance in the hangar?"

"You bet, I do the bloody thing is impossible to sell, I now know why it was cheap. I won't be buying one again maybe if I took the equipment, they left it out and fitted some seats, I could sell it as a big passenger."

"Is it airworthy?"

"Well, it was last week when it was tested. Why the interest?"

"Can I use it?"

"The problem there," he said, "legally it can only be flown by the owner as it's not registered as a rental."

"Well, how much do you want for it?"

"For you £2000, and I will throw in a full tank of petrol. But what are you going to do with it?"

"What about insurance?" I asked, ignoring the second question. "Do you still offer thirty days free?"

"You bet I do why the interest anyway what are you going to do with an air ambulance?"

Sensing there was no way of avoiding the question, I answered, "My brother has been injured in Wales, and he needs to be taken to Swansea, but all roads will be impossible, and the air ambulance will be too busy to be of any use we can't wait that long."

"I'm sorry to hear that, mate."

"How long will it take to get the paperwork done?"

"A few hours, if I rush," he replied, sensing the importance. "But there is no saying the weather will be suitable for travel, and you would have to sign a waiver as It won't have been tested prior to you taking ownership."

Looking at the time and the news report, just in time for the alert to be lifted, I said, "Can you have it ready for me when this is lifted."

"Sure, thing, I'm in the office now, I keep it in the shelter under the hanger so if I'm stuck down here, I can get some work done."

"You're a lifesaver. Maybe, literally."

"Where do I wire the money?"

Having got the wire info and him giving me the codes and aircraft registration I would need to register it with the helipad. "One more thing," I asked. "I will need somewhere to keep it while I'm there."

"Leave it with me."

I ended the call and opened my online banking luckily; I had been saving for some home improvements including landscaping the garden which was enough to cover the cost of the craft. Entering the info needed I watched as the money left the account and the digits disappeared off the screen and moved to Sean's account. Followed by a confirmation message that it had been received by the corresponding party.

Opening Skytel this time opting for the messaging page. I wrote a message to Sean telling him the money had been sent.

Chapter Twenty-One
A Family Conference – *Rob*

Taking June's advice I went to the kitchen where I left the gin bottle, I was halfway through pouring it when I realised, I in only a few hours could be flying a new aircraft and I would need a clear head. I poured it back into the bottle and opted for coffee instead. I cucked a pod in the coffee machine today wasn't going to get any easier, and I would need all the energy I could get.

Coffee in hand and a plan formed I sat back in front of the computer and started to compose a call entering Scott's number followed by Sue's as secondary, I took a deep breath and pressed call.

I took a sip of my coffee, black the way we all drank it apart from Jay and waited while the calls connected. Scott was the first to come though followed shortly by Sue's. I sat back and took another sip as I waited for the cameras to load and everyone to come into the frame apart from June.

Once I could see everyone all gathered around their computers. "Where is June?"

"She's just coming, Scott," said as she came into view.

"What's the update on Adam?"

"No change since our previous call, I put him on a drip to try and keep his fluids up, but he's still stable."

"You mean he's not even conscious," said Sue, alarmed.

He woke up once June interrupted but he was in pain so I administered a dosage of morphine and then he went back to sleep with head wounds he might drift in and out of consciousness."

"That is why it's important we get him to the hospital," I said. "June, have we got permission for the pad."

"Not yet," she said. "I've informed them of his condition and there ready, but they need the Reg and squawk code along with the make and description of the craft, but I don't see what use it will be the only craft suitable is the air ambulance, I'm still unsure why you need it."

"Okay, have you got some paper handy, I rattled off the code and Reg seeing her looking confused as to what I had planned. And what type of craft is that?"

"Helicopter. Air ambulance, to be precise." When she heard the description air ambulance, she looked shocked.

"You got them to agree to send the air ambulance for a non-emergency case!"

"No, I didn't even try it's a decommissioned one, only since last year used to run in Scotland used it for mountain rescues over Ben Nevis I believe."

"Registered keeper?"

"Rob Wolf."

"How have you got an air ambulance?" Sue asked.

"It's all well and good having it," June said. "But who the hell's going to fly it."

"He is," said Peter with pride.

"You?" June said, looking into the computer.

"Yes. I once wanted to be a pilot but backed out when the new carbon laws came in. I wanted to do my bit but I still hold a full license."

"But when was the last time you flew," asked Jay.

"Last week."

"How long have you had this helicopter?" asked Scott.

"You didn't tell us you could fly Uncle Rob came, Jake?"

"Okay, one at a time, yes, I can fly, Jake, it's never come up and about only about ten minutes. I've not even signed for it, Sean as it is at the airfield, he's had trouble flogging it and as it's now a decommissioned craft not registered for rental, the only person that can fly it is the registered keeper, so I had to buy it."

"So how did you fly it last week," asked June?

"I didn't, I also own a kite, I go once a month to keep my hand in and do my required hours to keep my license."

"Well, I'll be blown," said Jay. "I never knew."

"Anyway, the plan I said taking back control of the conversation, is as soon as the alert is over, I will head to the airfield sign for the craft, I've already sent the money and Sean's on the paperwork as we speak. He's even giving me a full tank on the deal. Weather permitting, I jump in and fly over to you."

"I'm coming too," interrupted Sue.

"I'm not sure; that's possible."

"I'm not staying here while you deal with it alone, if you're going so am I."

"Can you get her to the airfield?" I asked Jay.

"I can try," he said. "Okay then, if you're sure, Sue, then meet me there."

"Now there are a few things I will need to know, firstly if I have permission to use the helipad to drop Adam off. June, I would like you to accompany me on the flight."

"Of course, but we will need to proper equipment to transport him."

"As far as I'm aware, it's all there minus medication, I know for sure it contains a stretcher and support grips for it in the back they were in such a rush to get rid of it they neglected to take it with them. Second, I will need somewhere to land."

"The backfield," said Scott.

"Is it safe?"

"With the storm, I don't know till I'm out there but I'm sure me and the lads can clear a space big enough."

"Me to," interrupted Dad.

"Well, let me know if things change, lastly I need to know exactly what happened out there today."

We all stayed on the call for an hour all putting in our two pence on the matter, but one thing was agreed it was without a doubt the most utterly stupid thing we had ever heard each voicing that opinion to them. All except June who had gone to make the arrangements with the hospital regarding the craft returning just as we were finishing the story to tell me it had all been accepted.

"Well, I hope you've learnt a lesson," I said.

"I knew there was little more that could be said and they already felt guilty as sin so I left it at that all agreeing to say nothing more about it. And with that, I ended the call."

No sooner had I ended the call than Sue rang back.

Chapter Twenty-Two
The Great Outdoors – *Scott*

"He really is something, isn't he?" said June when the call had ended. "How does he do it? He's incredible. Who can just magic up an air ambulance, never mind be able to fly it."

"He's my son," said Ann. "Bursting with pride he was always blessed with being able to organise anything, got that from his dad," she said, taking Peter's hand and pulling it close.

"I can see that," said June, "tell you one thing, I wouldn't want to get on the wrong side of him in a kitchen. Just then the news flashed they had lifted the alert. It was now safe to leave the shelter."

I went to the shelter door hoping nothing was blocking the door, I opened it cautiously. Even though the all-clear had sounded I wanted to make sure it was safe before we all went out. It took a while for my eyes to adjust as I opened the door. Rex came bounding out from the kitchen and out the door as soon as it was open clearly as happy to get out as I was.

It was as bright and clear as a summer day with only a few clouds in the sky but still the wind was blisteringly cold. The end of the storm passing over us I took a look around and settled on the house at first glance it looked okay with only a few tiles off the roof and the windows broken you could see the turn the tornado took just heading away from the house and across the garden the exact route the Wolf took to the shelter, veering off just about where Adam was laying on the ground.it was like it was following them. It looked like it must have come straight across the shelter itself at some point stripping the earth covering it and exposing the steel sheeting underneath.

I went back into the shelter and told everyone to grab a coat or jumper telling them it was safe to leave but to be careful. "What about Adam," asked Jake.

"He will be okay," said June. "We won't be far and he's sleeping."

I grabbed my coat and headed for the door Peter was behind me followed by Ann, June and the kids.

Walking up to the house I could see more damage than I had originally spotted, a few loose bricks and severe structural damage it wasn't until I got closer and looked through a window frame that I could see all the way through the house and to the land beyond the tornado had ripped the front of the house to pieces leaving flying debris to destroy what was left. I felt a hand on my shoulder and turned round to see Peter. "Sorry, I know how much work you put into this place."

"It's only bricks and mortar," I replied, turning round and looking at June and the boys all standing staring at the house; the main thing is that we're all together. "All of us," I said looking him in the eye. And putting my hand around his shoulder.

We walked around the side of the house Rex at my side, trying to avoid what we could on the ground and looked at the Wolf house beyond there was nothing there just an empty plot of land where the house once stood. I looked at Peter, I knew it was all but destroyed. Anyway he said, "It was basically a ruin when we went in."

We stood for a few minutes, just taking in the surroundings and the damage that had been caused, Ann was walking across the garden to where their house once stood what was left of it was scattered over the garden. She stopped in front of the shelter the tree now gone leaving the entrance clear inside the roof of the shelter had caved in the hallway the only space you could even step foot in. and a massive hole above the living area. Where they should have been safe.

We stopped behind her as she broke down and started crying, Peter went to give her a hug and she melted into his embrace. Look at it Peter look imagine what would have happened if we had been inside.

We weren't so don't even think about it were safe.

Adam's not. She cried he might not even survive.

He will be fine, he's a wolf, he's a fighter, he will pull through Rob will soon be here and have him on the way to the hospital and it will all be okay trust me and if you don't trust me trust Rob.

I left them to it and walked over to the tree where I parked the rover a mound of brick, fencing and tree branches all covering the area I pulled away from the top and couldn't help but smile, as I saw It underneath the light on the head still light up a good sign that it was still functional. Jake appeared beside me noticing what I was doing started pulling away as well. Soon we had uncovered enough to see the rover I had parked it in a corner where it would be covered. The storm having pushed it back further created an alcove that it sat in. Taking one side and Jake the other we struggled to pull it out of the cove and eventually placed it on the ground. It looked undamaged apart from a few scratches here and there. I opened the back panel pulled out the remote and switched it to manual. I pressed forward and couldn't help but smile as it moved. As it rolled forward, I couldn't help but hear a sound somewhere between a laugh and a cry.

I looked over to see Ann and Peter smiling in my direction.

Ann walked over to the rover and placed a kiss on its head and thanked it. We all laughed and headed back to the shelter the robot leading the way. June was picking stuff up from the rubble photo frames containing pictures of her parents and a family portrait we had on the wall was at the side of her already creating a pile of belongings she could find as she went. She looked up as she approached, "You and that bloody robot," she said half laughing.

I pulled it to a halt at the side of her and put my arm around it, a bit of a clean and it's good as new.

Jacob came out of the shelter to say that Adam was awake again, dropping the belongings she had collected she ran to the shelter closely followed by Ann. Looking over towards the field I could see it covered and in no fit state for a helicopter to land placing the remote back in the rover. I headed in the direction of the field.

"Come on, boys, let's get a start on the field. I don't know how long we've got, but looking back I saw Peter unsure whether to help or go check on Adam."

"I will come as well," said Peter, noticing my attention was on him.

"Don't you want to go help June with Adam?"

"No, Ann's there, and I could help him more clearing the field for Rob than standing beside the bed."

"Should we take a corner each?" said Jake as we stood looking at the mess.

"No, I think, it would be better if we all started in the middle and made a pile in each corner to give him as much space as possible."

Two hours later, we had created a space the size of a small house in the middle when we heard a voice shout tea break! June was walking towards us with a tray of drinks sandwiches and crisps.

"I thought, you could use some refreshments."

"Thank you, love," I said, kissing her on the head before rubbing Rex's head who had been lying down chewing a stick he found as we worked.

"How are things?"

"Okay, he's conscious now, I've replaced his drip to keep his fluids up and keep him going with pain relief the best I can, but I'm nearly out we need to get him to the hospital as soon as possible."

"Will he be all right though?" asked Peter.

"I don't know the fact he's awake is a good sign, but I won't be happy till he's at the hospital and having a scan."

"As he said anything," asked Peter.

"Not really," said June. "He was either in too much pain or out of it on pain relief to say anything."

"PETER!" We looked around to see Ann running towards us.

"What is it?" he asked, failing to keep the worry from his voice.

"It's Rob, he's just rang all clears, come though," he said. "He should be here in the next two hours, if not sooner."

We downed our drinks and told June to leave what was left of the sandwiches on one of the piles. We're not far from being done if we get on with it now, we should have plenty of time to spare. "What can I do," asked Ann. "June can cope with Adam and she knows where I am if she needs me."

I looked at Peter who just shrugged his shoulders, saying, "Five hands are faster than four."

"Okay, start collecting as many little stones as you can.

You're going to spell out the letter H on the ground to help him land."

An hour later, we stood back and looked at the landing strip we had created. June had cling-filmed the sandwiches and bought a jug of juice over as well ready for when we had finished, Ann took a sandwich and a packet of crisps. "I'm going back to the shelter, to check on Adam."

"Does anyone want a hot drink?"

"No," we all said. "We would stick with the juice." June had put some ice in it to keep it cool.

We sat out in the field the sandwiches didn't last long and the juice soon ran out between us all. Peter couldn't stop thanking us enough for everything saying he didn't know how he would ever repay us. Fifteen minutes later, we heard the sound of propellers getting closer and closer we kept looking around but couldn't see anything all hopeful it was Rob and not another craft. Before long we could see a large helicopter appear from the distance. Even far out you could see it heading in our direction and it was clear it was an air ambulance. The boys were enthralled and moved closer trying to get a better look. Back here boys, come on stay out of the landing zone. They soon ran back, and we saw Ann and June appear behind us, obviously having heard the noise. "I have been on the phone with him," said June. "He knows we put the H."

We all stood there in admiration of such a plan coming together, I looked over at Ann and Peter both their faces covered in pride.

Feeling the power of the propellers I pulled the boys further back and held onto Rex's collar much to his reluctance as the aircraft got closer and closer eventually stopping above us before slowly descending to the ground sending up dust soil and pebbles. "Haven't we had enough tornados for one day?" I shouted.

All I got was a smack on the back of my head from June and a laugh from everyone else. Behave yourself I was instructed.

"Yes, nurse," I replied. This time ducking in time to avoid another hit.

The helicopter landed bang in the middle of the H with such skill you would have thought it was an everyday occurrence, we heard the engines stop as they were turned off and the doors opened when the propellers slowed down enough. What looked like an army of people came running out, all with their heads low and all running towards us. Ann burst into tears as she saw her entire family empty out of the aircraft. Sue and the kids were first followed by Peter and a guy I had never seen but June seemed to recognise carrying a stretcher lastly, the pilot who couldn't be mistaken for anyone else Rob was finally here.

Chapter Twenty-Three
A Plan in Action – *Rob*

I ended the call and sat in disbelief at what we had just heard. That didn't last long before the phone went again suddenly feeling exhausted, I looked at the screen to see it was Sue. Pressing answer, I saw Jay and Sue come on the screen. This time it was Jay's time to speak first.

"How are you getting to the airfield, as nice as your Tesla is? It's not exactly made for all-weather terrain."

"I will find a way," I said. "I think the quads are still in working order it was when I moved in. That should make it."

"Is it road-legal?"

"Not officially, but it's worth the risk, can't see the police doing traffic stops."

"But they may have roadblocks; look you're not far from us just get the quad to us and I will get us all there."

"Probably the best plan," I agree. "As soon as this is over, I will head straight to yours."

"Okay, see you then," I said, ending the call.

Finally, I checked the message screen and saw a message from Sean saying the paperwork was ready for my signature and the money had been wired over successfully. I asked him to have it ready and waited after the alert and thanked him for all his help.

I was about to stand up before remembering to ring Sam I knew he lived near the airfield than I did so it shouldn't be a problem for him to get there.

"Hello, again. I got after the third ring and was wondering when I would hear from you, you just can't leave me alone, can you?"

"Are you serious about going to Wales after this alert?"

"Deadly, I want to check on my dad, and I don't know, how else to get there."

"Sam didn't drive and preferred to cycle on days he couldn't get a lift. Relying on trains and public transport for all other journeys."

"Well," I said, "as soon as this alert clears, I will need you to head to the Leicester air base."

"The air base!"

"Yes, the airbase; I need you there ASAP after the alert."

"But why the air base," asked Sam.

"I'm flying over there the roads will be impassable and no use waiting for any other form of transport could take weeks."

"Well, who's going to fly us?"

"Me."

"In a one-seater kite, what am I supposed to do hold on to the wing? If you like," I replied, laughing as I did Sam always could make me laugh.

"Look," I said. "I have a plan just meet me there the air marshal is called Sean if you can't find me ask to see him if I've already left, he will let you know but you should beat me there. Unless you want to stay here?"

"Oh no," he said, "this is the most excitement I have ever had. You think I'm missing out on it you can think again. Will pack some rope so I don't fall off the wings."

With that all sorted, I packed a bag with some clothes for myself and made a second coffee before pacing the room once again staring at the clock and constantly checking the storm report for both areas.

Wales had now been given all clear. And no tornados or higher winds were expected to hit our area meaning that minimal damage should be caused not that it would help with the roads. The expected time for all clear was one hour satellite maps showing a clear path of the storm passing over and disappearing looking good for clear skies meaning there should be no issues getting in the air.

The hour felt like a day, I made myself more coffee than I usually drank in a week and made some lunch that I barely touched. I watched and checked the news and storm maps every second until at last the all-clear sounded. Now it was time to see if my half-baked plan would prove efficient it all depended on the air travel one thing, I knew was that I was getting in the air if it killed me.

First thing, first I rang Sean to check the condition of the base I knew he would have been given all clear before civilians so the base could be used by emergency services. All good, he said just seeing off a few crafts now, but I will get yours ready soon the weather is not the best up there, but it should be manageable.

Finally, I rang Scott's number, Mum answered the phone. "Hey, Mum, it's Rob; how are things?"

"Adams is awake," she said. "He is not really with it but at least he is awake."

"That is a good sign."

"I am just ringing to say I'm leaving now; the weather is suitable for flying so I should be there in the next two hours all being well, hopefully, sooner."

"Please take care. Just get here when you can."

I ended the call grabbed my bag I had packed my coat and

headed out the door.

I ran out of the cellar and up into the house taking the steps two at a time. Once in the house, the sun shone through the windows. I could see broken glass everywhere, but a few broken windows were the least of my worries. I headed outside to the garage opening it up. I could the Tesla still where I left it completely undamaged. At the side covered in a dust sheet was the quad bike. Opening the key safe on the wall. I grabbed the keys and pulled the cover off. I jumped on throwing my bag over my back and inserted the key, turning it, I couldn't help but pray it would start. Jay was right just the road outside my house was a mess The Tesla would struggle to make the few streets to Sue never mind the airfield. Holding my breath I turned the key. After a bit a splutter it roared into life. Leaning forward I put it in gear turned the throttle and sped out of the garage.

Using pavement and road to avoid everything lying in the way, I sped as fast as I could to get to Sue. Successfully avoiding fallen tree trunks and whatever else was around, it was only a few minutes later till I was rounding the corner to Sue's I could see a few of the older houses had received some serious structural damage. Everyone was on the street assessing what damage there was and what could be saved. I turned into Sue's street as I did all the neighbours looking around some in disapproval at some speeding past some in pure interest as to who it was and what was so urgent. As I approached I watched the front gates open, Jay, Sue and the kids were all getting into the car as I rode the quad into the garage beside the car, I slammed the breaks bringing it to a halt right beside Jay.

"Nice driving," he said as I extinguished the engine and jumped off pulling the bag off my back.

"Thanks," I said as I jumped in the back with the boys. Sue

and Jay getting in the front and the same time.

"Uncle Rob!" they both said excitedly as I got in and slammed the door shut. "Hello, you too," I said giving them both a hug.

Jay was driving fast out of the drive before I even had my belt on the car beeping angrily to show its disapproval. His driving was similar to mine on the quad using road and pavement to avoid the debris on the road but not fully succeeding. Making it one bumpy ride for all of us. The boys loved every second of it, Jay was known for being a responsible driver, so this was a new experience for them. Sue on the other hand was known to be a lot more reckless.

"Which is the fastest way to the air base," he asked as we came out of the town.

"Just stick to the main road for now." Taking the A6 out of Leicester we soon headed out of the houses and to the fields the air base was about thirty minutes away from Sue. It had taken five minutes to get from mine to Sue's.

The boys still loved the fast-driving, Jay also found it exhilarating but Sue was holding onto her seat and pressing the imaginary brake pedal. "Turn here," I said as we approached a side road, Jay only slowed down slightly took the corner way too fast nearly ending up in a ditch.

"Be careful!" shouted Sue. "Get us there alive. When did you learn to drive like a maniac?"

"When me and Rob went on that track day. You could tell from his voice that part of him was enjoying this."

"Hey, don't blame me," I exclaimed. "Take the third left," I said. "This time with an advance warning it would bring you out on the other side of the airstrip."

"Well, don't we need the main entrance?"

"No, he's expecting us so we can use the departure parking."

Driving past the fields, I knew we were close it had been a while since I had flown a helicopter so I was reading a manual I had downloaded on my phone looking for anything I may need to know about the craft. Finding nothing that I didn't already know I Locked the phone, just as the airfield came into view, Jay slowed down and stopped outside the gates. "What's the code?" he asked while winding down the window.

"0000."

"Well, that's secure," he said with a snort of derision.

We had barely stopped moving and parked before I had wound my window down and used the handle to release myself.

"Don't you get any ideas," I heard Sue say to the boys as I jumped out of the car and ran towards the office. Clearly, I had just blown their mind of this magical way to get past the child lock.

There was no sign of Sean, looking out I could see the helicopter on the landing strip. It was twice as big as I had imagined it, I knew it was a large craft with a twin-turbo engine and four rotor blades with a top speed of 160mph. for the first time, I had doubts over my ability to carry this off even from a distance it was daunting. I walked out of the office and towards the ambulance when I saw Sean running towards me. "What do you think?"

"It's definitely big enough," I said, sounding a bit worried.

"You will be fine once you're in the cock pit," he said, laughing slightly. "Don't let its size intimidate you; once it's up, you won't even notice, you may just notice a bit of added torque."

Having a quick look around I saw that as I expected the stretcher and other bits of equipment were still inside ready to be used.

I was looking it over when Sue, Jay and the kids walked over. The boys who were anxious to get a closer look and only just managing to stop themselves from running. Jay whistled as he got closer. "Are you sure, you can fly this thing?"

"Of course, I am," I said, trying to sound as confident as I could my own doubts whirling around my brain.

"I suppose, I better sign for it," I said, looking at Sean,

"It's already," he said, "just follow me into the office. Oh, I forgot someone came asking for you and said he was told to meet you here."

"That will be Sam," I said short, "thin with black hair."

"That's him," I told him to wait in the office as you hadn't arrived yet. We entered the office just as Sam was coming out of the gents.

"There you are, I'm ready for my glider experience," he joked.

"Will have to do that another day, you will have to settle for a ride in a helicopter first to get your head for Hight's."

"You mean that thing," he said, pointing towards the ambulance.

"Well, it's the only one around," I said. "Go have a look, Sue's out there waiting; I won't be long just need to sign some papers. Sam knew Sue from the restaurant where they were a regulars always refusing discounts. As Sam walked out to meet them, I sat at the desk opposite Sean."

"Now," he said. "I should really go through some safety with you first but I'm busy and you're in a rush so if anyone asks, we went through it over the phone earlier. When was the last time you flew a helicopter?"

"The finals exam, I'm hoping it's like riding a bike."

He laughed the previous year we had gone on a bike ride for

the first since my childhood and not only did I fall off I managed to break my arm in the process. But don't tell them that I said to point towards Sam and Sue, your secrets are safe with me.

"Have you got your pilot license," he asked as I handed it over, He handed me the contract and papers to sign shortly followed by the insurance. Adding my license to the flight pack he handed that over along with my copy of the documents. We stood up and headed for the door the whole process had taken all of five minutes. It's got a full tank in that should be more than enough for Wales and back but there's more fuel available at the air base in North Wales. I pulled a few favour's and cleared landing rights from a mate of mine he was all the aircraft details and they have a car at your disposal should you need it he keeps a few for hire as a side-line. Was thinking of doing it myself he makes a healthy profit.

Chapter Twenty-Four
The Flight – *Rob*

As we approached the craft, I could see Sue and Sam talking beside it. The boys inside were closely watched by Jay telling them not to touch anything even though it was hard to tell who was having more fun him or them.

"You both sure you want to come," I said, "because now's the time to back out if you're not."

"Sam was the first to say I'm coming if only to watch you fly this thing; it's a bit different to what you're used to, isn't it, it's no Tesla."

"Don't you worry, I know what I'm doing giving a warning glance at Sean to keep quiet as I did."

"On that note, I'm going to check on air control and inform them about your departure; it took some clearance to get approval and managed to swing by the type of craft it is though as far as they're concerned it's an air ambulance they're not interested If it's active or not too much going on at the minuet for their kind of checks. "Radio though once you're ready," he said as he walked off.

"Well, we already?"

"Yes," they both replied.

"Come on, boys, off you get."

"But, Mum, they complained why can't we come with you?"

"Because it's not a holiday," she snapped. "Tell them, Jay."

She looked at Jay the most he could manage was a cheeky

grin and shrug of his shoulders.

"Well," he said, "it's not every day you get to ride in a helicopter before looking at me."

I didn't have time for this so I asked Sam to look after the boys and told Jay and Sue I wanted a word. "Look," I said as they both joined me beside the doors. "I don't have an issue taking you all, but I don't know what condition Adam's in or any of the others are in not to mention what will happen when we get there. So, it's up to you, they are your kids it's your choice if you think they can cope with what they may see," I said before walking off to start warming up the engines.

I was halfway in the cock pit when Sue and Jay came up behind me. "We're all going," they said, hugging each other as they did.

"Okay, then get in shut the doors and strap yourself in helmets and headphones in the back. Anyone not on board in two minutes gets left behind."

I was clicking switches and loading the coordinates in the GPS system when Sam appeared, "Look like we have a full house," he said. "Mind if I sit in front with you pointing to the co-pilot seat."

"No," I said, "as long as you don't touch anything."

"You can rely on me," he said, jumping in beside me.

"So, when was the last time you flew one of these?" he asked.

I shoot him a glance before saying, "Do you want to ride in the front."

He understood instantly and mimicked a zipper on his mouth telling me he was going to shut up from now on.

Finally, fully loaded and with the ignition sequence initiated. I told everyone to put on their helmets they all have a radio in case, I said so we could hear each other while in the air. Then I radioed through to air control. Looking at the flight pack I got the flight code.

"This is Romeo Oscar Brava flying AA147 to control ready for take-off over," I said.

"Control to Romeo Oscar Brava – clear in two minutes," came over the reply.

Followed by Sean's voice. "Take it easy out there, Romeo. There's a lot of traffic around the area, so try to avoid crossing paths over."

"Understood," I said, now in full pilot mode.

I sat formalizing myself the controls while I waited for clearance.

"Control to Romeo Oscar Brava clear for take-off over."

"Loud and clear control over and out."

I could see and feel the boys and Jay's excitement behind me they were loving every minute and the anticipation of when we would be going up. I pressed the button on the mic activating the internal intercom and told everyone to hold on.

Now having the all clear I lifted to the collective to re-pitch the blades and used the throttle to increase the torque giving it pull.

At the same time use the right peddle to re-pitch the rear propeller to counteract the clockwise spin.

The trees looked as if they were moving as we rose up the field behind coming into view. It took both feet and both hands to fly the helicopter both feet on the pedals to pitch the rear propeller blades. Right hand on the cyclic that maneuverer the craft by changing the pitch of propeller blades up top and left on the collective that controlled the height of the blades higher it went up lower it went down all of these needed to be controlled to counteract each other and stabilise the craft stopping it from spinning out of control

Having reached the right altitude, I used the cyclic to turn the craft to the left turning then easing slightly off the right peddle as I did. The turn wasn't the smoothest as I expected the rest of the journey would probably be on the same line, but at least we were up I would worry about coming down later on. Having completed the turn, I pushed the cyclic forwards and set the helicopter on its course over the air base and to the fields beyond.

Shrieks of joy and excitement came through the headset as the boys whooped in delight. Sam's voice came over the intercom. "Wow, look at that view," he said as we left Leicester behind us following the directed course. The radar scanner showed no approaching craft in the vicinity or at my altitude. I always knew you could fly but it's not till now that I realised what it meant this is amazing.

"More than I did," came Jay's voice, "How is it? I've never been told this before.

"I don't know," I said, "suppose it's never come up you weren't around when I was learning and since then it's just been a hobby with little importance."

"Well," he said. "You certainly know, how to surprise us still," he said.

"How long will it take to get there?" asked Sue

"We should be there in the next twenty minutes," I said.

We flew in silence apart from the odd sound of wow and ohh coming from the boys and Jay. Sam had adjusted well to flying and sat just staring out the window. Sue mainly worried about Adam to really care about what was happening.

As I got nearer to our destination, I gave Sam my address book and asked him to dial the number into the control panel. "The phone connected to my headset started to ring before," June answered.

"Hey, June, this is Rob, just to let you know we are approaching and will be there in a few minutes' time is the field ready?"

"Yes," she said. "They even made a H in the middle of it not sure if you can see it from up there though."

"That's great," I said. "I'm locked onto the location anyway, but it will help with landing I should be low enough to decipher the letter. How's is Adam?"

"He's still awake but out of it on pain relief so isn't aware of much I've just used the last of it though, so we have about an hour till it completely wears off."

"Okay," I said, "well, get him and yourself as ready as you can, and I will be there shortly."

Ending the call, I used the intercom to announce we would be landing in the next few minutes. "Sue when we land, I want you to take the boys, Jay and Sam. I want you to grab the stretcher and take it to June. But wait till I give all clear before you go, okay?"

"Yes, Captain." They all echoed back.

Apart from Sam who went with, "Yes, chef."

It was only a few seconds later that, I saw a field below with the faint sight of the letter H spelt out on the ground. "Look down," I said.

"See that H that's where we will land."

"Romeo Oscar brava to control," I said, "ready to land over."

The coordinates were on their screen so knew exactly where the craft was to sit.

" _

As I approached, I used the cyclic to slow down our rate of acceleration and used, the collective to lower the craft bringing it to more of a hover potion as I descended until we were on the ground. Lowing the torque fully and the collective completely I released the pressure on the pedals before turning on the brake and shutting off the propellers completely. I waited till they slowed right down before I said off you go but keep your heads down the blades are still moving.

Sue was first out with both boys holding on to either side of her. Sam moved to the back and with Jay lifted the stretcher and moved out the door. I stayed in while, I shut off the helicopter completely before leaving via the cab and walking around.

Chapter Twenty-Five
The Welcoming Party – *Rob*

I pushed open the door and stepped out grabbing my bag and chucking the headphones on the seat as I walked off. I walked around the side of the craft and was instantly greeted by Rex who had come running over. Rex had taken an instant shine to me from the minute we met, he was so friendly and happy you couldn't help but love him. Patting him on the head and ignoring his jumps trying to get my attention. I walked over to where everyone was gathered in a group. Mum was hugging Tyler and Declan so hard, they might burst, Sue embracing Dad and crying with happiness. June was in conversation with Sam and Jay. Scott was with Jake and Jacob as I walked over. Before I even got close, they were asking if they could go look at the helicopter.

"As long as you don't touch anything," I said them, running off in an instant. Soon followed by Tyler and Declan who had managed to wiggle free from mum's clutch. Holding my hand out to Scott as a greeting, "Hello, Scott, sorry for causing all this hassle."

"Don't mention it," he replied, "anything to help a friend that was a brilliant landing by the way how long have you been flying these things?"

"About half an hour," I replied, "not touched one in twelve years."

"Well, you haven't lost it."

"DAD! You have to come to look at this," Jake shouted from

the helicopter. Looking at me I laughed. "Go ahead," I said you can keep an eye on them for me, while I get Adam sorted.

As Scott went to see what the kids were doing Mum and Dad sheepishly walked over. "We're so sorry, Rob," Mum said.

"It's done now, let's just forget it and move on," I said before hugging them both.

"Now I need to sort Adam. Where is June?"

"She went into the shelter with the stretcher. Jay, Sam and Sue went with her," said Dad.

"Well, we had better join them," I said, walking to the now exposed shelter. "I tried not to look at Scott's house which I could already tell had suffered some serious damage."

"Why is Sam here anyway," Mum asked.

"It's a long story," I said. "He's basically here to check on his dad, but he knows June from a previous encounter that he never got to thank her for so insisted he came."

I dropped my bag by the door and went to where June was standing, by this time they had pulled Adam onto the stretcher and June was fastening the straps. She was holding what looked like a bag of water I assumed was a saline drip. "I'm impressed," I said. "All I have is some plasters and bandages for first aid."

"Well, I'm always prepared," she said. "Fail the prepare, prepare to fail, it's what I tell everyone at work can't ignore my own rules, can I?"

"Well, thank you for everything; I'm sorry I can't just relieve you of it now and let you focus on your family."

"He's my patient now, I will see it through to the end," she said as I went over to Adam.

"Hey, bro, what mess you been getting yourself into," now I joked, but he was too out of it to even notice who was around. "Let's get you sorted, shall we?" I said.

"We ready to go," I asked.

"Yes," she said, grabbing her bag and a coat. Jay and Sam took one side of the stretcher while me and Dad took the other, June followed holding the drip high enough to keep it working. As we walked to the helicopter, we saw the boys and Scott sitting outside of it with Rex beside them. Tyler and Declan were talking probably raving about the ride from the looks of the excitement on Jake and Jacobs's faces.

Scott had a big smile on his face trying not to laugh as they told their story. When they saw us coming, they stopped and looked as we carried the stretcher over to the ambulance. "Come on, boys," Scott said, rounding them all up and out the way, so they couldn't see what state their uncle was in. "Let's get out of the way and let Rob and your mum get to work."

We placed the stretcher in the back and fastened it down so it wouldn't move around as June attached the drip to a hook above the roof of the helicopter.

"Okay? All set?"

"Yes," said June.

As I went to shut the door, I felt movement behind me, I turned round to Scott and the boys, can we come asked Jake and Jacob. The story from Tyler and Dylan sounds too amazing to miss. "Sorry, boys," said June. "I'm afraid this journey is better with just us."

"What about me?" asked Mum. "You hate flying I pointed out you never want to go in a plane."

"Well, sometimes you have to make sacrifices," she said already climbing in.

"Okay," I said.

"Do they know we are on the way?" I asked June.

"Yes, I rang them when we went to the shelter."

"Then let's go," I said before I shut the side door behind me.

"I need to get Adam to the hospital and things sorted," I said to Jake and Jacob, who were standing next to Scott, frowning, but when things are sorted and settled, I will take you for a ride. Their faces soon changed from a frown to sheer excitement.

Getting in the cock pit again. I looked out to see everyone heading away from the helicopter and Scott holding onto Rex's collar. Sam wasn't around his dad's farm only being a few streets away I assumed he was heading there. June was shining a light into Adams's eyes. "Is everything okay?"

"I don't know, he's stable but he's not as responsive as before."

As soon as I heard that I started the engines and got ready for take-off June was giving Mum a helmet to wear and showing how to converse through it, before strapping them both in.

"Romeo Oscar brava flying aa147 to control – request immediate take off to Swansea hospital over," I said while inputting the coordinates into the GPS.

"Control to Romeo Oscar brava – what's your emergency over."

Server head wound on the left side due to impact, the patient is breathing but unresponsive over. This had a visual impact on Mum who got distressed but impressed June. "Who gave me the thumbs-up sign?"

"Hold tight, Romeo will have you off as a priority ASAP over."

I switched to the intercom. "How we are doing back there?"

"Not too bad, but we need to get moving."

"I'm waiting for authorization, when was the last time you were in one of these?"

"Not since training, we all had to do a course in case we were ever called upon."

"Just as well as, you did." I saw a plane flying over us and it wasn't long till I heard control.

"Control to Romeo Oscar Brava – clear for take-off over."

"Romeo Oscar Brava – to control. Understood loud and clear over and out."

"Here we go," I said. "Through the headset before taking hold of the collective and lifting us up into the air sending a swirl of dust up off the ground as I did."

"Once up, I spun it around and was soon pushing forward, it was only a short journey but it would still take five minutes to reach. How did you get approval so fast asked June once we were moving?"

Repeating what I heard from Sean earlier, I said, "AC doesn't care if the craft is currently active, I said all they see is an air ambulance and that's all they care about. It decommissioned not deregistered."

"Smart move."

"It wasn't planned, I didn't even think about flight approval from AC it was Sean who sorted it for me adding the clout of it being an air ambulance to get them to grant permission."

"Clever," said June, laughing as she did.

We were three minutes into the flight when June came back on the mic. "We have a problem," she said. "He was unconscious again and was getting no response."

"What happened?"

"I don't know, his pulse is still strong, but I'm not happy with his blood pressure."

"Okay, hold on," I said as I increased the speed and contacted air control.

"Romeo Oscar Bravo to control two minutes out from

Swansea request immediate landing over."

"Control to Romeo Oscar Bravo – what's the status over."

The patient now lost consciousness and with fallen blood pressure.

"Hold tight, Romeo, landing will be priority over."

"AC have us as priority landing," I said, "though the mic shouldn't be long till we're down."

"Control to Romeo Oscar Brava – area clear for immediate landing over."

"Romeo Oscar Brava to control – understood loud and clear over."

"We're clear for landing," I said, and I can see the hospital now get ready to go and remember to keep your heads down. I could see the lights of the helipad up ahead slowing it down I got ready to land dropping the collective and easing the throttle. Until I was firmly on the ground. Turning off the blades I let them slow enough to release the doors.

June pushed the doors open the propellers still moving outside two doctors and a nurse were gathered together around a trolley to place the stretcher on. The power from the propellers blew there lab coats and hair all over the place. As the propellers slowed more the doctors ran towards the door grabbing an end each Mum and June both taking the other, they kept as low as they could until they were out of the way of the propellers and put Adam on the stretcher before disappearing into the hospital June briefing them on his current condition as they went Suddenly AC came through the headset.

"Control to Romeo Oscar Brava – helipad required for immediate landing over."

"Switching the engine back on and getting ready," I replied.

"Romeo Oscar Brava to control – understood permission for take-off over."

"Permission is granted to Romeo."

Grabbing the collective again once again rose into the air.

"Romeo Oscar Brava to control – navigating the path to air base over."

"Control to Romeo – path clear over."

The air base was only two minutes away from the hospital upon landing and handing the aircraft to the crew. I went in search of the marshal in charge.

"You must be, Rob," he said, "when I found him in hanger one. It's not very often, I get a call from Sean asking for a favour it is usually the other way around I'm Carl. He spoke with a clear American accent was tall with blonde hair muscular and looked to be the age of about twenty-one."

"Nice to meet you, thanks for letting me use the base."

"Don't sweat it, buddy. All in a day's work."

"So, this is the craft," he said, walking out of the hanger to where the helicopter was being prepared to be moved.

"I have to say, I'm amazed you can fly it. They take some skill when he told me what was happening; I had my doubts but the way you landed it. I am not ashamed to admit I was wrong. Have you had any training?"

"Thanks," I said following him to the office, "no simply basic license training first time I've flown one in twelve years."

"Then you're a natural, pull up a chair," he said before pulling out the paperwork to check in the craft.

"I produced my license and flight pack up for inspection." But he just glanced over them obviously Sean having made them was as much confirmation as he needed.

"How long do you need it stored?"

"A few days, maybe more. Is that a problem?"

"Naww, man, you're good, it's a quiet base. Take your time." He pressed a few keys on the computer and scanned the code on the flight pack. Producing a second document. This is for the rental.

"Ahh, yes," I said, pulling out my bank card ready for a credit check.

"Put that away," he said, "this is on me any friend of Sean's is a friend of mine. Just sign here and here," he said, pointing to two crosses.

"That means you took ownership and claimed the insurance. Got your driving license?"

Having produced the license and signed paperwork. He handed me the keys with a Land Rover logo on them. "When do you need it back?"

"When you're done with it. All I ask is it comes back with the same amount of fuel she left with and undamaged."

Having finished all the formalities, he stood up in time for a member of his crew to turn up to get his attention.

We left the office. And he pointed to where I would find the car.

I shook his hand and walked in search of the car desperate to get to the hospital. As I approached the lot there was a selection of cars, a mixture of old and new, and in all different sizes and styles. Looking around, I saw a few land rovers standing in the middle of the lot, I pressed the open button. And the lights flashed on a new one fresh out the showroom or as close as be with this year's plate on its e+ identical to Jay's. I made a mental note to ask Sean what kind of favour Carl owed to be this obliging.

I got in a started the engine felt right out of my comfort zone in a vehicle this size. But I needed to get to the hospital and if I could fly and helicopter, I could drive this bus.

I adjusted the seat and mirrors and pulled up to the gates they must have been on a sensor because they automatically opened up allowing me out and onto the too the road ahead.

Chapter Twenty-Six
Rubble, Rubble and More Rubble –
Sue

We stood watching as Rob flew away with Adam, June and Mum in the back no one moved until they were out of view. I wasn't sure what was more impressive. Being in it while he flew it or watching with what skill he took off and spirited away I know which the boys would have chosen and Jay.

Jake and Jacob were with Tyler and Declan who were full of excitement that Rob had promised them a ride in the helicopter later. Rex was in the middle desperately trying to catch a stick they were all throwing between them. Jay put his arm around my shoulder and fell into him. "Everything okay," he asked.

"Yes, I just feel so lucky to have the family I do, I don't know what I would do without them, it's sad that it takes things like this to make you release it."

"Me neither," said Jay. "Only one problem now we're here what are we going to do, it was all good for the ride in a helicopter but now we were stuck around the rubble".

We turned and looked at what was left of Scott's house. "It's such a shame I remember last summer when we came here for dinner it was so homely."

"It's not severable either," remarked Jay. "It will have to be demolished and then built from scratch."

"We didn't see Scott behind us until now. I'm so sorry," Jay said. "I didn't see you there."

"It's okay, I knew anyway deep down just to have it confirmed seems so final that's all."

"Well, it will have to go through a building regulator first."

"Yes, I know, but you're right it's gone but it survived better than your parents did."

"What do you mean," asked Sue?

"Have a look for yourself."

We walked no more than the corner of what was left of Scott's house before we saw it. There was nothing left but a few timbers sticking up through the ground just an empty space where their house once stood. I stood still unable to move just staring at it. "Don't say it, Jay, don't you dare say it. I don't need to," he said before walking off ahead.

We made our way towards what used to be the dream retirement house my parent had dreamed of for so many years. I saw one of Mum's ornaments on the ground, and picked it up it used to belong to my grandmother and had been in the family for generations. Dusting it off, I held it close at least this survived.

Jay reached down and pulled a photo album from under a roof beam it was one that we had given Mum as a gift after the wedding so she could look back. "It was identical to ours and this," he said.

We opened it up to see photos of our wedding and Mum in her dress and big hat looking proud as punch. Rob and Adam standing behind Jay. Both giving him the eyes that said you dare hurt her. I know Rob wasn't sure the day we got married that I was doing the right thing or that Jay was right for me.

We saw something move behind us and locked back to see Dad and Scott coming up behind us. "What have you found?" Showing him the ornament and album, he smiled. "Your mum will be glad you found that."

"Well, at least you haven't lost everything," Scott said.

"Come on, let's go get a cup of tea. Scott's promised to make lunch. Before walking off."

I stood where I was looking at Jay. But what if there's anything else?

"We will come back later and salvage what we can," he said. "It will still be here. Until then I think we all need a good break."

Reluctantly, I turned round and headed towards back. Clutching the statue. We ate in the kitchen of Scott's shelter Scott proved to be a worthy cook and cooked spaghetti Bolognese which he claimed was his speciality. Eating lunch, the kids all playing together the adults all chatting it was easy to forget what had happened, it wasn't till we were clearing up that we all remembered the circumstances that had brought us here.

As Jay helped Scott with the dishes. I excused myself saying, I was going for a walk and went back to the house and sat staring at it all scattered over the garden I couldn't help thinking of what could have happened, how much worse things could have been.

I stood up and once again started to clear space and create a pile pulling out anything I found and putting it to one side, I was determined that I would salvage everything I could and return my parents' loved possessions. I don't know how long I had been out there before Jay found me. "Thought you would be here," he said instantly joining in the hunt. It wasn't long before the rest joined us as well and before long, we were all mining for gold, Even Rex was getting involved more destroying things but it wasn't long till he found the cookie jar from which helped himself.

It wasn't until the sun went down completely that we realised how late it was, we grabbed what we had found called it a day and headed back to the shelter. We still hadn't heard anything from Rob or Mum about Adam, and even June hadn't bothered to check in with us yet. Scott rang the hospital but failed to get an answer as expected the NHS were stretched to the limit and answering the phones would be the least of their worries.

It was approaching nine p.m. now and the boys were getting tired it had been a long day for everyone, especially the younger ones. Having looked at the sleeping arrangements we agreed that each boy could share a bed with his brother, which left the main room for Scott and June and me and Jay would have one of the sofa beds and Dad the other. It was agreed that when they returned Rob could have the use of the sofa in the games room giving him some privacy to relax properly. But as the night drew on there was still no sign or contact from them. Scott tried the hospital again and got a response from the receptionist who could only tell us that Adam was in ICU but stable after having to have an emergency operation but couldn't give us any information on the whereabouts of the others.

Having agreed there was nothing more I could do. We decided to put on a film, but before we were even a quarter of the way through, Dad was asleep, followed shortly by Scott, then me and Jay, and even Rex, who had managed to squeeze himself between Dad and Scott on the sofa couldn't stay awake any longer.

I awoke to an empty space at the side of me, I was alone in the room, my neck hurt from sleeping in an uncomfortable position, I had a blanket draped over me and the door was shut. I heard voices coming from the kitchen and the smell of bacon and coffee. It took me a while to remember where I was, and it wasn't until I was stood up that the horrors of yesterday. As I opened the living room door the light hit me the sun shone down through the open door to the shelter. I stumbled to the kitchen half covering my eyes.

As I entered the kitchen, I could see Dad, Jay and Scott sitting around the table with the boys, all eating a full fry-up. Seeing me come in Jay stood up. "Here you go," he said, giving me his seat. "I will get you some coffee."

We saved you some breakfast, Mummy," Tyler said excitedly.

"We sure did," said Jay.

"Now how do you like your eggs in the morning," he asked, handing me the mug of coffee with a kiss.

I replied a slight smile coming across my face. An old joke we always made. He gave me a kiss before saying, "I meant scrambled or fried." I settled for fried and Jay broke an egg into the oil.

"As anyone heard from them yet?"

"No, not yet. We rang up again this morning, and Adams's condition hasn't changed, but still no word of the others, they seem to have disappeared," said Jay.

"Their probably just sitting in the family room waiting."

"That doesn't explain why they haven't tried to ring," replied Scott.

"Rob's there," Peter said. "Everything will be fine."

Rob pulled a plate out of the oven and placed the egg on the plate before bringing it over and placing it in front of me.

"It wasn't till now I realised how hungry I was. And attacked a sausage with full force."

"Even so," said Jay. "You would have thought Rob of all people would have made sure we knew what was going on, it's most unlike him."

Having finished their breakfast, Scott placed the kids in front of the TV while they cleaned up and finished off what was left of my breakfast and washed it down with a gulp of coffee.

"What are we going to do about the others? Now I feel more alert."

"If we don't hear from them by dinner, I will ring the police," said Scott. "But until then I say we just wait, what's the worst that could have happened? We know they made it to the hospital, so odds are that's where they are."

"So, where just going to sit here, and wait?"

"No," said Jay. "Where going to go outside, and salvage what else we could from both houses."

"We worked in groups, me, Dad and Jay would work on our house, leaving Scott and the boys to work on his, Rex roaming between the two mainly finding food. And pieces of wood to chew."

By mid-day, we each had a substantial pile and although we had cleared a decent space, we still hadn't touched the surface of what was left. Looking at what we had found I felt a flood of memories come back to me a mixture of childhood memories and times spent together.

Scott came up behind us. "Come on," he said, "tea break." We had to agree the heat and the sun had left us quite dehydrated. So, we stood up and headed back to the shelter. As we approached Scott and the boys had made seating out of some wooden logs and on the one in the middle was a jug of water and a plate of sandwiches.

As we sat, and talked about all that we had found, and was amazed at some of the stuff that had survived, like Mum's porcelain doll, and June's glass clown which had somehow managed to be completely unscathed. We had found clothes and books all salvageable while a few were beyond hope. We had nearly finished when we saw a Range Rover E+ edition pulling up outside Scott's house three people got out, and it took a while to recognise them Rob especially. They all looked as if they hadn't slept, Rob and June more than Mum. June was covered in what looked like blood and Rob was far from his usual smart self all dishevelled and ragged.

"What happened?" we said, standing up so they could sit down.

"No thanks," said Rob, walking straight past as I offered him my seat. "I need a wash first."

"Me too," said June who followed after. "And coffee lots of coffee."

Chapter Twenty-Seven
Your True Calling – *Rob*

The car felt strange, I had never driven a car this size and it felt like driving a truck. A few minutes earlier, I was at the command of a large aircraft, and I felt right at home, but now driving this 4*4 I felt completely out of my depth. Turning right on the road out of the air base, I followed the signs to the hospital for those who had survived. I was one of the only people on the road. I suspect most vehicles had been severely damaged and put out of commission by the storm, taking a swift left as I saw a sign, stating that the hospital was that way and 10 miles away.

I followed the road staying away from as much debris as possible, utilizing the pathway when needed. Wales was notorious for having tight lanes which wasn't helping. I wished Jay was with me, he could do the driving; after all, he was used to handling a vehicle of this size. And after the way he handled his on the way to the airbase earlier I could definitely use him now.

Even taking it slow it didn't take long till I was approaching the hospital. The barriers were missing, leaving the car park clear to enter, I stopped to get a ticket anyway, but the machine wasn't working, obviously damaged from the storm.

I pulled into an empty space a jumped out of the car, using the key fob to lock the car as I ran towards the entrance to the accident and emergency department, the doors automatically opening as I approached. I ran up to the reception desk. There was a receptionist who was clearly overwhelmed with the extra demand, having two phones ringing at the same time. I waited while she dealt with the calls and placed a tonoi announcement for Dr Jenkins. Before I spoke. She looked at me trying to keep as professional as she could, but still sounding flustered. "Yes, sir, what can I do for you?"

"I'm looking for my brother Adam Wolf, I dropped him off about forty minutes ago in a helicopter," I said.

"We've had a lot of helicopter admissions this evening, there stretched beyond belief tonight," she said while typing his name into the computer. "Mr Adam Wolf," she said, "admitted with a head injury?"

"Yes, that's him."

"And who are you in relation?"

"His brother."

"In that case Mr Wolf. He's in the theatre. Was rushed straight in, the rest of your family is in the waiting room I believe just outside ward four." Instantly, running off towards ward four.

"Thank you," I shouted after me. Just as her phone went again. I ran towards ward four and saw Mum sitting outside in the seating area. "What's going on?" Mum was clearly crying and trying to act as if she wasn't.

"Oh, Rob, thank god you are safe," she said, dabbing her eyes with a tissue. Before she could speak June walked towards us with a cup of tea in each hand.

"I didn't know you were here, Rob. Here take mine."

"I've only just got here," I said while holding up a hand to refuse the offer of coffee. "Well," I asked. "What did they say?"

They've taken him straight to the theatre. "I didn't want to worry you back then, but he had a clear bleed on the brain, and it ruptured while we were on the way here, I didn't know till we were in the air."

"Could it have been the change of altitude that caused it?" Suddenly, I got that sickening feeling in my stomach. "Had I just done the opposite of what I intended and killed my brother?"

"It may have exasperated it, but it was only a matter of time till it would happen, if it's any consolation I still think we did the best thing we could have done."

I sat down before I fell. "Oh god," I said, holding my head in my hands. "What have I done?"

"You've done the only thing; you could reply to June. It's my fault I should have spotted the bleeding sooner."

"No one's done anything but their best Mum argued, and I'm grateful to both of you, who knows what could have happened if we had just sat there waiting, at least this way we have given him a chance."

We sat in silence for what seemed like hours, but a glance at my watch told me it was only minutes. I stood up and started pacing the waiting area, looking out for a doctor or anyone who could give us any information. "How long has he been in there?" June looked at her watch, about half an hour, they practically rushed him straight in, but these operations could take hours.

I let out a deep breath and started pacing again. I sat back down and picked up a magazine. Flicking through but not actually looking I couldn't find anything of interest I stood up again. "I'm going to get a drink." I looked at Mum and June's. Mum hadn't touched hers and June was halfway through hers. "Want another one?"

"You stay here, I will go get you one."

"Its fine, gives me something to do."

"Okay," she agreed as I walked off, it wasn't until I reached the machine that I realised I didn't get an answer as to whether she wanted a refill or not. Deciding to get her one anyway I put in two pounds and selected tea. Looking at the machine next to it I realised I hadn't eaten since lunch and it was dark now, guessing Mum and June hadn't either. I got more coins out and selected three ham sandwiches. Three dairy milk bars and pack packs of ready-salted crisps.

Holding a cup in each hand I balanced the rest between my arms holding the crisps in my mouth. I walked back to the seating area and passed them out. Take these, sounds like it's going to be a long night and we will need are strength to get through it. We had only just finished when we saw a doctor and a guy in a suit walking towards us. June tapped my shoulder pointing to the guy in the suit, that's the director of medicine for North Wales. "That's not good," I said suddenly regretting eating anything.

"Mr Wolf and Mrs Dunlop," he asked as he took a seat in front of us.

"Yes," we replied as he held his hand out for us to shake. "I couldn't help but notice that he only asked for me and June and not Mum who was Adams's next of kin. June must have picked up on it too because she beat me to the question. "What can we do for you? Is there any news on Adam, because surely you need his next of kin?" Pointing to Mum as she said it.

"Unfortunately, not, I don't know what's happening there. I'm afraid, but rest assured he will be in the best of hand."

"My heart skipped a beat as I heard the word unfortunately as I'm sure, Mum and June had as well. Then what do you want?" June was as unsure as to where this was going as I was.

First of all, let me introduce myself, my name is Harry Silks, I'm the chief of medicine for North Wales and this is Toby Whitehall my head of staff, we have a few questions as to, "How you got here," he said. "My heart felt like it was about to burst as," he said it. Me and June looked at each other both sensing where this was going. "I hoped I hadn't caused her any trouble getting her to use her contacts to grant us access to the hospital."

"I'm sorry," I said before June could say anything. "It was all my idea, I didn't think of anything but getting my brother here where he could be looked after, I didn't mean to cause any trouble."

"What do you mean?"

"I could see his game getting me to tell him everything without having to ask."

"Well pretending to be an air ambulance on active duty."

"Well, of course, that is very severe in normal circumstances and wouldn't be tolerated by myself or the aircrew themselves. I was about to speak again when he cut me off, but these are not normal circumstances and I think we could turn a blind eye to that."

"So, what's this about," asked June while I was still too relieved to say anything.

Turning towards me, Harry spoke. "I was told, and you just confirmed that you used an air ambulance to transport your brother here, I'm also told that you did it with a level of skill not seen by half of our current crew. That's not to say there are not good pilots but some are Rockies and could use more airtime, despite which we are under a certain amount of stress to accommodate a significant increase in patent numbers and ambulances are becoming a matter of supply and demand.

"I see where this is going," I said. "You want to know whether you could have use of the helicopter. Well, sure," I said, by all means.

"Well, it's not quite that simple," he said. "It's one thing having the use of it, but not much use, if you don't have a pilot to fly it."

"You want Rob to fly it for you!"

"That is where I'm going with this Mrs Wolf, look I know it is a big favour to ask under the circumstances and not one we wouldn't usually ask under normal circumstances, but as I just said these aren't normal circumstances, there's a heavy demand out there with the roads closed and impassable the fire brigade are clearing as much as they can as fast as they can, but it's putting a massive strain on the air ambulance, and it simply can't cope, with every second comes another call demanding its attention." I looked over at Mum and then back at Harry.

"I'm sorry," I said. "I simply can't just leave Mum here to deal with this alone."

"You go," Mum interrupted, "you can do more good out there than here with us, the end result will be the same if you stay here or go there's nothing more you can do for Adam now and it is time to answer your true calling go back up and save someone else. Me and June will hold the fort here."

"Well, that's the other thing," Harry said. "You could tell by his face, he was having trouble asking what he was but to buts, that's how desperate the situation had become."

"You want June to go with him, don't you?"

Harry stood up rubbing his hands threw his hair so tight. "I thought he was about to pull it out."

"The thing is," said Toby, taking one for the team and saving Harry the trouble. Just like the air ambulance and the increase in cases arriving in the hospital, the staff on the front line are being stretched just as thin, with everyone working full throttle to get us through it, and a nurse of June's experience. "Well, we need all the help we can get. We've managed to free up one other trained nurse who's on her way in; we can divert her to you, but even with the three of you and no doctor, it's the bare minimum required to take on an operation like this."

"Skeleton staff," said June.

"Correct," replied Toby, looking over at June we simply can't afford not to utilise everyone or miss an opportunity like this.

"I know, it's a lot to ask announced Harry having regained some of his composure. I promise, I will take a personal interest in Adam's case, and personally see to it that your mother is taken care of in your absence by taking her to my office where she will made comfortable and I can keep a close eye on her the whole time." I looked at June who in turn looked at me.

"They will do it," Mum announced not waiting for us to reply. "Go do what you both need to do; don't let anyone else suffer like we are. It's the right thing to do I will be, okay."

"Fine," we both said at the same time. "But I want to know as soon as anything happens, and I want to retain the right to call the whole arrangement off at any point."

"Agreed," said Harry, shaking my hand. "I don't think you know how much you will be helping," he said before grabbing his phone and dialling a number.

"Looks like we're going back up," I said to June.

"Sure does, we're gluttons for punishment."

Chapter Twenty-Eight
Back in the Air – *Rob*

We just stood unsure of what to do as Toby and Harry walked off, waiting to be told where to go and what to do. Soon Toby returned with a small blonde girl who wore tortoiseshell glasses. she looked about eighteen and was as confused and startled as us, as she got nearer Toby introduced us, this is Rob Wolf he will be the pilot, and this is June Dunlop, head nurse at St Lenard's, June, this is Sally she's your number two. She's done all the training required, I think you will find her very efficient and resourceful; I've never known her to flap under pressure.

"Nice to meet you," I said, offering my hand.

"You don't look like a pilot," she said, "well, not one of our usual pilots anyway."

"I'm not, I'm a chef, unsure what a pilot fit to fly an ambulance was supposed to look like." Just then Harry returned.

"Okay, I have an ambulance on its way to drop off supplies to the helicopter and instructed the air marshal to have it prepared and refuelled immediately, ready for take-off. So, if you would follow me, I just have a few papers for you to sign and we will have you on your way." We followed him through a series of corridors and doorways. Until he stopped outside a lift and pressed the button for the top floor.

"Always good to a friend in high places," I said as he did. "I thought, if I made a few jokes people wouldn't realise how nervous I had become, flying it here for Adam was one thing but here I was about to join the front-line people literally putting their lives in my hands."

The doors opened up to what was clearly offices this is a strict staff-only zone, not many civilians have made it up here. Harry said as he led us to his office. Which was situated at the end of the corridor. Inside was a woman sitting behind a desk typing on a computer. This is Jade, my personal secretary. Jade, I want you to ring down to theatres and get me the progress report on one Adam Wolf. She instantly grabbed the phone and pressed a button on the phone, it was pre-programmed with what must have been at least fifty buttons on it, what was more surprising was there was another one beside It.

"Come in." He held the door open to his office for us to walk in. It was a large, open-planned office with large windows giving magnificent views you could have mistaken it for a penthouse, a drink cabinet with crystal decanters and matching glasses stood in one corner, a large TV was mounted on the wall, a large desk stood at the end of the room facing the door it was very minimalistic just a phone, pen stand, laptop and nameplate where visible. In front of the desk were two chairs and behind them were two leather sofas both facing the TV. Take a seat.

Sitting down I couldn't help but feel how comfortable the seats were.

"Make yourself comfortable, Mrs Wolf."

"Please call me, Ann."

"Of course, Ann, make yourself at home."

Mum took a seat on the sofa and instantly sunk into it, with Sally at her side. Just as Harry collected some paper from the printer on the sideboard behind him. Took a seat behind the desk and sunk into a big black desk chair that looked like it was tailored to fit him. "Your mother is welcome to have access to this office at all times and will be more than comfortable and will be looked after, if not by me then Jade will be in the other room the whole time if I'm not here, just in case she needs anything. There's even a kitchen and a sleeping area for them long shifts, which she's entitled to use when she pleases."

"Thank you. I could tell he meant every word that or he was one hell of an actor."

"It's the least I can do," he replied as the phone blurted into life pressing a button, Jade's voice came through the speaker.

"I have theatres on the line one." Pressing another button, a man's voice came on.

"Hello, sir, what can I do for you?"

"I want a report on Adam Wolf. I believe he's currently in theatre, showing the authority in his voice as he did."

"Yes, sir, I can't tell you much at the moment. I'm afraid still too early to tell."

"I want to know as soon as he's out," he demanded, "and I don't mean in recovery, I want to know the second you're done and what the prognosis is understood?"

"Yes, sir," he said before hanging up.
"There you go. As soon as I hear anything, I will be straight on the phone you will know before he even hits recovery. I will be taking an active interest in his condition from now on and continue to till I know he's out of any danger."

"Now," he said, handing over the paper from the printer. And opening a draw, pulling a folder he took out a form and handed it to June.

Turning to me, he said, "This is just a simple authorization form used when we outsource to contractors, I just need you to sign it just so you are covered and insured to carry out work on our behalf. And June if you could sign this release form, just to say you're working for us on loan from St Leonard's till a time undisclosed. I will clear it with your chief of medicine but that shouldn't be a problem I have the right to second any member of staff under my jurisdiction as I see fit. I will see that any of your shifts until then will be covered leaving you free to help."

We signed the papers as quickly as we could and passed them over.

"Perfect," he said. After casting a glance to make sure they were all in order, then opened a draw and placed them in before locking it and removing the key. "Now did you get here from the airbase?"

"Rental, from the airbase."

"Reliable?"

"Very," I said, showing him the keys.

Standing up I went over to Mum and kissed her on the cheek. "I will be back soon, I promise. "Love you," I said, giving her a hug.

"Love you too."

"One thing confused me," I said as I met Harry at the office door. "How did you know where the helicopter was stored?" It had only just occurred to me he had never asked.

"Lucky guess, the only one airbase near here that's capable of taking such a craft mixed with the time it took you to get here after dropping him off I simply edged my bets."

Harry saw us to the elevator. All in agreement that he should go back and see to Mum leaving Sally to show us the way out. "Thank you for this," he said as the doors shut.

As we got off at the ground floor and headed for the car park Sally was in front. "You okay, Sally?" She was looking a bit worried.

"Yes," she said, trying to make it sound believable but

failing, I wasn't at all surprised she was anxious. Ten minutes ago, she didn't know us from Adam. Even now, all she knew is that I was her pilot, who can cook up a storm in the kitchen. June picked up on it straight away.

"Don't worry, you're in good hands, he's already flown it from Leicester to Wales, then from a field with his brother in the back to the hospital before dropping it off at the air base." Hearing this she cheered her up slightly reinforcing her confidence in her pilot.

We walked so fast almost running through the double doors they only just had time to open. The same doors I hadn't long arrived through, the secretary was still looking as busy and flustered as when I arrived. I took the lead and walked towards the car using the fob to unlock it as we got close.

"Nice car," Sally remarked just as she got in and shut the door.

"It's only a rental from the air base," I repeated, "and it's way too big for me I'm used to my tesla." Starting up I backed out the space and followed the one-way arrows to the exit. The barriers where down preventing exit without a ticket. I immediately put the car in reverse and tuned it round what are you doing asked June, I don't have a ticket the entrance terminal is broken, and I couldn't get one.

Backing into a space I used it to turn the car around and drove the wrong way up the one-way system. I will get a ticket said June, winding down the window as I approached the front entrance was still missing the barriers, but a security guard trying to fix the machine. "No time," I said as I shot out past the entrance. The security guard held out his hand in protest. Ignoring him I just drove straight out onto the road. Looking back, I saw him talking into the radio.

With the roads now being partly cleared I drove like the wind, with no traffic around and me finally getting the feel for this monster of a car, I was soon on the main road heading back to the airbase. As we approached the turning for the entrance to the airfield, we saw an ambulance speeding past with its lights flashing and the siren blaring. I took the turning and drove down the lane leading to the entrance. The gates opened as If by magic as I approached, I could see Carl standing there as I slammed on the brakes the car suddenly coming a halt, I jumped out leaving the engine running. Well, I appreciate the speedy return but there was no rush he said smiling as he reached in and turned the engine off.

"I will probably need it again, any chance you can keep hold of it for me?"

"It's yours, now follow me, she's all ready and waiting for you. I've done the security and safety checks already there's nothing to cause any concern. Also, you just missed the ambulance that stocked it up, they told me to say sorry it's not organised and put away, but they were needed elsewhere."

"We will survive," June said.

"I must say, you certainly proving to be one of the most interesting visitors I've had first you arrive right after a historic storm, and in nothing more than a decommissioned ambulance of all crafts, then just under two hours later you now actually going out on duty in it fully stocked, I'm impressed."

"Thanks," I said as I walked round to the cock pit, not really in the mood for chat but not wanting to appear rude. "If I'm honest, I'm surprising myself today."

I got in the front as June and Sally climbed in the back. "I saw what they meant," she said, looking at all the equipment in boxes sitting on the floor. It wasn't long before she and Sally were ripping open the boxes and sorting the equipment the best they could. Carl shut all the doors. While checking everyone was well out, he way gave me the thumbs-up sign and stood back. As I started the engine grabbing my helmet, I pressed the intercom. "Here we go again," I said, "you ready."

"As always," said June as if this was a regular occurrence. "What about you, Sally?"

"All good," she replied sounding unsure.

"Then here we go," I said contacting AC at the same time.

"Romeo Oscar Brava flying aa147 to control – ready to take off over."

"Control to Romeo – clear for take-off."

"Romeo to control – understood loud and clear over and out."

Taking hold of the collective I once again lifted us off the ground and into the air for the fourth time today.

Chapter Twenty-Nine
My Duty – *Rob/Joan*

Once we were in the air, I looked at the GPS giving me the location of the first call on active duty, looking behind me it looked like Sally had lost all anticipation she may have had and was going thought the supply with June. Sorting them into piles and checking what we had on-board. Counting out amounts of different medication and names that meant nothing to me, but they understood each other.

Sitting at the controls of the helicopter again, I couldn't help but recall what Mum and Harry had said earlier. Mum had said it's time for your true calling to get up there and Harry had said I'm also told you flew it with more skill than half the pilots we currently have, maybe it was just the excitement or maybe it was my true calling. I had to admit it felt right I was comfortable with the controls they fit like a glove in all that had happened I was excited to be back in the pit again and this time I not only had a mission to complete but a job to do.

"Everything okay back there?"

"All good," said June.

I estimate we will be there in about five minutes. We had been told earlier that due to our reduced staff and lack of training in difficult situations, we would be solely used as a carrier plane, meaning we would always land before taking on patients, not having the right training or ability to tackle hillside rescues and use the equipment even though it was still on bored.

"So how many of these you flew?" asked Sally. "You seem to be well experienced."

"Only one and you're in it," I said, trying not to scare her. "But don't worry, I have her figured out by now."

"The smoothest ride I've ever been on, and I've done a few runs."

"Thanks, means a lot. Hold on looks like we're on the approach."

"Romeo Oscar Bravo to control – on the approach request permission to land over."

"Control to Romeo – you're clear to land over."

"Understood over and out."

Lowing the craft, I hovered around looking for the best place to land, with the absence of the marker I had before it was more difficult to find the exact spot, using the light on the front to illuminate the ground below, I spotted an empty playing field with plenty of space in which to land.

Moving closer and hovering over it. I began the decent to the ground. Once again blowing dirt and dust everywhere.

June

As we got in the ambulance, we started to look though the supply's the mainly consisted of two medical bags with a few boxes containing spares should they be needed a new stretcher and been placed in more robust and modern with better fixings. A spinal board and neck brace was also by the side as well as a heart monitor, blood pressure kit and a defibrillator. Although basic I felt confident that with a bit of improvisation and resourcefulness, we could put up a good fight to anything tonight could throw at us.

Robs flying was as excellent as it was before. This helped Sally settle quickly, she had shown hesitation before take-off. Which was only natural considering she knew nothing about Rob other than he was a chef. And that he would be flying the helicopter she was to travel in, it was incredibly brave of her to even step in at all under the circumstances, especially as she didn't look old enough to have much experience.

We were nearly done checking supplies when Rob's voice came over the intercom checking up on us. Having insured him everything was well. I started to look at the brief for the mission, as Sally started chatting to Rob.

Rob had he coordinates that being all that he needed meaning the rest was down to me and Sally. Looking at the tablet that was left for us with the rest of the equipment I looked at information that as being fed to us from the paramedics on the ground. It was short and brief but gave me all the information I required to get an understanding.

Case number: #A14JG2

Name: Paul Andrews.

Sex: male

Age: seventy-two

Injuries.
- Broken leg
- Suffering from COPD
- Long history of heart trouble.
- Suspected diabetic.

Treatment. 10cc of glucose, 20cc morphine.

Notes. No sign of spinal, back or head injury, fully alert coherent. Blood pressure stable.

Risk level – yellow

The risk levels where in a traffic light system green being low risk, yellow meant medium and red high. Looking around I quickly complied what I thought, *We would need and added I to the medical bags handing one to Sally.* And giving her the tablet so she could formularise herself with the case notes. I suspected most of our cases would be like this tonight. But it suited me easy come and go cases with very little danger or risk. Simply as promised just patient carrier service.

"You ready," I asked Sally as she put the tablet down. "I could see what Toby meant when he said unflappable, apart from the worry of putting her trust in Rob, she had bounced back full of vigour and ready to go as soon as the doors opened."

"I am going to use the playing field to land Rob informed us It may be a bit further out than we would like but I don't see anything closer that's remotely suitable."

"That's fine. Just get us down we can plan our next move from there." I felt the air and atmosphere change as we lowered to the ground grabbing both bags and the tablet, I put them on the stretcher, and we waited for the propellers to slow enough to allow us out.

It wasn't long till we were out on the ground and running avoiding the propeller blades as we went, both holding a one end of the stretcher. Rob staying behind ready to take us up again as soon as we were ready. We could see a large group gathered around watching as we left one person calling us over directing us to the patient. I could see an ambulance parked further down the paramedics having done everything they could for the old boy now having a laugh trying to keep his spirts high.

"You air ambulance," the younger one asked. "It hadn't occurred to me that neither of us were in any form of uniform with no identification on us."

"Sort of. More a decommissioned line helping out. You could see they weren't too sure but with the helicopter only feet away with us running out with medical bags and a stretcher it was hard for them to dispute."

"What have we got? It was always best to get the information direct in case anything was missed, or miss communicated in the patient notes."

"This is Paul, he's seventy-two, suspected broken leg and showing signs of breathing difficulty. Glucose levels are stable now, and he is fully conscious we were going to take him by road to the royal, but control insisted, he be sent to Swansea because of his underline health issues."

"Ever been in a helicopter, Paul," I asked, pulling on some gloves as I knelt down the check is vitals myself. "They had put him on oxygen to aid his breathing, which prevented him from talking." Paul shock his head. "Well todays your lucky day, we're going to take you for a little ride.

I attached the blood pressure cuff to his arm and inflated it. Taking his arm, I checked his pulse as I let it out. After checked the reading I established although slightly high it wasn't anything to worry about. Probably down to stress. Taking the cuff off and putting it back in my bag. I turned my attention to the leg. Which had already been strapped up in a support. Turning to the two paramedics. "Can you give us a hand moving him to the stretcher?" Between Sally and the two paramedics I was beginning to feel old none of them looked a day over twenty-one and all instantly jumped to action at my command.

With the help of the paramedics, we carefully transferred him to the stretcher and taking a side each slowly walked him over to the helicopter. I've never done a shift in one of these said the youngest clearly interested and excited at actually getting a closer look, I'm due on the course sometime in the next few months, but it keeps getting put back. Me and Sally entered the helicopter and pulled him as the other pushed. I strapped him in and transferred his oxygen between ours and the one supplied by the paramedics.

The paramedics said their goodbyes and shut the door as their radios blurted into life. Rob waited for them to step back before starting up again it wasn't long till we were up in the air. Spinning around and heading back to the hospital at full speed.

"Are you okay there, Paul?" A nod of his head was all I needed good. "How you are feeling?" I could tell by his face he was in pain. Using your fingers show me out of ten how bad this is. Seven fingers came up.

So, I dug out the morphine and hypodermic. And took a dose of 25mg. Just something to ease the pain, I said before injecting into his arm.

Sally was tracking his pulse and looking at her watch when Robs voice came over the intercom were approaching but not clear for landing. Will have to hover for a bit while the pad clears.

"Okay," I said, "no rush." Before taking the tablet and adding the dosage to his notes. "How's the pain?" This time only two fingers came up. So, I sat back and waited as we hovered. It was only a few minutes later, we were moving again and lowering down onto the pad. As the propellers slowed the doors were pushed open and we unstrapped Paul from the fixings. Two doctors arrived to help us carry him out and onto a trolley I gave them the rundown of all medication and pain relief and conditions we knew of. We were heading to the door to the hospital when we were handed another stretcher. "What was this for?"

"Your next case requires immediate attention; get back on board." We ran back to the helicopter and shut the door before once again rising to the skies.

Chapter Thirty
Down to Earth – *Rob/June*

The clock and gone five a.m. by the time we heard Rob's voice come over the headset informing us that he had been told to stand down. We flew back to the airfield in silence all too tired to talk, it had been a long night taking us all over Wales's further distances than we had expected. In the course of the night, we had attended to twelve rescue and relief missions. Every one of them safely delivered. And undergoing treatment, our list of injuries consisted of five broken limbs, one heart attack, four suspected spinal cases from people trapped under rubble and two head wounds. The head wounds where the worst, one of which was so sever. He nearly died on the way there, but we were informed later on that he was in ICU undergoing treatment.

We had made four refuelling stops at the airbase. Each one takes ten minutes. We had a few intervals between cases where managed to find a half hour of rest bite before being called upon again. It was during one of these that Rob received a message from Harry, telling him Adam was in ICU after undergoing four hours in the operating theatre, but he was expected to make a full recovery.

"Sally, it turned out was a trainee nurse, just about to take on her finals and applying for permanent employment in the area. I insured her that wouldn't be an issue after her performance today, and I would personally see that she would get a glowing reference even implying she should apply to ST Leonard's. It occurred to me as we left the helicopter what an odd team, we had looked a trainee nurse a head nurse and a chef, all working together to save twelve lives. We were treated with more respect after every mission we went on, the word had got round that a group of volunteers were running a taxi service for patients to help free up the actual crew for more serious work, and we were admired all the more for it. But it wasn't till we finally stood off the helicopter to Carl, who had also been up all night running the base I thought what a mess we looked."

My god," he said, "you look like the living dead."

"You to," replied Rob. Tired and rundown from lack of sleep not to mention food and subsistence we politely, avoided starting a chat and asked for the keys to the car before heading in that direction to make our way back to the hospital.

Rob

As we headed back to the car, I knew I shouldn't be driving, I was tired and very fatigued. But I was the only one on the insurance and we were all as beat as each other. I had considered asking Carl if I could crash in his office for a while, but I wanted to know what was happening with Adam and knew I needed to go see mum.

The day and night had merged into one, leaving nothing in between the novelty of flying had worn off now. The thought of ever getting back in it now made me queasy. I opened the car and jumped in the driving seat. Taking a second before starting up, the first thing I did was open the window allowing the cool morning air to hit me in an attempt to wake me up. June had jumped in the seat beside me and Sally in the back. Looking out the window I felt Junes had touch my shoulder. "You, okay?"

"Yes," I said, suddenly being pulled out of my daze. And starting the car.

"You did good today, no one could have done more."

"I know. Let's get going; shall we see what happening?"

Keeping the window open I was barely paying attention as I pulled out the gates and on to the road. It was by some miracle we made it to the hospital alive, we had driven in silence the whole-time Sally, I'm sure had drifted off a few times, and June was also struggling to keep her eyes open. I noticed the barriers were still missing as I pulled up to the car park, but the machine now in full working order I pressed the button and took a ticket before finding a space to park. All three of us sat for a few seconds before stumbling out the car and heading for the door, all of in need of some coffee anything to perk us up.

As we walked in, we heard clapping and cheering it took us a while before we realised it was for us Harry and toby where in the front. With a few members of staff nurses, doctors, orderly's and cleaners anyone who was spare had gathered to form a welcome party. "Well done," Harry said, walking over to us. "Well done, some of the best teamwork I have ever seen. Come on, up to my office, I will have some food bought up for us all."

"I need to check on, Adam," I said.

"There's no change, Ann's been there half the night before I finally convinced her to go use one of the sleeping quarters."

"Too tired to fight." I simply followed him to the lift and stepped in as it opened. In the elevator I was struggling to stay awake and feeling very lightheaded. I leaned against the wall of the lift and watched as the doors shut before everything went black.

When I awoke feeling weak and funny a bright light shining

in my eye. I was laying on something soft. The light suddenly disappeared, and I took me a few moments its effect to dissipate and for me to realise I was laying on the sofa in Harry's office. A doctor in a white coat was standing over me putting his ophthalmoscope in his top pocket. Harry was standing at the side of him June and Sally sitting on the other sofa a mug each in their hands. I jolted up as I come to. "Easy," said the doctor, placing a hand on my shoulder pushing my back to sofa. "What happened?" I was feeling out of breath now and slightly panicked.

"It's okay," said Harry, whose relief was clear to see, "you passed out in the elevator it's not a surprise you've been under a considerable amount of stress and I expect been up for over twenty-four hours." He heading for the drink cabinet and poured some water into a glass, and flying that helicopter you're bound to be suffering from mental and physical exhaustion, you certainly flew longer and more miles than regulations stated. I should have pulled you out the air earlier. Looks like I timed it just right.

The doctor now holding my wrist and feeling my pulse, Harry walked back over with a glass of water. Here have this it will help. The doctor placed one hand, on my arm, and slowly pulled me up till I in a sitting position. Before taking the glass from harry and putting to my lips. Feeling like a child being spoon fed, I lifted my hand and took the glass from him before I took a sip and instantly started coughing. I looked at the doctor who I assumed had finished his examination, as he was now sitting down drinking from a mug himself. I recognised him from reception, he was standing beside Harry and toby as we walked in. "He will be fine," he said to Harry. "As we expected just a simple case of exhaustion like you said. A bit of a rest and he will be fine. He drank what was left in his mug and put the cup down on the coffee table."

"How long was I out? I was still feeling slightly dazed, but more alert and able to function now."

After about five minutes, Harry informed me pulling over a chair as he spoke.

"Don't do that again," June said to me, holding her head in her hands a rubbing her eyes as she did.

"Where's Mum?" Looking around I couldn't see her anywhere.

"She asleep in the on-call room, and I didn't want to wake her."

"Please don't tell her," I pleaded she has enough worry with Adam.

"I think we can do that," they agreed.

"Anyway," said Harry. "This is Dr Jenkins, I originally asked him up here to give you a report on your brother as he's the doctor in charge of his case."

"Good job I did in the end wasn't," he joked.

Stretching out my hand we shook hand. "So, doctor, how is he?"

"Please call me, Jamie. Well, there's not much change so far. He's been in the same condition since coming out of theatre. But that's good because although he's not got any better it means there's been no deterioration either. He came through the operation with flying colours. He said, there were no complications and we managed to control the bleeding. We have arranged a scan for later this morning, but I must stress this purely formality, there's no evidence or indication that he won't make a full recovery."

"So what's the scan for?"

"It's just a simple cat scan looking for any abnormalities in the brain. But like," I said purely formality.

"Could it have been the change of altitude that caused it? I wasn't entirely sure, I wanted to hear the answer but if I didn't it would bother me."

"Your mum asked the same thing, I will say the same, I said to her. I'm not saying that it won't had an effect, but there's no saying that it caused it to rupture. As I told Mrs Wolf, I'm under the impression it would have very little effect, and certainly what saved his life. The quick response he received certainly gave him the best chance of survival. With the best chance of making a full recovery, you saved his life," he said, looking at me. "And the treatment that he received beforehand as well," he said, looking at June. "He owes you both his life."

We looked at each other and gave each other a smile. I had gained so much respect for June in one day, and owed her more than I could say in words, I would make it up to her if I ever could.

Jamie's beeper burst into life. "I have to go," he said. "There's only one other thing," he started.

"You go," interrupted Harry. "I can fill them in on the rest."

"Thank you," I shouted as Jamie ran towards the door. "For everything!"

"No, thank you," he replied before leaving the room.

"One other thing?" I looked over to Harry for further explanation.

"Yes, it's possible he might have to go back into surgery."

"What!" I jolted up at hearing this in a desperate attempt to go to Adam. Nearly spilling the water as I did. Suddenly going lightheaded and dizzy again Harry was up in an instant ready to catch me with one hand a taking the glass with other.

"Sit down! You're not going anywhere till I'm sure you're ready. Falling more than sitting, back down he waited for a few seconds before handing me the cup back and starting again.

"It's not serious and may not be necessary. We won't know till he's had the x-ray, but we think we may have to reset a bone in his leg before we plaster it. It's a very simple and routine procedure. I'm not saying there's no risk but the likelihood of anything happening is slim to none the main cause of problems with a procedures like this is a reaction to the aesthetic and having just been under, it's highly unlikely he will react to it."

Chapter Thirty-One
The Hospital – *Rob*

I don't know how long we had been in the office, but we were now left alone as Harry went downstairs to attend to a call he had received. He had made me promise to not to leave the office and do nothing but rest, almost daring me to move.

Informing his secretary Jade on his way out that I was to stay where I was, effectively putting me on house arrest, Jade came in soon after offering us a drink, I asked for tea June was already asleep on the sofa Sally looked like she wouldn't be far behind not wanting anything. I was daydreaming when she arrived with the tea. "Extra sugar, give you some energy," she said, handing it over.

"Thanks, how long have you worked for Dr or Mr Silks?"

"Professor? He's one of the highest rankings in his field. Worked for him for two years started after I finished college; a friend got me the job." The phone started to ring in the office.

"I will be back. Don't you move," she said as she headed out to answer the phone.

I sat holding the mug in both hands. My head hurt and I could feel my eyes straining to keep focus. I took a few sips of the tea the added sugar causing an explosion of sweetness. In my mouth, I set the mug back down and rested again on the sofa before drifting off.

I woke up to the sound of the phone ringing and opened my eyes to see, Harry jolt up from behind his desk where he had also fallen asleep, quickly grabbing the phone and failing to hide the fact he had just woken up he answered. "Hello," he whispered into the phone.

June and Sally were still both asleep as I assumed Mum was as well. Sitting up and reached for the mug of tea still front of me and still barely touched. Picking it up I took a sip. I was used to drinking cold tea I was forever making tea at work and forgetting about only to find it two hours later. It had become that regular I had stopped heating it up drinking it cold worked just as well.

Draining the cup, I started to stand.

"Hold on a minute," Harry said into the phone, turning his attention to me.

"Carful, don't want you fainting on us again."

"I will be fine," I promised using both hands to pull myself up.

All my muscles hurt. My head was pounding, at least the pain in my eyes had nearly gone having rested for a while. Looking at the clock, it said, Nine a.m. I figured, I must sleep three maybe four hours maximum.

Seeing that I was okay, Harry resumed his conversation. Keeping his eye on me the whole time. I stretched my legs and walked towards the window the sunlight now was lighting up the spectacular view. Standing there looking out it felt like a bad dream. The view had some magical effect on me and for a few minutes I was lost in for the first time forgetting, all about the events of the last forty-eight hours and was blissfully unaware of the troubles we still faced.

"Sorry about that," he said, placing the phone back into the cradle and breaking the moment all the feeling and memories flooding back.

"I thought, I had put it on silent. I didn't mean to wake you."

"It's okay, it's your office," I said, walking over to the chair in front of his desk and taking a seat.

"How are you feeling?"

"Like I've been hit by a bus?"

Leaning back in his chair he let out a laugh. "Yeah exhaustion will do that for you."

"You hungry?"

"I'm fine, don't trouble yourself on my account."

"I'm not, I'm starved, I will ring down to the canteen and order breakfast for five," he said as if we were in a hotel complete with complimentary room service. Picking up the receiver he pressed a button.

"It's Harry silks, can I have five full English breakfasts complete with tea, coffee and orange juice brought to the conference room."

"That's fine," he said before hanging up.

"Be about twenty minutes?"

"That gives me time to go toilet," I said, standing up. I was still a bit uneasy on my feet but the effects of last night still taking their toll. Straight out past the office and its first on the right?

I left the office and walked into the secretary's office, Jade wasn't at her desk instead sat an older woman with auburn hair; you're up then. "I'm Jackie, Rob," I said, shaking hands as I did.

"Is it true, what everyone's saying?"

"About what?" I leaning against the desk for support.

"That you flew your brother here by yourself before volunteering to go help others?"

"Didn't quite work like that, but it's true that I flew the helicopter yes, I flew my brother in for treatment."

"You're a hero."

"I wouldn't go that far, just doing my bit."

"You did more than your bit."

"Well thanks, it's nice to be appreciated now I would love to stay and chat but I must use the facilities."

"First."

"On the right," I interrupted as I walked out the door.

As I crossed the corridor, I saw a door slightly open. Pushing the door slightly I could see Mum fast asleep, I wondered how many hours she had managed to get during the night. Quietly shutting the door, I walked to the bathroom. I was expecting a room with a toilet and a hand basin, but as I walked in, I was surprised to see a full shower cubical in what was a family sized bathroom, it was ice white with a black tiled floor. The toilet hovered off the ground and towels were placed on heated towel rails. There was a large window that was frosted to stop people seeing in quite pointless for a room so high up but with cameras now a days you could zoom into a room from 10-miles away, and NASA could take a clear picture from space.

As I washed my hands in the basin. I looked in the mirror. And could see I needed a wash. Finding a face flannel, I soaked it in water and pressed it to my face. Instantly feeling refreshed. I stood for a few moments enjoy feeling the water on my face. Before drying off and heading back to the office.

I re-entered the office, June and Sally where now awake, Harry having woke them up ready for breakfast. "Sleep well?"

"Yes, thanks," she said, yawning even though June was the first to fall asleep she still would have only had four hours at best only enough to slightly recharge. Being a nurse, she was used to long hours as was as I. Neither of us a stranger to burning the midnight oil.

Jackie went to wake Mum and was told to meet us in the conference room. We followed out of the office and down the corridor, he stopped at the door facing the lift and entered a code. It was a large room with an oval table with what must have been thirty chairs around it. There was a speaker in the middle of the table with a dialling pad built in for calls. Pressing a switch on the wall a projector screen came down from the roof and a projector appeared form a hidden compartment above us.

Grabbing a remote from the side table he turned on the news, a presenter was in the middle of asking questions to the health secretary.

"So, we don't know how many fatalities this storm as claimed?"

"No, but it's expected to be in the hundreds. Many shelters just simply weren't up to the task of protection from such high winds."

"Surly that begs the question that we should finally be looking at changing the regulations regarding the level of protection shelter can take isn't it," a reporter asked.

"It's something that will certainly be bringing up with secretary of defence, and the prime minister himself. But its clear something will have to be done if we are to avoid a disaster of this magnitude again."

"But what happens in the meantime, many thousands have lost their homes and lucky to come out with their lives. What do you have to say them?"

"I would like to reassure everyone that we are in the process of looking into where the storm as caused the most damaged and arranging some form of support and housing the those most in need. But let's not forget that some shelters although damaged are still accessible with supply of up to two months if not longer inside, we ask people to take refuge in them, were safe to do so and help those in need of shelter if there in a position to. Working together we will get through this," he said.

Harry muted the screen leaving the subtitles running it was only then that we saw Mum leaning against the door. Staring at the screen.

"Mum," I said getting up and giving her a hug. "You, okay?"

"Yes, just glad you're back safe."

"Of course, I'm back safe." I walked Mum over to the table where she took a seat next to June.

"You look terrible."

"Thanks." I smirked back.

"How did it go last night?"

"Fine," we all said in unison not wanting to upset her with the details.

"More than fine, Ann," Harry said. "These three saved a dozen lives more if you include Adam."

"Which I do." She took June's hand. "Rob, the doctor says that the helicopter wouldn't have made any difference to Adams condition. In fact, it's what saved him."

I knew that wasn't quite what the doctor said, but either she was trying to clear me of any guilt I was carrying or had made herself believe what that's what the doctor had said either way I let it go.

"I know." I spoke to the doctor as soon as I arrived back.

"What time did you get back?"

"They were called down around five a.m.," said Harry. "The roads had been cleared to allow ambulances to pass and the demand on the air crew was significantly reduced."

"No wonder, you look tired."

Just then a knock came at the door a canteen server was pushing in a trolley. Which contained five plates with lids on, two thermoses, five mugs and glasses and a jug of orange juice.

"Room service," she said as she walked in. Harry thanked her and told her to leave the trolley where it was. He handed us each a plate, cup and glass, putting both thermoses in the middle of the table.

"One thermos," said coffee the other hot water. He pulled a wicker basket off the trolley containing tea bags, sugar and more coffee powder in little sachets. We all took the coffee apart from Mum who opted for tea not being a big coffee drinker.

"Please accept this as a thank you on behalf of me and the hospital," he said, "for everything you did."

"To you," he said, toasting with his mug.

Lifting the lid off the plate there was two slices of toast, two sausages, two rashers of bacon, a grilled tomato and a ramekin of beans. It didn't take long for any of us finish. All eating way too fast for our own good. "Don't know why they complain about hospital food," Mum said, sitting back as she finished the last of her breakfast that seemed perfectly all right to me.

"Well, Harry, I did order from the staff canteen and I insist they always cook a fry up fresh. So, I wouldn't judge all the meals on that."

The phone started to ring, Harry pressed a button and Jackie's voice came though the speaker. Message from Dr Jenkins sir, he says that a Mr Wolf as just gone down for his scan then said he would let you know when he's out. "Thank you, Jackie," he said before ending the call.

We won't know any more until later today, the scan will take a while and then a while to analyse the results. You're more than welcome to wait here if want, but if I'm honest there's not much point. It will be late this afternoon that the results will come back. If it's agreeable with you I will arrange for someone to drive, you home where you can get some rest and freshen up. I'm going to get my head down here. And I will ring you as soon as I know anything?

Looking at June, she could certainly do with a change of clothes, and so could I. I had left my bag behind when we picked Adam up. "Agreed," I said, apart from the lift.

"You sure you will be okay to drive?"

"I'm sure, the food and ample amount of coffee had boosted my energy levels and I was more than capable of driving. Besides, we will need to get back again and there's no helicopter to get us here this time."

"How about you, Sally, do you want dropping of anywhere?"

"No, thanks. I don't live far away I could do with some fresh air." We exchanged numbers with Sally. Harry gave us his card containing his direct line should we need him.

Having all finished, we stood up and headed for the elevator. We pressed the button and waited for it to open. "I will see you later," Harry said as we got in, and security has permission to let you out without charge. He said, "There's no need to drive out the entrance this time," as the doors shut. I hung my head in shame as June and Sally looked at me a smile across their faces. Mum just looked confused.

Chapter Thirty-Two
Facing the Music – *Rob/June*

Rob

"Where's the car?" asked Mum.

"This way," I said, leading past the row of cars and round the corner. I walked towards the car and unlocked it as Mum went to walk past.

"Were you going?"

"Sorry, was looking for your Tesla."

"Isn't this Jay's car?" Looking confused as she got in the only difference being the absence of booster seats.

"Same model, different vehicle."

I started up and backed out the spot. As I approached the exit, I saw the same security guard I had driven past yesterday.

"Hello," I said, pulling up beside him apparently. "We have permission to have the barriers lifted," I said, hoping he didn't recognise me.

"Name?" he said, looking up. "Oh, it's you."

"Yes, about yesterday," I started.

Holding up his hand to cut me off. "Don't mention it, it's all been explained."

Without even looking at the sheet he lifted the barriers and said, "Thanks."

"Anytime."

With the barriers now open, I pulled out onto the road as

June struggled to load her post code into the satnav, before giving up Insisting we didn't need it as she knew the way.

"It's not knowing the way; it will direct us round the diversions and road closures I argued The last thing I want to do is sit in traffic."

"Don't worry, we won't be using the main road." Mum fell asleep in the back not long into the journey and June was content just staring out the window, occasionally giving me directions, and managing to avoid any traffic.

Even missing traffic and taking every shortcut possible it still took us over an hour till we arrived pulling up outside I could see everyone sitting on a pile of wood all eating lunch, Rex waiting patiently for any food to fall. We got out and headed towards them Sue, Jay and Dad instantly stood up. "What happened to you," they exclaimed, sounding shocked. "Here take a seat."

"No thanks."

"First, I need a shower."

Me echoed June, "Coffee lots of coffee."

We both headed for the shelter, Scott wasn't far behind us followed by Sue, Mum was hugging Dad and insuring him she was fine.

June

Rob had the right idea; shower first talk later, I was still beat from yesterday and I was a passenger for most of it. How Rob was still standing I don't know. I wasn't surprised when he had fainted earlier. Luckily Harry was fast with his reactions and caught him just in the nick of time. I felt bad about not telling Ann, but it was a simple case of exhaustion and it would only cause her more worry even so after everything had calmed down, I would try and get Rob to tell her. Scott followed as we went the shelter.

Once we were in Scott gave me a hug. "Don't," I said. "Already too late, I'm filthy."

"I was worried about you. Why didn't you call, he let go and started prepping the coffee machine?"

"Didn't have time."

"I can see that I suppose once there you jumped straight into the ward and started taking over."

"Something like that."

Rob came up behind me holding the travel bag he had brought with him before.

"You go first, you need it more than me."

"You sure?"

"Yes, go on your covered in god knows what."

He took a seat as I walked out. "Coffee, I heard," Scott ask as I walked out.

I headed to the bedroom and collected some fresh clothes. Before entering the bathroom. Turning on the shower, I started stripping off what I was wearing I realised some of it was stuck to me. Blood had seeped though, and my entire torso was covered in blood.

I put the old clothes into a bag from which I would put them in the bin I wasn't even going to try and save them, they weren't anything special anyway.

It felt like I was washing away the last few days as I stood under the water. The water turning red as it washed off all the blood. Most of it was from one patient, the one with the uncontrollable head wound. It was impossible to control the bleeding. I doubted whether he would make it. Reports where that he was in ICU but unlike Adam there was no way he would escape some form of brain damage.

As I washed my hair, I could feel it clumped together from sweet and whatever else was in it. I indulged in the feeling as hot water rushed over my body. Before remembering Rob would be needing a wash as much I did. I grabbed a towel off the rack and started to dry myself off. I placed the towel in the washing hamper and replaced it with a new one.

I quickly got changed and headed to the kitchen. Rob was sitting with Sue and Scott all had a mug of coffee. "It all yours? Take as long as you like."

Grabbing a mug, I poured myself some coffee and took the seat Rob had just vacated.

"You look beautiful," said Scott.

"Please don't," I said. "I haven't done my make-up or sorted my hair yet."

"It doesn't matter, if you are hungry, I can cook you something."

"No thanks, I've already eaten too much."

"I suppose Rob's already explained everything."

"No, won't say a word said, he's not saying anything till we're all together."

"So, what did happen?" asked Sue.

"If Rob isn't saying, then neither am I." I stood up mug in hand and headed for the door. "But I will say this your brother is a hero in the eyes of everyone at that hospital and mine. And I walked out the door."

"That's exactly what he said about you," they both said after me.

Rob

I entered the shelter and headed straight for my bag founding it in the hallway, it was surrounded by piles of possessions that had obviously come from the wreckage of both houses. I stopped as I saw a figurine. It was completely white and in the shape of a woman holding a child. I recognised it instantly it as mum's it had been in the family for generations it had supposedly been given to my great, great grandma as a wedding gift from a prince who had attended their wedding. Although it had never been tested it was rumoured to be made of pure ivory. And made especially for her. It was modelled on one that was kept at his palace, although it had never been proven we had never seen another one like it. If the story was true not only, was it worth a fortune not that any amount of money was worth more than the sentimental value it was only one of two to exist. And it had somehow survived.

 I saw Sue coming up behind me. "You found it," I said, looking at her. I could feel my eyes beginning to water.

 "It's the first thing we found?" It was like it was just waiting for us saying, "Here I am."

 Placing it back I grabbed my bag and headed towards the bathroom. Afraid of showing how emotional I was getting in front of Sue. Stopping outside the door for a moment I realised June needed it more than me and changed my direction to the kitchen. "You go first," I said to June as I walked in you need it more than I do.

 "Are you sure?"

 "Yes. I was already taking a seat and putting my bag down."

 "Want some coffee," Scott asked.

 "Love some."

"You look beat mate."

"I feel it."

"What have you three been up to, you can't have got in that condition from sitting in a waiting room."

"Well, I started, before stopping."

"You know what, it might be better to wait till were altogether save us going though it twice."

"Come on," said Sue as she joined us in the kitchen. "Just the highlights."

"No. Sorry you will have to wait. But I will say this June worked miracles today she's a real hero."

"Fine," she said sulkily.

"She always is," said Scott. "Nice car by the way."

"Thanks, it's a rental."

"Looks like ours. Jay will be impressed."

"Exactly the same. How have things been here?"

"Okay, we got worried when you didn't call. Been checking with the hospital all they said was Adams stable but had to have a brain operation."

"Yes, he deteriorated while in the helicopter they rushed him straight into theatre."

"Will he be all right?"

"Well, I haven't actually seen him, Mum spent some time with him during the night."

"Well, where were you?"

Sounding annoyed, "I wasn't around."

I shot her a warning look.

"I know, I will have to wait."

"Anyway, the doctor and professor seem to think we got him there just in time. And that he should make a full recovery. We came home to get sorted as there was nothing else, we could do while he's having a scan and then an x-ray there's a possibility he might have to go back in theatre to reset his leg. But I've been insured its purely just procedure."

"Shouldn't someone be there?"

"No, he's in good hands and Harry is taking a personal interest in the case. He will let us know as soon as anything happens."

"Who's Harry?" Scott asked.

"The director of medicine."

"For the hospital?" Sue said, sounding shocked.

"No, Wales," I replied, just as June walked in.

"All yours, take as long as you like," June announced.

I grabbed my bag and headed straight out the door. Leaving his mouth wide open in shock.

Chapter Thirty-Three
Another Family Conference – *Rob*

I stepped out the shower, feeling refreshed, as well as cleaning myself the shower had also washed away all the stress leaving me calm a fully in control ready to get us through the next stage.

I grabbed the towel and rummaged through my bag grabbing what clothes I had packed. My outfits consisted of some light blue jeans a black top and blue striped top. I also took out my denim sport jacket and exchanged my boots for trainers. Placing everything else into a plastic bag, I kept for my dirty clothes, I stuffed into the bag.

As I walked out of the bathroom, I could hear June's hair dryer going. Looking in the bedroom she was sitting in front of a mirror, doing her hair and makeup.

"That didn't take long, either that or I've been very slow."

"Not at all." I laughed as I walked towards her and sitting at the end of the bed.

"I just want to thank you for everything, I don't know how but one day I will repay the favour."

Putting down the mascara she turned to look at me, taking my hand in hers and holding it tight, she looked me in the eye. "You don't owe me anything," she said. "What you did was extraordinary. I couldn't have done it without you."

"And I without you."

"Now," she said, turning back round a picking up the mascara again we need to tell that lot out there. "I was informed you refused and who was I to counteract you."

"It's our story, we shall tell it together if Mum hasn't already."

There will be plenty of questions, yet Ann doesn't know over half of it remember.

Laying down on the bed as I waited for June to finish her makeup, I wanted to fall asleep, but not wanting to face them alone I stayed till she was ready.

"Ready?" I looked up to see her looking back to her usual self, she looked as if she had just got up from a full night's sleep.

"The powers of makeup," I remarked suddenly feeling like I was letting the side down.

"Come on, let's go get it over." With that, she walked out of the room.

Leaving my bag where it was. I followed her out the room everyone was now back outside sitting around the log seating two more logs had been added waiting for us. As we approached, I saw Sam and his dad sitting with the others. I had only meet his dad a couple of times, but he was the spitting image of Sam just older.

"There they are," he said, getting up and coming over.

"What's this? I hear about you coming back looking like you had just been run over. Why do I always miss the fun?" We sat back down on the logs.

"I've Rang work," he said.

"I completely forgot about that. They will go mad."

"No, they won't."

I got hold of Harry apparently the whole place is wreaked they don't think it is even worth fixing up. We're going to need new jobs I'm afraid.

"Okay, enough," said Sue. "Tell me what happened last night."

"You mean Mum hasn't told you?"

"Thought it would be better coming from you, I don't know a lot of it myself."

"Where do I begin," I asked June.

"From the moment you took off," Jay suggested.

We retold the story detailing the event from the moment we took off to the second we parked up and June took it in turns. It turns out our efforts had gotten us a mention on the news, Sam having watched it with his dad although they didn't mention names it was rumoured that a Sevillian crew had assisted in the air operation, reports from locals thanking them for their help deeming them a blessing in disguise. Some kind of hero turning up to save them all from the villain that was wreaking havoc.

"Well," June said. "Looks like we've gone from heroes of a hospital to a living legend of Wales. We had just finished when my phone started to ring."

"Hello?"

"Rob, it's Harry, just had the results back on Adam he's showing signs of improvement he's even opened his eyes. The scan shows no abnormality other than some swelling that's consistent with a blunt-force trauma like he received. The x-ray shows a break so we will be prepping him for the op now he should be out of recovery by six p.m. and we feel confident enough with his progress that he can be moved from there straight to a ward. This means he's out of the ICU."

I let out a deep breath as he finished. "Thank you so much, for everything."

"Any time, I hope to see you soon. Tell reception when you

arrive. You have a full access pass to the entire hospital within reason."

"Will do. Bye."

I ended the call to see that everyone was looking at me. "He's fine," I said. "He's being prepared for theatre to sort his leg; they say he will be out about six p.m. and into a ward they don't think he requires ICU any more."

"That's great," said June. "What did they say about the scan?"

"Just that there's nothing abnormal but swelling consistent with blunt force trauma. He's even opened his eyes."

"He's going to make it." Sobbed Mum.

"I told you, he would," Dad replied.

Turning to June, apparently, we need to inform reception when we arrive. He said, "We have all access pass to the hospital within reason."

"You know what that means don't you?"

"No, for once I don't."

"It means staff canteen."

"It was now three p.m. and we wanted to be back at the hospital by the time Adam was out of recovery."

"We don't have long."

"And I only have five seats."

"Seven," said Rob.

"I only counted five."

"What about the ones in the back?"

"Didn't know there was any."

"Give me the keys," he said. "I will sort it."

We decided that me, June, Mum, Dad, Jay and Sue would go to the hospital leaving Scott with the boys. Sam and his dad would go back and shelter at his.

Chapter Thirty-Four
Sleeping Beauty – *Rob*

We had nearly two hours to spare before needing to leave out. Everyone decided the best way to kill some time was to get back to work trying to salvage anything they could.

As we stood up to start rummaging through the rubble. Me, Mum and June were told to go the shelter and get some rest. Too tired to argue, Mum headed for the living room being informed that the sofa bed was made up ready. June escaping to hers. And I was told the bed in the games room was for me. and that kids had been told not interrupt alternatively I could use the other sofa bed in the living room, in the end I decided against either preferring to settle in the kitchen with a cup of tea. It was no use even trying to sleep. I was too wired from the coffee and having gone past tired long ago. I was replying to a message from Sean. He had heard of the heroic actions, having called Carl at the air base to check I had landed safe. He finished saying Carl was impressed and allowing me to use the base as long as I needed. I was halfway through a reply when Sam came in. "Didn't think you would sleep," he said, taking a seat facing me; I could see something was wrong. He clearly wasn't himself.

"Penny for them," I said, putting the phone down.

It's Dad he's acting as if everything's okay when in reality it's not. He won't accept that the house is gone he's out there now helping saying he can't wait to get home and put his feet up.

I take it the house is gone.

Completely, the entire street as gone, the shelters a communal that houses the whole street are on bunk beds.

"So, what do you intend to do?"

"I don't know, I was hoping you would know."

"Well, the obvious choice is taking him back with us. Doesn't have to be permanent just until we can get him back on his feet."

"I've suggested that. But he won't. Saying there is no need."

"It's shock, it will sink in soon and when he starts to evaluate his options he will come around."

"I suppose you are right."

"I always am remember."

We sat in silence for a while finishing my reply to Sean, eventually, Sue, Jay and Dad walked in that's enough for today. I'm going to clean myself up looking at my watch time had flown by and it was already reading four-thirty. "Better hurry," I said, "after them we don't have long."

Turning back to Sam as I stood up. "Go back with him tonight and tomorrow we will look into it more let him sleep on it. I'm not going anywhere anytime soon. Especially if works shut."

"Thanks," he said as I headed out the door.

Half hour later, we were walking back to the car Jay still had the keys and although he wasn't on the insurance I didn't protest when he automatically jumped in the driving seat. I set the sat nav this time hoping it would divert and take us the route we took like last time. But putting it on silent navigation in case June took over navigating.

Mum was desperate to see Adam and kept asking how long it would take. June who had come hoping to not only get an update on Adam, but also hoping to find out the fate of her twelve patients as she was now calling them. Jay's driving was significantly better than mine. And he managed to make the journey in half the time.

As we approached the gates a security guard appeared stopping Jay as he was about to take a ticket, he saw me and June. And lifted the barriers before waving him though. I saw him salute the vehicle as we passed.

"Well, that was strange," he remarked as he watched the car behind us take a ticket. "Hope he didn't think we were someone else."

"No, he knew it was us," said June as Jay found a space and pulled in with ease.

Getting out once again me and June took the lead and walked towards entrance, hoping we didn't get a welcome like last time. To our relief there was no one to be seen as we walked through the glass doors and headed for reception. The Staff had changed and someone else was now manning the desk.

"Can I help?"

"Yes, my name's Rob Wolf, I was told to report to reception on arrival."

The name clearly having rang a bell she instantly picked up the phone and pressed a button.

"Hey, Jade, it's reception. Mr Wolf has arrived."

She stopped as she waited for a reply. "Okay," she said before hanging up.

"If you would take a seat over there." She pointed towards the waiting area. "And Mr Silks will be right down."

"Mr Silks?" she asked. We took a seat.

"Also known as Harry," I replied.

"Ahh, your friend in high places," Jay said, earning him a punch on the shoulder from Sue.

As we sat, we saw a few doctors from the night before. "Have they been on all this time?"

"It's more likely shift change," June said, looking at her watch it's about time. Every so often people would stop point to us and whisper something and the other person would look shocked.

"What going on?" Dad said clearly, looking uncomfortable.

"I don't know, but I don't like it."

I wasn't long till Harry walked round the corner he had changed his clothes and clearly had a good nap since we last spoke his eyes still red as if. He had only just woke up. "Look at you, don't you both scrub up well. It hadn't occurred to me what a state we must have looked at are last meeting."

Standing up, I shook his hand and started the introductions. "Harry, this is Jay."

"Hello," followed by handshake.

My dad Peter—another shake—and my sister Sue got kiss on the cheek and everyone this Mr Silks.

Harry to friends. And any friend of Rob is a friend of mine. "I have your all access passes here," he said, handing one to me and one to June. "Let me take you to Adam, sorry I took so long I had to find where they had moved him."

We followed him to ward seven, which was on the second floor. And specialised in head wounds. Swiping a card like the ones he had given me and June, you have twenty-four hour access, you can come and go as much as you please. All the staff have been instructed to not prevent your entry.

The ward looked more like a hotel hallway with plants on wooden tables and leaflets sitting around. A few soft chairs were around with neatly stacked pile of magazines.

We put him in here where he would be comfortable it's

usually reserved for private patents, but the odd VIP gets in from time to time. Harry explained as he stopped outside a room and opened the door for us to go in.

Mum walked up to the side of his bed before picking up his hand a kissing it. "How's he doing?"

"No change since my phone call this afternoon, I'm afraid but he's showed good sighs of response. Don't worry, Ann, he will be fine. Now I'm going to leave you I will be in the office if you need me."

"Don't you have a home to go to?" asked Jay as a joke.

"As a matter of fact, as of last night I don't," he replied before heading towards the door. Stopping by at my side as he did, when you have a minute can you a June meet me in the office.

"Sure, in about an hour?"

"Whenever suits you," he said before heading out the door.

"Well done, Jay," said Sue, after he left.

"Well, how was I to know?"

Dad was at Mum's side who was still clutching Adams hand he was her youngest, her baby and if she could have picked him up and cradled him in her arms, she would. He looks so peaceful she said remember when he was young and wouldn't sleep until you sang that song, or how when he fell over, he wouldn't stop crying until I kissed it better, suddenly standing. Before bending down and kissing his forehead. "There we go," she said it's all right mummy's here. As if he was little child.

Adam although unconscious wasn't stuffed full of wires having being deemed safe to breath unaided and not require life support. All he had was a pulse monitor connected to his finger a blood pressure cuff loose around his left arm, and a cannula connected to a saline drip. His leg was in plaster and elevated a bandage was also wrapped tightly around his shaved head holding a pad in place on the right side of his head.

I walked over to June. "Harry wants us to meet him in his office," I whispered.

"When?"

"Whenever were ready."

"Did he say what it was about?"

"No, just asked us to come up."

"Sounds ominous," she said as Sue who hadn't moved since she walked in, suddenly walked out of the room. "I could hear her crying, I will go," said Jay as I turned to leave.

"I will come with you."

Chapter Thirty-Five
Press Harassment – *June/Rob*

Sue was leaning on the wall outside the room. Jay walked up and pulled her into a hug.

"He will be fine," Jay said.

"I know it's just seeing him like that, I knew he was bad, but it wasn't until I saw him I realised how close to death he was."

"He's not going to die," I said. "The doctors say he will make a full recovery. And with Harry taking an interest they will be paying close attention."

"Hello, again, Mr Wolf."

I turned around to see Dr Jenkins, his hand on the door handle to Adams's room letting go he came closer.

"How are you feeling now?"

I could feel Jay and Sue turn their attention from him to me.

"I'm fine. I would still like to keep our secret," I whispered. "Hoping Jay and Sue wouldn't hear. And there's no need for formalities," I said. "Just call me Rob."

"Of course, sorry I forgot. I'm just going to check on your brother," he said. "He's made brilliant progress considering his injuries."

"See," said Jay, turning to Sue. "He will be fine."

"Sorry, I should have introduced you this is my sister Sue and her husband Jay."

"Nice to meet you, he stretched out his hand to Jay. I'm Dr Jenkins your brother's primary physician. But you can call me

Jamie. I'd better go in once again placing his hand on the door handle. Have you spoken to Harry yet he asked half in the room."

"Yes and no. He brought us to Adam but asked me to meet him in the office when I was ready."

"That's okay," then he said before heading in the room shutting the door behind him.

"What's all that about?" Sue asked.

"I don't know. Don't suppose I will till I go up and speak to him."

And the bit about you feeling better, Jay asked, "What do you want kept secret."

"I was hoping you hadn't heard that."

"Come on, no secrets remember, you said you told us everything earlier."

"Only if you promise not to tell anyone else, especially Mum."

"Why?"

"Because she would only worry and there's no need."

"Just tell us."

"It's a bit embarrassing," I said, sliding down the wall till I was sitting on the floor. We returned to the hospital after dropping the helicopter back off, and we told you greeted by a welcome comity.

"You went up to Harry's office," Sue interrupted.

"Yes, well, I passed out in the elevator on the way up and Harry had to catch me and carry me into the office. That's where I met Dr Jenkins making probably the worst first impression of my life. It was just exhaustion from all the hours of flying, after that Harry put me on office arrest till he was sure I had recovered."

"Why is that embarrassing?"

"Well, I was here to see Adam not be a patient myself."

"Yeah, but it's only natural after the day you had."

"Exactly, hence the reason for keeping it quite didn't seem worth mentioning you know what Mum like if she heard that she would hit the roof one son in ICU and another passing out. She's better of not knowing so don't say anything only a few of us know."

Sue looked at Jay. "It's only a white lie," he said to Sue, "who didn't like keeping secrets?"

"Okay," she said this once.

"We stood up. But you're all right, now, aren't you?"

"Of course," he said. Jay looked at him. "Does he look like he's about to fall down," he said jokingly, punching my arms as if to knock me over. "See solid as a rock," he said as June came out the door.

"Why wouldn't he be?"

"Dr, Jamie let it slip about the incident in the elevator."

"Ohh, looking at me so I suppose that means."

"That it's now their secret as well."

"Okay, well, the Dr's just checking Adam's vitals, I thought, this would be a good time to go and see what Harry wants."

"Something's definitely going on, even Jamie asked on his way in if had spoken to him yet."

"Then we had better go find out."

"Can we come?" asked Sue. "I'm not ready to go back in there yet."

"Don't see why not, do you remember the way?" I asked June, looking up and down the corridor completely lost.

"Yes, follow me."

As it turned out she didn't know the way and after fifteen minutes of walking around, we eventually ended up at reception.

I walked up to the desk, and the receptionist recognised me straight away. "Hello again."

"Hey, Professor Silks asked us to meet him in his office, and we can't seem to find the way."

"You will need the staff elevator and it requires a card you I will ring up for you."

"It's fine." June held up her card. "We have the card it's the elevator we can't find."

A look of shock came across her face, "Where did you get a card?"

"Professor Silks."

"He gave you his card."

"No, just a card," he said, "to use around the hospital."

"Well, the elevator is down the corridor take the first left followed by the first right."

"Thanks," I said before walking off.

I get the impression that these aren't given out freely, I said, following the directions, "We had been given, we soon found the elevator and was on are way up to the top floor." As the doors opened Sue stared at the hallway with its thick carpet.

They followed as we walked towards the office admiring the art on the walls, I knocked on the door and Jade looked up from her computer. Looking up and noticing it was us, it took her a while before it clicked who we were.

"Oh, it's you, come in." We entered her office as she pressed a button and informed Harry, that we had arrived. Before she could even put the phone down, the door opened and Harry was telling us to come in. Jay and Sue held back. "I think we should probably stay out here," said Sue, feeling intimidated.

"Don't be silly, come on though," Harry said, holding the door open as they walked in, instantly looking impressed with the office. But with the sun having only just going down you could the whole sky was lit up red, large floor-to-ceiling windows mixed with the highest give a spectacular view of the sunset.

"Can you arrange some coffee and tea? Please, Jade," Harry asked before shutting the door once we were all inside.

We all stood standing, not sure where we should sit this time. Sue still open-mouthed taking in the view. "Take a seat," he said, pointing to the sofas; we all took a seat me and June taking one sofa and Jay and Sue the other. Harry went to the end of the desk and dragged a chair over, so he was sitting facing us. The TV was on mute. With *BBC* news presenter giving the headlines.

"So, what can we do for you this time? One more patient needs transporting with no crew."

"As desperate as you are to get back in the air, I'm afraid not. As you can imagine, were under considerable amount of stress from the media for information regarding the storm," he said. The phones won't stop ringing with reporters trying to get a story out of us about the impact its having on the NHS and all other types of questions.

Jade entered with a tray of coffee and placed it on the table in front of us all. Before backing out the door we all took a cup.

"I get what you asking, and don't worry we haven't said anything," June replied after taking a sip of her drink.

"That's right, we haven't even heard from them but rest assured if they do, we won't tell them anything."

"Well, you wouldn't have, because most of the calls are about you and your achievements, they all want a name. I even had to ring the airbase and speak to the air marshal, man he likes to chat, asked him not release any information took a while to get to that point though."

"So, what's the problem," June said, trying to hold back a smirk and failing.

"The problem is that every reporter and journalist is after name and story to explain how these three heroes that randomly flew into the area yesterday and started saving lives."

"They obviously don't know the whole story," I said.

"Well, no they don't know anything, and they don't like that. So, they will continue to dig and sooner or later one of them is going to get a lead and start piecing it all together."

"So, let them, we will tell them to sling their hook."

"Well, the health minister and press relations office want to try a different approach and have you quite the opposite approach," he said. "They want to name you both along with Sally at tomorrow's press conference, they will hand out a prepared statement regarding what happened in an attempt to keep them at bay make sure your actions are acutely reported in the papers."

"Won't that make things worse and just make them come looking for us?"

"Well, after they want to do a photo shoot with me, the health security and the three heroes at the airbase they want you to tell your story to the media."

"What! They want us to go out there and be harassed by a load of reporters." June's nurse's voice came through with her anger.

"We will have a police presence, and it will all be tightly regulated all papers will be informed that they aren't to bother you on personal numbers and not to be seen appearing at your homes, or invading your privacy, you would be assigned an MRO (media relations officer) who will deal with all the requests and harassment for you. Leaving you to get on with your lives as normal as possible."

"I don't know. I didn't do any of this for attention I would feel more comfortable just waiting for it all to blow over."

"Me too, I'm just a normal nurse, with a family."

"Well, it's up to you, I promised the health minister I would argue the case, and I feel that I've explained all there is to know in regard to what you would be required of you, and what help you would receive. Why don't you think on it for a while, it's a big thing to just agree to, I do need an answer before you leave so we can prepare the press conference."

"We will think about it but I feel we will be letting you down on this occasion."

"You won't be letting me down at all. It's the healthy minister's idea I feel we have already imposed on you enough."

Standing up we promised to think about it and get back to him with our answer later.

"Are there any updates on the cases we brought in last night," June asked as headed back to the elevator. "I can't stop wondering what happened to them."

"They're all still alive, thanks to you, although all in different stages of recovery, but I've been too busy to keep a check on them all. Toby, would be the best person to ask?" he said, digging out his phone.

"Toby?" Sue whispered so Harry wouldn't hear.

"He's the chief of staff."

"Is there anyone you don't know in this hospital?" Jay whispered in my other ear.

"Loads, just seem to be well connected with the highflyers."

"Toby said if you head back to reception, he will personally give you a tour of the hospital and review the cases with you as you go."

"Thank you," we said, stepping into the lift.

"Anytime," she shouted back, as the door shut.

Chapter Thirty-Six
Ward Rounds – *June*

The lift started to head down to reception we had only gone a few floors when the elevator stopped. As the doors opened, we could see Toby waiting to get in.

"That's good timing," he said as he got in. "I hear you want to check your charges."

"I can't stop thinking about them. I usually see all my patients through from start to finish. I can't seem to get used to just dropping them off and leaving them behind."

"That's the sign of a dedicated nurse, not all people care so much about their work. It's a good quality to have, I wish half my staff had the same dedication."

The doors opened and we followed Toby around as he headed for reception. "Thought it would be better to start from here."

"The patients will come in through that door, and across to the accident and emergency department this is where most walk in will be seen to, unless like in Adams case they require immediate surgery. Would you like to see it or move on. Everyone you admitted yesterday will be onwards. It will be today's intake in there now."

"I think we can move on."

"Okay then, this way."

We followed as he approached over room's pediatrics, triage and respiratory ward covered ninety per cent of the first floor.

Apart from ward four, also known as ICU (intensive care unit) he said mainly for Sue and Jay's benefit.

We walked into a sea of beds some in rows others in rooms. Going behind a desk he greeted the ward sister. And picked up a clipboard scanning though he indicated for us to follow.

We walked fast as he passed a row of people nearly all on life support. This is where Adam would have first been admitted after his operation. He stopped behind the side of a bed he pulled the curtain to one side looking in.

"Sorry, Mrs Peterson. I just have a few people here who wanted to check on your husband's condition. Is that okay?"

She must have agreed because he pulled back the curtain fully.

In the bed lay a man with a bandage wrapped around the whole of his head tubes coming out of every orifice he was the most major case of the night with the uncontrollable head wound.

Mrs Peterson looked up wondering who was so interested in her husband's condition. She had accompanied us to the hospital, we weren't entire sure weather regulations permitted us to carry her at the time, but to concerned about his condition to argue we just let her jump in. we were soon informed after that it wasn't allowed.

"It's you." Her eyes filled with tears as she stood up and ran towards me giving me a big hug.

"I don't how to thank you," she said, "you saved his life, you and the pilot that brought him here will you thank him for me?"

"It wasn't a surprise that I would be recognised instead of Rob which didn't seem right he was as much a part of this if not more than I was. But he had spent the whole time wearing a helmet facing the opposite direction in the cockpit. I doubted if anyone would recognise him now. I wouldn't have in jeans, t shirt and denim sport jacket his short black hair neatly combed, he looked completely different."

"Thank him yourself," Toby said, not taking his eyes off the chart from the bottom of the bed. "Rob, this is Mrs Peterson, and Mrs Peterson, this is Rob Wolf." He piloted the aircraft last night. Finally looking up from the chart and putting it back.

More tears escaped her eyes as she ran to towards Rob giving him a hug as big as if not bigger than the one, I received. I'm so happy I can thank you in person. I'm so grateful. We stayed for a few minutes. Mrs Peterson expressing her thanks and telling Sue and Jay what a hero their brother was. Sue was beaming with pride. Toby soon pushed us along saying we had better make a move. Having said our goodbyes and promised to call again.

"What are his chances?"

"All evidence points to a recovery, it's still unsure on what condition or how much damage has been caused yet, but he will live."

He took us to a bed a few rows down. The curtain was already pulled back with no visitors. As with Mr Peterson, he was unconscious. Picking up the chart from the bottom of the bed. He gave us a run down. Mr Harris as spinal fusion once again were still waiting for some test results but early indicators show damage to the lower right weather it will cause permanent paralysis is still unsure. He looks like he with some work he will gain some feeling again. If not all.

"At least he's not requiring life support."

"He's due to be moved to a ward, another successful rescue." He dropped the file back and luckily that is it for the ICU.

We left struggling to keep up, headed for the elevator to take us up to the second floor. Finally, I caught up as the doors opened. "Do tell me if I'm going too fast."

"Just a tad," Sue said.

As the doors opened, we walked out this time at a slower pace past ward five and six and stopped at ward seven, scanning his card again we entered. He looked at the board on the wall detailing the lay out of the ward and patent names I recognised three names.

Mr P Andrews, Mrs G Hatter and Mr S Thump all of which I remembered had-broken arms or legs.

We followed to the room there was six beds and at the far end sat a man reading a book. "Hello, Mr Andrews, how are you feeling?" Already picked up the chart and examined it. "I have some visitors for you I'm sure you recognise them. I remember you," he said, pointing to me. "You were in the ambulance that flew me here."

"Correct, and this is Rob the pilot," I replied, wanting him to get the credit he deserved straight away. "We thought, we would come check up on some of you while we were here."

"Nice to meet you." He shook Rob's hand. "You did a fine job up there it was almost worth breaking my leg for the ride."

"Looks like your due to be released," Toby announced.

"Yes, tomorrow morning," they said, "they're just waiting for an ambulance. Don't suppose the helicopters free?"

"Unfortunately, not."

"You take care," we said as toby walked off.

"You too," he said after us. "Thank you."

"Sorry to cut it short," he said.

"It's fine," I said. "I know how busy hospitals get."

Entering the next room Mr Trump and Mrs Hatter where side by side.

"Hello, I'm Toby the chief of staff, obviously he hadn't meat these two yet either, I brought some visitors to see you."

"Mrs Hatter had her arm in a sling and we were told it required surgery. Mr Trump had both legs in plaster and we were informed due to be quick response the right had been spared amputation."

From there we went to ward eight. Where Mr Black and Mrs Smith the last of the limb patents who were both due releases tomorrow before going up the next floor.

We were taken to ward ten. And once again followed Toby till he stopped at bed twelve. Mr Patrick our one and only heart attack of the night. It had been diagnosed as acute angina. And he was now sitting up in bed eating his meal which didn't look appetizing at all.

"Hello, Mr Patrick, how are you feeling?"

"Like I've been run over."

"Well, let me introduce you to Mrs June Dunlop and Mr Rob Wolf, they were your flight crew last night. And wanted to check on your condition."

"Well, in that case, thank you," he said, leaning over to shake our hands. "I owe you both my life, and I was informed you were only volunteers."

"We were simply happy to be able to help."

"More than most would have been and them few minutes were the difference between life and death for me."

Over halfway Toby announced dropping the chart back and walking back out and heading towards twelve.

This is where we found Mr Spike. He was one of our other suspected spinal injuries and although in pain he had been cleared of any spinal damage.

From there we went on to meet Mr Pass and Mrs Roper in beds ten and fifteen. Both being admitted with suspected spinal injury Mrs Roper had been given the all clear but was being kept under observation for underline issues, and Mr Pass had lost the feeling in his right leg although it would be a long road to recovery he was expected to recover. Having chatted with both and said are goodbyes we followed toby out of ward twelve and heading back to the lift. Where we saw the sign for theatres. Passing the lift toby headed straight for the entrance. Entering a code, the doors opened. Stopping to sanitise his hands and put on a plastic apron, gloves and face mask, he instructed us to do the same.

Once suited up he led us down the corridor and into a room. It consisted of four chairs facing a two-way mirror (the kind of thing you would see in a police interview room) the room was used for observing surgery. With the mirror facing into the theatre so the surgeon wouldn't be distracted.

Thought you would like to see this. Holding the door for us to enter.

"Is this where Adam was treated?"

"I don't know, for sure which one he was in, there are five altogether and all identical; so it would have been in this or one just like it that the operation would have taken place."

"Apparently, it took over four hours."

"Yes, well, its delicate work. But we are home to specialists of brain surgery the neurology building being across the car park, so he would have been well looked after. I believe the head guy personally helped in the operation once he found out, professor Silks was interested."

We could see the doors being opened and equipment being brought into the room. And that's our cue to leave. Leading us out the room and to the exit. Where we disposed of all our PPE and headed for the lift, this time we took the lift back down to floor two. Thought we would leave this till last.

We walked and entered ward seven, after seeing the rest of the hospital it looked even more grand. Adams door was shut as we walked past and headed for the last row on the ward before stopping at bed twenty-one. Mr wrote worthy. He was our last patient and final head wound, subsequently also our youngest at seventeen and from a wealthy family. he had climbed a tree that been damaged by the storm, a bet placed on him by his friends he was over halfway up before it came tumbling down him with it, you could say wealthy but not smart proof that money couldn't protect you in life but could make you very comfortable.

"How are we doing?"

He was in bed watching TV with his headphones in he had a big pad stuck to the side of his head and you could just see a row of stiches underneath. Pulling out his headphones he looked at up.

"All right, Dr Whitehall, come to see me off."

"No," he said. "You're not leaving till tomorrow once the forty-eight hour observation period is up. It was customary with all head injuries to allow forty-eight hours to let any symptoms show after a period of that length it became highly unlikely that any complications would arise."

"I know you in particular expressed a wish to thank those responsible for your nice helicopter ride. Well, let me introduce you to Mr Wolf the pilot and Mrs Dunlop the nurse on-board."

"Really," he said, jumping out of bed and shaking Robert's hand.

"Yes, I'm glad to see you up and about."

"I certainly won't be climbing any trees again," he said that's for sure.

"Glad to hear it," replied Rob.

"I want to ask," he said. "How long have you been a pilot for the ambulance and how do I apply?"

Rob informed him that he wasn't the best person to ask and explained how he had come to be flying it that night. But fully supported him in his new dream of becoming a pilot. Even offering his service to help instruct should he need it, they exchanged numbers, he was only just old enough to gain his license and it would take a while for him to get the stage where he would be permitted airtime.

Saying goodbye and leaving him to his TV we walked back down the corridor before stopping outside Adams's room.

"And you're thirteenth patent," he said. "You know it supposed to be an unlucky number don't you." His pager sounded and he glanced down, looks as if I had better get going, "Take care," he said, walking off and out though the doors.

Chapter Thirty-Seven
The Decision – *Rob*

Mum was still sitting by the side of the bed talking to Adam begging him to wake up. Dad was sitting on the windowsill. "Where have you been?"

"Everywhere," said Sue, sinking into a chair. Now officially tired from trying to keep up, I think, we visited every ward in the hospital.

"Why?"

We checked on the patients we brought in last night June explained, I wanted to check they were all right.

"Did you go speak to Harry?" Mum asked not looking away from Adam.

First thing we did, I was walking over I put my hand on her shoulder. "Come on I think it's time you had a break let's go find the canteen. And get some food."

"It will be shut." Dad looked at his watch.

"Not the staff canteen." I held up the card as if it was a magic key.

Once again, we got lost and had to ask for directions from a passing doctor. It turned out to be on the fourth floor. That created another problem of finding the lift again.

Eventually finding the lift and the canteen. I scanned the card and held the door open as we were granted entry. I saw Sally sitting at a table near the door as I walked in.

"Hello, you back on shift?"

"Not yet," she replied. "I don't start for an hour, thought, I had better eat beforehand, I slept most of the day not long got up. Thought, I would be better eating here than cooking. Not to mention faster."

"What are you lot doing in here?"

Been visiting and thought it was time for a break we took a seat at the table with her pulling to chairs over. "Harry was kind enough to give us these," I said, pointing the pass. "Have you spoken to Harry?"

"Yes, he's asked me to think about it," he said, "He was waiting for you to get back to him as well."

"Yeah, we're not sure what to do."

"About what," asked Mum. Taking a seat at my side. We explained what Harry had said and got two different responses Mum was of joy and pride Dad of doubt and worry, Mum thought being in the paper and getting the acknowledgment we deserved was the right thing, Dad afraid of publicity and the negative effect it could have on your life. Although being public acknowledged as hero was flattering, I shared Dad's miss giving's as did June. Sally agreeing that she was 50/50 and saying she would go along with whatever we decided. Getting up before we started debating too much and heading for the serving line everyone else following.

I decided on pie and chips followed by cheesecake and a can of coke. Usually, I would have been more reserved swapping the chips for potatoes and cheesecake for fruit even the coke for orange juice, but I was craving comfort food I would worry about health later. I waited for everyone to go though and paid for the lot by card. We arrived back to the table just as Sally was getting up. I have to go start my shift I'm working on ward ten today. "Can you get Harry to ring me when you reach a decision."

"Of course, I hope it easier than last night."

"Well, should be a lot less eventful for one." I'm staying firmly on the ground. "Catch you later," she said as she headed out the door.

"When you due back on shift, June?"

"Well, I'm seconded here until told otherwise but I should really bring it up with Harry."

"So, what we doing about his press thing Mum," started again.

"I don't know. I was hoping Sally would be against it and that would decide it for us but now were deciding for her."

"I would do it," said Sue. "It's not every day you get and offer like it."

I agree with Sue interjected Jay, "Although I understand what your dad's saying it's still an achievement to be proud of."

"Dad was the only one against it but having been in the media arguing the case of global warming most of his career, he had the most experience and it was hard to ignore."

"What do you think," said June?

"I'm still on the fence, but I am leaning more towards doing it if only for the protection from the media they can't keep it hidden forever, let's face it twelve people now know what we look like and our names. I won't take long for the press to find them. And once they do the trail will lead straight to us."

"That's true, and I don't suppose it will be as easy as just going back to Leicester to get away from them."

"Talking of that, you're not the only one that's been busy I sent my guys over to your house they boarded up all the broken windows and erected scaffolding to fix the roof it's still structurally sound and they should have it done in the next two days."

"When did you sort that?"

Jeff rang after the storm, I asked him to check both the houses and make sure they were secure I know I didn't check, and I was certain you just gunned it out. He also said when you leave a shelter your supposed to turn the air supply off. And it's a good idea to shut the door to garage if you don't want the car to drive itself off without you.

"Was too busy gunning it out?" Using his own words against him.

"So, you decided then," Mum asked. "You're going to do it."

"I think first of all, June, should ring Scott and see what he has to say. He has as much right as us to an opinion."

"He will go along with whatever I decide, but your right I should run it past him."

Having finished eating, June excused herself to go ring Scott.

The convocation turning to me. "How long till you have to go back?"

"As long as it takes, works destroyed beside which I would now be on holiday. But we can't just impose on Scott and June forever."

"What about you, Jay?"

"Compassionate leave. The CEO is very generous. Told me to take as long as I liked he joked. Him being the CEO had given himself the time off directing his men to fix up both houses. While he was in Wales."

"Won't you need to be there to check on the sites and sort incoming work?"

"That's what the foreman and site manager are for. Let them earn their wage for once. The accountant can do the wages and the rest can wait."

"So, it's just the boy's school," I said. "Well, under the circumstances I think they will understand, I will ring them tomorrow and explain."

"Scott thinks it's a marvellous Idea," June said suddenly, appearing behind us. Apparently, were fools for even considering turning it down.

"That's it then? Looks like we're doing it I suppose we had better go and inform Harry."

"And we had better go and see Adam," Mum said.

We all went our separate ways, me, June and Dad who instead on seeing this office Sue and Mum had been raving about clearly feeling left out. Mum, Sue and Jay going to see Adam I gave Jay my card so he could gain entry as visiting hours were well over, June keeping hers to allow us to gain entry to the lift.

Chapter Thirty-Eight
Flashing Cameras –
Rob/June/Harry

We sat in Harry's office waiting for him to return.

Dad was admiring the view although dark the moon still made an amazing backdrop. "You're sure you want to do this," I asked. I was already having second doubts.

"We made up our minds everyone is now expecting us to do it, so now we have to it can't be that bad."

Jade had offered us tea or coffee but neither of us wanted one. Apart from Dad who now had a cappuccino complete with sprinkles. The phone hadn't stopped ringing since we arrived, always the same response sorry he's not here can I take a message.

Suddenly, Harry burst into the room, breaking Dad from his daydream, Harry was the one looking tired now, the stress of the hospital weighing him down. In his hand he had a stack of post it notes in three different colour's pink, yellow and blue. "You have seen this madness," he said, showing us the notes.

"Blue is private," he said, "of which he had one."

"Yellow was hospital business, there were about three of those."

"'Pink' is media. These made up the bulk of the stash containing roughly twenty to thirty. As he flicked through them, he dropped most into the wastepaper bin. He picked up the bin and showed us its contents. It was nearly overflowing with what were nearly all pink notes."

"This has been going on all day," he said, "almost all of them about you."

Jade walked in with a mug of coffee and handed it over. "Thanks, Jade," he said. "Isn't it time you went on a break yourself."

"With the phones the way they are," she said. "I thought, it would be better to stay here."

"Don't be silly ring reception and tell them all non-essential calls are to be told to ring back it's mainly reporters hoping for a scoop anyway."

"If you're sure."

"Yes, just divert the phone lines into here."

"I will only be half an hour," she said as she left, shutting the door behind her.

"Well, I can guess what you're doing here, what have you decided?"

"We will do it," June said before I could speak. "She knew I was still unsure of going into a situation I couldn't control."

"Thank you," as he replied. "You could see the stress drop from his face instantly." Picking up the yellow notes, to which he had added four more from the desk. "All these are from the health minister, and I only spoke to him an hour ago."

"Better ring him back then."

"Yes, just need to get hold of Sally first."

"She's in ward ten; we meet her in the canteen. She will go along with whatever we decide."

"That's brilliant, I will ring and confirm first, just in case she's changed her mind." He picked up the phone and waited for the ward to answer.

"It's Harry Silks, can I speak to nurse partridge, please."

"Hey, Sally, it's Harry. I have Rob and June here," they said. "They will go ahead with the conference tomorrow."

"Yes, that's what they said just wanted to confirm."

"Of course, what shift are on tonight?"

"Well, put me onto the ward sister."

We waited in silence as he was being transferred back.

"It's Professor Silks. It's about Nurse Partridge; she's needed for an important meeting first thing tomorrow, and I need her at her best, she's to be sent home with pay as soon as you can arrange the cover."

"No that's all," he said as he replaced the receiver.

Opening a desk drawer, he pulled out a black book and opened it up using the marker. He once again picked up the phone and dialled the number.

"It's Professor Harry Silks from Swansea hospital I need to speak to the minister."

"Yes, I can hold." Placing his hand over the receiver he offered us a drink telling us to help ourselves to the drink's cabinet. We both declined. I was just managing to stay awake and alcohol made me tired.

"Hello, Patrick, yes, I have good news for you they agreed to participate."

"Yes, is it?"

"Of course."

"Then I will speak to you later, bye."

"He's delighted," he said, putting the phone down. He's sending the press release now so hopefully all this can stop, looking at his watch, made us look at the clock it was eleven p.m. Dad was now sitting on the sofas looking tired. I suggested we all go get a goodnight sleep.

"Good idea," he said. "We have to put on a good show tomorrow we can't go looking tired. We agreed saying we had better get going anyway, after all it was a long drive back. And got up heading for the elevator, dad following close behind. We were informed that we would be collected at ten a.m., the shoot not starting to twelve. I told him we have a car that it wasn't necessary but he insisted saying security would require it adding that if anyone wanted to follow in our vehicle and watch the show, they were more than welcome."

Harry

I watched as the doors shut creating a barrier between us before I walked off hearing the elevator go down as I did. I had more respect for Rob and June than I could describe. They had so much strength and bravery but yet so modest with it, most people faced with the offer of a media story hailing them as heroes would jump at the chance. But instinct told me the second Patrick first came up with the idea that I would have to sell it to them, he couldn't get his head around why they were being so difficult I only hoped that when he meets them, he would. And not hold it against them.

I walked back to the office and poured myself a whiskey, it was time I called it a night, but I would wait for jade to return and man the phones as promised. Never one to be late she arrived bang on half hour. Anything she asked getting settled behind her desk again. "No."

"I expect it will go quite now."

"How come?"

"Well, it is getting late. And the health minister has just released a statement for tomorrow's conference."

"They agreed then."

"Yeah. Luckily, you know they truly don't want any recognition for their actions. It so heartwarming to see."

"You can see it in them, that this is truly done out the goodness of their hearts."

"Yes, anyway. I'm off to the shed. Hold all nonemergency calls, you working tomorrow?"

"Evening again. Julie will he be here when you get up?"

The shed was what we called the sleeping quarters we kept for those nights; we burned the midnight oil a little too long. It was also where Ann had slept last night. It had previously been an office but with cutbacks recently creating a significant loss in staffing numbers we found we now had fewer staff working more hours and empty office space doing nothing, so the shed was invented. It had gained its nickname as a way of saying. Although you were there you weren't on duty just like a piece of furniture in your house that's not being used it goes in the shed for storage. It had two bunk beds and one single bed. As well as nightstand. I dropped into the unmade single bed I had found my way here a few times in the last twenty-four hours each time having a power nap. And given up any attempt to remake it. But this time I set the alarm for eight a.m. and settled under the covers.

I woke up the sound of ringing in my ear flowed by a voice grumbling at me to turn the dam thing off. Although Id, had an uninterrupted night sleep I didn't feel like it. I reached for the alarm and only succeeded in knocking it to the floor. Still half asleep I rolled out of bed and started searching. Finding it under the bed. I pressed the off button.

"Got it," I said. "Sorry for waking you." I sat up my back against the bed. As my eyes adjusted to the light, I could see it was Toby sitting on the bed opposite. We were the main occupants of the shed and the worst for never leaving the hospital.

"It's okay." He yawned. "I should be getting up anyway."

"What time did you get here?"

"Just gone twelve, not long after you I expect, I saw Rob leaving just as I came up, I checked the alarm and decided to get up with you."

"In that case how about breakfast," I said, picking up the phone what do you want.

"Usual."

After placing the breakfast order, I got up leaving Toby to get changed. I'm going for a shower we will eat in the office after.

I grabbed my bathrobe and some underwear I always kept here in case and headed to the room next door. In the shower I could feel myself become partly human again. I may have indulged a little too long because when I walked past Julie on my way into the office, giving her sheepish good morning, she informed me breakfast had already arrived. Julie like all my secretaries having being used to me in a bathrobe now didn't batter an eyelid I showered more here recently than at home. A habit that was only going to get worse now.

Toby was sitting on the sofa a cup of coffee in his hand watching the news, both breakfasts were still covered on the trolley.

"You didn't have to wait."

"I didn't, she's only just gone surprised you didn't pass her in the corridor."

"Must be my lucky day," I replied as I walked behind my desk. Although it looked like a white gloss wall it was actually storage cupboards that opened when the panel was pushed. Behind It was a wardrobe where I kept at least six sets of clothes.

It also had a mirror and several body care products. I pulled out a white top and put it on then pulled out my best suit and hung it on the door before putting on the door to hang. Then found some bottoms to a track suit.

"Too much?"

"Not at all, but if I was you, I would wear the suit. You know how the press is about appearance."

You know fully well what I meant. I picked up a breakfast and handed it to him, then poured myself a coffee and some orange juice picked up my plate and took a seat next to him. It's already on the news, he said looking at the TV the morning press conference was in full swing with the health minister answering questions. He still hadn't released the names yet telling them all would be made clear at a later interval.

"I don't want to be in your shoes today, facing that pack of vultures."

"It's not me I'm worried about, I've had my fair share of relations with the press, but the others haven't it's going to come as a bit of a shock I already regret talking them into it."

"Well, it's too late now. You will just have to muddle through together."

Finishing breakfast Toby stood up. "Well, I better be going," he said. "Harriet's already bleating on about how much time I'm spending here. Let's hope she's understanding this time, I will catch you later he shouted as he walked out the door. On the news."

Noticing the time, I got changed and had a shave before grabbing my keys and phone. "Did you get that address?" I asked on the way out. Julie handed me a piece of paper with June's address on it. I'm on the mobile if you need me.

It wasn't long till I was on the road my new electric jag

hitting the highway and bursting into life it was a company car provided by the hospital for all the meeting across the country. I would usually have had a driver but decided to drive myself today I was in the mood for a drive and there was something about them that made me want to be with them as much as possible their presence was infectious. Besides which I was too tired to think last night and had forgotten to book one. I turned the radio over the country station my guilty pleasure. They were playing a song from the shires—ahead of the storm—*Well that's fitting,* I thought.

Sitting back into the new leather seat. I could feel the lumber support me. And made a mental to drive myself more and rely less on a chauffeur. Following the satnav, I followed the main road out of town and towards the hills. I hadn't driven this way in ages and always forgot how beautiful it was. Music playing and enjoying the view it wasn't long till I released I was nearly at my destination.

I was pulling up outside June's, it was the first time I had seen the damage first hand and finding the street was harder than I anticipated. But finding the house was even worse I was surrounded by fields and all houses in the area were destroyed. Only seeing one car parked that looked like it was roadworthy a new Land Rover. Having never actually seen Rob's rental but knowing the make. I took a gamble and pulled in behind it.

A group of kids were out front of a house that was half standing half completely gone. One ran towards the back of the garden. I was halfway across when Rob appeared.

"I wasn't expecting you," he said as we shook hands. "I just thought, you would send a driver to fetch us."

"Well, usually I would but I didn't book one besides it's the first time I've left the hospital in four days the drive did me good."

June appeared from what looked like the opening to a shelter she looked glamours in a simple white dress with small flowers around the hem paired with some wedged heels. Her makeup was floorless and her hair looked like she had just come out of the hair salon.

"What are you doing here?" I leaned in and kissed her cheek.

"Thought, you might like the personal approach."

"He forgot to book a driver," Rob replied. "You should have rung, we could if made our own way."

"Told you the drive did me good."

"Well, go get ready Then. Go and See what of Scott's you can use." "Coffee," she asked once rob had walked off.

I looked at my watch 9.45 I had made good time. "Suppose I can have a quick one," I said and followed her in the shelter.

I took my coffee outside and sat on a pile of logs. Everyone was busy running round getting ready all wanting to come and fighting to use the bathroom. As I sat and drank my coffee, I couldn't help but feel envy towards Rob and June, not because of their hero status but because they had the one thing worth fighting for family. My dad had died last year leaving me with little to no family those, I did have lived to far away or hadn't been in contact for years. I didn't have any friends I could lean on either. When it came down to it, I was a workaholic even more so the last year. But no one noticed all the friends, I did have where employees at the hospital and could be classed more as colleagues. Toby was the only one I shared anytime outside of work with and that wasn't very often.

"Everything all right," June asked.

"Yes," I said, snapping myself out of the daze.

"What about this," Rob shouted over.

Rob was trying to find something to wear June having disapproved of his shirt and jeans from the previous day, saying, "They weren't suitable for such a big event."

"It's better," she said. "But it's too big."

Rob was roughly the same size as me similar build as well if not more muscular from a few extra hours in the gym than myself. I looked at my watch. I hadn't considered what they would wear having no clothes on them.

"Why don't I lend you something from the office? We should have time if were quick."

"Are you sure?"

"Yes, can't have you going looking like that, can we?" His shirt was two sizes too big. It was clearly made for someone with a bit of a belly. Mix that with the fact his jeans that fit perfectly. And finished off with some pure white trainers. And a dark sports jacket. The whole thing just looked odd.

"I have a spare suit you could use and some black shoes. What size are you?"

"Eight."

"Same as me, but that means we have to leave now," I said, standing up and drinking the rest of my coffee.

I got in the car. And waited for June and Rob to join me. Everyone else would meet us at the air base in the cars the range rover and a pickup Scott, June's husband had managed to borrow. Wasn't long before they both came running towards the car and got in Rob in the back and June as passenger. I Started to programme the sat nav to return. Before June stopped me. "You won't need that you have me and I'm faster."

I pulled off and headed for the main road I wasn't on it for long before June was directing to turn left and head for the bypass. "Then right just before we reached it. Must say this is a very nice car. Between you and Rob's rental I feel spoilt."

"It belongs to the hospital. Company car if you will. But it's at my disposal at all times."

"Must be nice to have use of it though. Turn here," she said, nearly missing the exit.

We drove to the hospital none of us saying much, but directions. June proving to know the way better than any sat nav. The roads still being clear and free of traffic helped and we were soon back at the hospital and heading up to the office.

Opening the wardrobe, I pulled out a white shirt and my blue suit. He quickly got changed while I dug out my spare black shoes. Once changed we couldn't help admit although he looked smart it still didn't look right, you could also tell he didn't feel comfortable either, okay June said throwing his jeans back at him and his sport jacket. Lose the suit.

After changing yet again, he now wore a simple white shirt that fitted perfectly, showing his high shoulders and broad chest, it fitted so you would have thought, it was tailor made. Paired with his dark denim jeans, that reluctantly we had to admit fitted better than the trousers and looked more his style. And finished off with his navy sport jacket. Looked good. Which just left the trainers looking out of place. So we switched them with black shoes. Standing back, we had to admit he had the right balance of smart and casual. "Hell." He looked better than me or June. "Who had clearly put in some effort?"

"I didn't mean you had to show me up," said June as we finished you will be fighting the women off dressed like that.

"I have to admit, it puts me suit in the shade."

We were just finishing off with a spray of cologne and some hair wax to style his short but thick black hair. When Sally walked in.

"Wow! Hot alert," she said, fanning herself.

"What about you?" June said, looking over Sally outfit. She

wore a black dress that hugged her hourglass figure and was longer at one side than the other. The dress and strip of metallic blue ribbon running down the longer side. That matched a ribbon in her hair she had also switched the glasses for contacts and paired the dress with black stiletto heels and a black velvet clutch bag.

"You really pushed the boat out," Rob said. "I wouldn't have recognised you without the glasses."

"Thanks," she replied, blushing. "I used it at my college graduation it was a treat from my mum for getting into medical school. Might as well show it off."

"Well," I said, brushing some dust-off Rob's jacket. "Now we're all here we had better be going."

There was no doubt that Rob, June and Sally caused quite a stir as we made our way out of the hospital, it started with Julie who wanted to know if it was a dinner party or a press conference. Then Jamie who we caught in the elevator on the way down ended with stares from everyone in the waiting area. As we made our way back to the car, I received a text from Patrick asking where we were. I fired off a quick reply telling him we would be there in ten minutes. Bit of a lie as I knew it would be more like twenty.

As we approached the airbase, I could see a swarm of reporters almost blocking the gates. Warning them as we approached and told them to keep their heads down especially Rob who was in the front June and Sally in the back had blacked out windows to offer some protection. Police were on crowd control duty. And pushed the reporters aside as we approached while one of them opened the gates. As we drove through the camera caused such a flash of light that I nearly lost control of the car.

Chapter Thirty-Nine
The Press – *Rob*

The lights were blinding as we drove thought the gates, the car swerved as Harry slightly lost control. He drove round the corner following the signs for staff parking and rental returns. We were waved though as we past the office and round the back where a sigh said staff parking, I could see the helicopter on the pad it had been washed and polished and sparkled in the sunlight, as we drove in, I could see the land rover and borrowed pickup already in the car park, Harry pulled in beside them and switched the engine off.

As we stopped a door opened and Patrick walked out, he was the health minister for England and Wales. He walked to the car as we got out. Before I could even acknowledge him, his hand was in mine shaking it with such force and vigour. "You would have thought, he was trying to break it."

"You must be, Rob, I'm so happy to finally meet you, although I must say you don't look at all like," I imagined.

"Nice to meet you to," I said, not sure whether to take his last remark as a compliment or an insult. He moved off as Harry introduced June and Sally, he greeted both with a kiss on the cheek before giving Harry a friendly handshake.

I just want to express not only my thanks but those of the prime minister. He would be here himself but as to head a meeting at number ten. He's promised to try and make an appearance. What I can only assume as a guard appeared at the door. "Excuse me, sir, but the front gates are asking permission to allow the press in."

"Right, follow me and we will get this show on the road." The guard taking this as yes picked up his radio telling them to let the reporters in.

We followed Patrick down the corridor and into what looked like a staff room. It was a dark room with some old yellow nanotube lights, but well proportioned, with a kitchen top on one wall. On top was a microwave oven, air fryer, toaster, kettle, and coffee machine. In the middle directly under the light was a six-seater table, a large three-seater sofa that had seen better days, sat against the wall, a coffee table was in front of that and an old TV stood on a stand near the door. Three other people were in the room. One being Carl.

"This is Janet as promised she will be your press relations officer during and after this time." She was sitting on the sofa with a laptop and papers on the coffee table. "And this is Lucy she's the media adviser for North Wales." Lucy was leaning against the counter. Top, a mug of coffee at the side of her, just finishing a phone call.

"Nice to meet you," I said after each introduction.

"And finally, Carl, who I'm sure you've already had the pleasure of meeting." Carl was close by Lucy clearly trying to impress.

"Only by name and one phone call, it's nice to finally meet, thanks for the help," said Harry, leaning over and shaking hands.

"Take a seat," Patrick said, pointing to the table. "We will just go through some preliminaries before we go through." We sat for ten minutes while we were talked through. "What would happen and what we needed to do if we felt uncomfortable."

It was agreed that Harry and Patrick would start the

conference, detailing the rules to the press and explaining how we had come to carry out such a rescue. After he would introduce us, and we would take our places. We were told that all questions would be one at a time, and we were not to panic if we struggled or couldn't answer one. A simple look at Patrick, and he would take over either answering the questions for us or killing them stone dead. Afterwards, we would take a break before continuing to the photo shoot.

We were all given a piece of paper to sign stating we had been briefed and consented to take part. Before we got up and headed out the door. You ready he asked stopping outside the door to hanger one, where the conference was to be held. Now all now unsure and all nervous we nodded.

I must tell you that the turnout was fifty per cent higher than expected, not only is every local rag and national papers present, but amateur reporters from all over the UK from as far as Scotland have come to get their story. I expect a crowd of about a hundred, if not more, some will be photographers and be taking pictured though out. And most will be voice recording the conference. It's only going to televised on the major news channels mainly *ITV, sky and BBC*. It won't be live, but broadcast soon after. So, if we're already its show time. Patrick opened the door and walking in followed by Harry. The noise rose instantly with shouts of questions and the flashing of cameras going of crazy. Patrick and Harry worked the crowd well having been in the public eye on numerous occasions and having a good relationship allowing for banter. We could hear him speak as he took his seat.

"Ladies and gentlemen, firstly, I would like to thank you for your time, and for coming out with such eagerness, you will have a chance to not only meet but talk to the three individuals who performed these heroic acts. But first, we must ask you to be considerate and have patience. They are after all civilians and not used to such scenes we have here today. We ask that you give them time while they answer your questions to the best of their ability."

"Who are they?"

"We will get to that in a moment."

"What are their names?"

"First off all," completely ignoring the question. "I would like to begin with an explanation as to how these three individuals came to play the vital role they did."

"What are their names?" Came the question again.

Concluding that, telling them would be the fastest way of shutting them up he gave in.

The plane was piloted by Mr Rob Wolf, a chef who lives in Leicester, he was assisted by Mrs June Dunlop head nurse at St Leonard's Hospital, and finally, trainee nurse Miss Sally Partridge of Swansea Hospital.

"What was a chef from Leicester doing in Wales?"

Losing his patience with the reporter he bluntly stated. We will be getting to that in a moment if, given the chance and any more disruptions you will be asked to leave, all questions will be answered at the end. Now these three individuals were recruited thanks to the quick thinking and resourcefulness of Professor Harry Silk's director of medicine for North Wales. "Who I will now hand you over to?"

"Hello," like the minister just said, "I was responsible for getting these three together. I was originally alerted to such as possibility by my chief of staff, Toby Whitewall, who approached me after seeing to an irregular admission of a serious case just brought in by an air ambulance. Having personally attended to the patient after his arrival from the hospital's helipad." He remarked on the skill of the pilot. But his suspicions weren't aroused until the nurse aboard the craft stayed and the craft took off again soon to be replaced by another ambulance only a minute later, such was the demand on its services. The one thing he remarked was the skill with which the pilot maneuvered the craft. Being unsure as to what happened we soon found out from air control that two crafts, matching the description of an air ambulance, were in the air only one using the squawk code of the official ambulance, the other one being flown by a civilian. It was registered as a decommissioned craft and that the craft was now down at the airbase. Giving us the name of the pilot, we gained the name of Nurse Dunlop from the attending. It was then that we found them in a waiting area, where we approached in a successful bid to try and help relieve some of the demand currently putting a strain on the current craft.

"How did Nurse Partridge come to get involved?"

"Nurse Partridge was assigned once both Mr Wolf and Mrs Dunlop had agreed, having been called in as all staff were as the all clear sounded, we simply redirected her to join them making up the numbers required to undertake the mission."

"Who was he dropping off?"

Patrick took this question. "He was dropping off his brother Adam Wolf, Adam had suffered a life-threatening head injury from which he's still recovering. But what's more remarkable is that after this one act, he went on to perform twelve more successful rescues. Ending the night with a hundred per cent survival rate that's yet to drop. Mr Wolf along with Nurse Dunlop and Nurse Partridge are responsible for saving the lives of thirteen people in the course of one evening, that alone eased the demand on the air crew working allowing them to perform more vital and challenging rescues which a total of thirty-two lives were saved. That number would have been significantly halved without the help of these three individuals. I would also like to take this moment to thank everyone else who took part or was on the front-line night. Either in the air or on the ground. We must not forget that many more people across the entire country have pulled together, saving hundreds if not thousands of lives in what can only be described as the biggest crisis this country has seen this century. Now before we bring them out. Are there any questions?"

"Did the craft have landing rights?"

"Yes, nurse Dunlop had previously rang and arranged for the craft to land AC permitting."

"Where did he obtain the ambulance?"

"That's a question best put to him directly, anyone else?"

"No? Okay then allow me to introduce Mr Rob Wolf, Mrs June Dunlop. And Miss Sally Partridge."

I was given the signal to go as my name was called. I held back for a split second frozen to the spot. I had never wanted any of this all I had wanted was to save my brother. Having felt a hand push me forward I walked in as the room light up flashes from every camera blinding my eyes not having enough time to recover before the next flash. Eventually, I took my seat next to Harry, June was soon beside me followed by Sally. A large desk had been and placed on a platform creating a stage. On the desk was five chairs all with their own mics and bottle of water, behind the table was a banner, on which held two pictures of the air ambulance and the coat of arms in the middle, the hanger had been emptied to make room, and where there would have been air crafts, there now sat a crowd of people all there especially to see us.

"The three musketeers," Patrick said as we took are seats, Patrick was sat in the middle. Harry to his left I look as seat as instructed next to Patrick's right, June next to me and Sally taking the end seat next to Harry.

I know we've spoken in person but allow me thank you on behalf of the nation for the service you did. I'm sure everyone here would agree and like to join me in a round of applause. We sat as the whole room erupted to the sound of clapping. Once it had died down Patrick turned to the press. Now one question at a time please.

"You in the red," Patrick said, picking someone from the crowd.

Question for Mr Wolf. "Where did you learn to fly?"

"I started at the age of seventeen, when me and mate Toyed with the idea of being pilots, we were told to try and keep answer brief and to the point. Not to give too much detail."

"And why did you give it up?"

"At the time there was no green energy provided for aircrafts and I didn't want to contribute to the worlds carbon emissions?"

"When was the last time you flew prior to this?"

"Last week, I kept a small craft as a hobby?"

"Guy in the blue jacket," Patrick said as the questions stopped.

"Gary from the times." Question for Mr Wolf. "How did you obtain the craft?"

"It was kept at the same base as my other craft and had been up for sale for a number of months, I simply brought it and obtained the right to fly it."

"What was it like to fly?"

"No different than any other helicopter really, obviously the speed and size had an impact, but I just kept it slow."

"What are you going to do with it now?"

"I haven't thought that far."

"Women in the pink hat." Came Patrick.

Bernie from the sun. Questions for Mr Wolf and nurse Dunlop. "Firstly, What did you think when the professor approached you? And secondly to Mrs Dunlop, how did you come to know Rob?"

I looked over at June who signalled for me to answer first.

"Well, I originally thought, it was news on my brother so relieved."

"Originally, we had our doubts," said June, taking her turn. "But we soon came to see where we were needed the most. As for your second question I'm good friends and neighbours with his brother and his parents, so when Adam was injured, I was on hand it made sense for me to accompany Rob to the hospital. Having been at that point his primary care giver."

"How did you feel about being on board nurse partridge?"

"Originally, I have to admit I was a bit anxious. But Rob is very efficient pilot. And I was insured, I was in safe hands."

"Guy in the brown tweed."

Scott from the mirror – question for nurse partridge. "What went through your mind when you were asked to fly with an inexperienced pilot?"

"Like I said my first thought was to be a bit anxious, but in general I was happy to go where I was needed the most and it certainly made for an exciting shift."

"Nurse Dunlop and nurse partridge, was it the first time you had ever been up?"

"I take the training although many years ago, so it had been a few years since I had experienced it."

I took the basic training only a few months ago as I

approached my finals. "But yes, it was the first time I had been up on an actual call," said Sally.

"And to you both, how did you feel with Mr Wolf at the controls?"

June took the lead again clearly getting a feel for the format now. "Well, I had been on the journey to the hospital and seen him arrive from Leicester, so I knew he was more than capable I was more concerned about the patents than myself."

"It soon become very clear once up that I was good hands and like June. My primary concern was for the wellbeing of the patients."

"Finally, to you all how do you feel about being hailed as heroes?"

"It's not the case at all," I replied. "The real heroes are the true doctors and nurses that face this everyday so in my eyes nurse Dunlop and nurse partridge are and always have been heroes, but I'm just a normal person that was privileged to help and watch them work."

"Well, like," Rob said. "There are real heroes out there that save lives on a daily basis, especially last night we simply took the cases that need transport."

"I agree, with both Rob and June," replied Sally, "there are people out there that deserve more recognition than us."

The conference went on this way, for what must have been over half hour, the five of us taking turns to answer questions on everything from what cases we had admitted to how we saw our futures after this. Only at one point did we have to use our get out of jail card, getting Patrick to answer a question on if we thought, it was irresponsible to send an unqualified team out to people in need. His answer floored the journalist when he replied although irregular. The crew were more than qualified on the medical side and my license having been checked before taking off proving I had the qualifications. Finally, saying sometimes, you have to act fast and waiting to have my flying assessed by the regulator would have taken too long. Eventually, we stood up and made our exit.

Back in the staff room we were congratulated by Patrick on how well we handled it, before they both slipped out the room to check their phones.

"That's the hard part over, now all we need to do is smile for the camera."

"That or jump in and fly away," said June. "Who had previously said she hates her photo taken."

Carl joined us in the room heading straight for the coffee machine. "Sorry about all this," I said, "hopefully it will be over soon."

"Don't worry, its good publicity, and I've already managed to get Patrick to agree to some public funding maybe even set it up with an air ambulance of its own. Even been called on by the press for my opinion. I may be on the news later as well."

"Well, some goods come out of it then. Where the others?"

"Well, the minister and professor are both on the phone, Lucy is talking to someone and directing media ready for the photos and Janet is bogged down with the phone and laptop since your names where released I gave her my office."

Carl poured us all a coffee and brought them over with a tray containing milk, sugar and biscuits

Soon Harry walked back in. "Julies not happy, the phones melting again," he said, grabbing a biscuit.

"I thought, Janet would deal with all that."

"Only on your behalf these want me. It's fine though I have good media screening."

He poured himself a coffee and prepared another one for Patrick.

"Good news," said Patrick, walking in. The PM as finished and is scheduled to arrive later today.

"We only have the shoot left," June said, not seeing the point.

"Yes, but we have a little surprise for you back at the hospital."

"Although we insisted on being told what, he wouldn't tell us, and it wasn't long till Lucy arrived to tell us the photographers were ready when we were."

Finishing the coffee, we made our way to where the helicopter stood. The cameras started going again as soon as we appeared. The reports where in rows there being to many and the photos were taken in stages consisting of five photos one of me, June, Sally, Harry and the minister outside the helicopter we waited while the press worked though the rows re-joining at the back until the first lot were back at the front.

Then one of me, June and Sally in the same spot once again the row's moved round. Thirdly, I got a break and June and Sally were pictured standing in the back of the ambulance now empty the hospital having collected all its supplies, one of me sitting in the cockpit. And finally, me in front of the craft shaking Patrick's hand. As the photographers finished the final shot, they all disappeared, within minutes there was no one there as if nothing had ever happened. I climbed out as Tyler and Dylan ran towards me embracing me in a hug. Behind them was Scott, Jake and Jacob. "Can we go for that ride?" now they asked.

I looked over to Carl who was standing with the rest of them. "Carl is it all right, if I take the boys up for a ride?"

"Don't see why not. I will just go clear it with control."

"Anyone else for a ride?"

Patrick looked at his watch before deciding he had time for a quick trip along with one member of his security, finally Harry not wanting to be left out. Jumped on board. Carl brought more headphones and safety straps to fit them all in, and half hour later, I was back at the controls and in the air flying over fields. Harry at the side of me, Scott, Jake Jacob and Patrick in the back.

We flew across the hospital and over towards the house I hovered over the fields still showing the letter H made out of stones.

"Can we land," asked Scott. "Might as well let Rex out while I'm here."

Having landed back on the H we all got out. And Scott went to let Rex out.

I found Patrick and Harry looking at the extent of the damage to the house and area beyond as Rex was let out of the shelter instantly finding a tree to prop his leg against. Before bounding over to me for some attention.

"I've seen pictures," he said as I came up beside him. "But they don't do the damages justice." Walking around he got a clear view of what was left of Mum and Dad's house. Before heading over.

I take it this is what's left of your parents he bent down and picked up a roof tile. Before seeing the shelter. Look at that, suddenly standing up and walking over he looked in at what was now the uncovered living area.

"I do hope no one was in there at the time."

"No, they were in with Scott by the time it hit."

"I will see what extra funding, I can drum up for the area, the council are going to need a cash injection to start rebuilding. I will consult the PM about upgrading the legal requirements for shelters. Make sure nothing like this happens again."

Scott was locking Rex back in the shelter as we walked back. "All ready?"

"Yes," they all said in unison.

As we landed Carl's crew instantly jumped to work to move it back to the hanger. Leaving the pad ready for the PM. "Well, was it worth the wait," June asked as the boys got out.

"It was amazing I took a video and put it on Instagram. You should have been enjoying it not recording it," she scolded.

"I can see why Harry recruited you," Patrick said as we walked towards the cars that were the best flying. "I think I've ever seen you should consider coming back to it."

We got into the cars in the same order we arrived in only Patrick got in with us leaving his driver behind to drive the PM when he arrived.

Chapter Forty
A Job

We were sat in Harry's office still no sign of the surprise, I was beginning to wonder whether it was the visit of the PM, who we had been told a few minutes ago had landed safely but secretly. And was heading over to us now. Harry and Patrick had decided to go down and meet him.

Security now had been drafted in and now stood at the doors two monitored the elevator although we had been given clearance to pass, we decided to stay and wait. As I sat looking out at the view from the window again, I couldn't help but think of one question from the conference (where do you see your future after this) my answer had been that I expected to return to normal as soon as possible. But I'm not sure, I believed it the pub was gone with little hope of it being rebuilt. So, I would need a job. It wasn't until the last few days I realised my dream of flying was still alive, another thought came back to me just a comment Mum made earlier in the week (your true calling) it was my true calling my dream job. "What you doing, Uncle Rob." I looked round to see Declan walking over. Just thinking.

"What about."

"What to do next."

"What do you mean?"

"Well, we can't stay here forever at some point we have to go back home."

"Then you fly us home."

"Yes," I said. "That's what we will do."

"Somehow, he had just told me everything I needed to hear in five words (then you fly us home). That's what the future held that was my next step to get my family back home."

It was then we heard voices coming into the office. Harry was first in, followed by the PM then Patrick, I stood up and met them halfway in the room.

"You must be Mr Wolf, I'm Daniel Wells, the labour leader."

"It's a pleasure to meet you," I said, shaking hands. "Please call me Rob."

"And you can call me, Dan, when I heard about the press conference, I was desperate to meet the person responsible. I'm just sorry I couldn't be here sooner."

"Well, it wasn't just me." I moved aside showing Sally and June behind me.

"This is June Dunlop and Sally Partridge there are as many to thank as I am."

"Absolutely true, it's lovely to meet you all and I wanted to come in person to tell you how thankful I am."

"If you would all follow me," said Harry from the corner of the room. "I think it's time to get the party started."

"Party," we said, looking at each other before walking out.

As we followed, he stopped outside the conference room as he opened the door, we could see it had been decorated with thank you banners and balloons the table was full of food and drinks in the room were Toby, Jamie, Carl and Jade Harry handed round champagne flutes and raised a toast to the three heroes, he said.

The party as it was called went well with staff coming and going, the PM stayed for a few hours and although we spoke, and had a photo taken together later to be released to the press. No doubt to help his public image. He mainly used the time to network with a few people and tour the hospital to drum up support during visiting hours. All that being done, and his mission achieved he announced that he should be heading back to London. The health minister vowed to spend the night and travel back the next day. He found me later on looking out the window watching as the sun went down. "What's up," he asked, taking a seat next to me.

"Nothing. I'm just thinking of what's next, got to get this lot back home, at some point."

"And after that?"

"Look for a job I expect I don't think the pub will re-open. It was badly damaged."

"Have you thought about what I said earlier about taking up flying?"

"Yes, I would like to but not sure there's much call for a pilot in Leicester."

"But there is here, if I arrange it will you sit an exam for air ambulance pilots, it will be a written assessment and with practical but judging by your skill earlier I don't think that will be a problem. And we always need a good pilot."

"Are you serious?"

"Yes, I'm looking into splitting the area in half with a second base nearer here to cover this side while the other ambulance covers the southeast. It's clear we need more resources. In the area that means an opening for a full-time pilot."

"When?"

"I don't know, but I will be in contact with a date."

"Okay, just one thing could we not tell anyone yet?"

"You got it," he said as he stood up now. "Why don't I get us another drink?"

I sat and thought, *Could I actually do it and make a living out of flying.*

He returned with more champagne and we toasted to the future.

Chapter Forty-One
Nothing like Normality

The week after felt like a daze as we tried to find some normality, Harry had driven us home from the party and we had insisted he spent the night with us instead of driving back. We had become close over the last few days; our business arrangement having come to an end. It had now taken the form of a friendship. Yet we still knew very little about his family life. And as we sat eating breakfast. The boys argued over who was having what. It was clear that Harry was in deep thought. June had noticed it too. Him being in no rush to leave we invited him to take Rex for a walk. As we walked Rex bounded on ahead. We stopped at what used to be a picnic area with a view of Snowdon in the distance. Finding a bench that was still usable we sat admiring the view.

"What's the matter, Harry?"

"It's nothing, just been thinking."

"Want to talk about?"

"Nothing to talk about, just been thinking of my dad."

"You not heard from him since the storm?" I asked.

"He died last year," he said.

"I'm sorry. I didn't know."

"What happened?" asked June.

"Lung cancer. Terminal by the time he got around to having it checked he survived six months."

"June, but her arm round his shoulder, that's horrible."

Since then, he said, "I just threw myself into my work

spending every day at the hospital with the staff as a company. Being with a family again just makes me realise what I'm missing."

"Surely, you have family still somewhere."

"Only distant closet is an aunt who hasn't spoken to us for years she lives in America. She didn't even bother to fly over for the funeral if it wasn't for all his old work friends it would have just been me."

"What about friends?"

"A few acquaintances from college but no real friends."

"Well, what are your plans for today?"

"Go back to the office and work I suppose."

"Are you needed there today?"

"There's always something I can do."

"I know but are you able to take a day off?"

"Well, if I wanted to, I have no appointments."

"Then why don't you spend the rest of the day with us it's not going to be anything special, but if Scott can fix it up, we're planning a barbecue later we have enough bricks. Me and Rob are going to go shopping. Stock up on food."

"No, I would just be intruding."

"Don't be daft you're welcome to stay as long as you want." In the end, he spent the whole day with us he joined me and June on the shopping trip even helped Scott build the BBQ using the damaged one from their garden and bricks For support. He had taken to the kids as well, teaching them how to build a den from the wood and rubble lying around. As the day went on you could see him relax stripping back the professional persona and embracing being a part of the family. Although he did ring the office a few times and spoke to Jade who was shocked to hear he would be taking the day off. She promised to hold all calls that weren't important.

Jay took Mum and Dad to the hospital over lunch for a visit, but they stuck to visiting hours and were back by six just as we lit the barbecue. We ate and drank way past sundown and after drinking a few glasses of wine it was decided Harry would stay the night again joining me in the games room.

The next morning, he declared he should be leaving. But before he left, he pulled me to one side. I just spoke with Patrick.

"How is he?"

"He's fine apparently there's been a dramatic increase in support for the party so Daniels running for PM again, he's gained some support with the fast response to the clean-up from the storm."

"That's good."

"He also mentioned that he's starting up a new air ambulance service and splitting the region to improve response times."

"He did mention it at the party," I replied, trying to sound casual.

"He also said that, he wanted you to head it."

"Between us," I said, looking around to make sure no one was behind us; he wants me to have my flying assessed with the idea of me being authorised to be a pilot for the ambulance, running from the air base nearby would mean moving to Wales and it's not exactly the right time to be house hunting.

"No, well, if I can help let me know and I look forward to when you start work."

"You mean, if I start work?"

"Oh, you will, I know it."

"We saw him to the car telling him to drop by anytime and that we would be at the hospital later."

The next week, was a whirlwind of television appearances and interviews from journalists for magazine articles. We turned down offers of reality and game shows only appearing on morning TV and two chat shows, it wasn't till the end of the week that June was able to start back work at St Leonard's, Harry insisting she would be paid as a consultant for the last week. Her first shift back was spent answering questions and retelling the story of the rescue. She even dragged me in on her second day to meet them all.

Harry had visited us every couple of days sometimes spending the night. But always staying for dinner. I hadn't been at the hospital much with the media hype leaving that to Mum, Dad and Sue to look after Adam. Sam was also a regular visitor his dad had finally come to realise the extent of the damage and accepted what he had lost. But he was determined to stay put. So, after much deliberation, he had come to the conclusion that if he couldn't beat him, he was going to join him. Arranging to sell up in Leicester and buy with his dad in Wales. He admitted that it would be difficult to start with and finding work would be a challenge, but he never was one for the city anyway.

By the second week, we were getting worried about Adam there was still no change, even Harry had arranged for a second opinion from a London specialist who agreed with the in-house doctors that no abnormalities were shown on the scan; and he would wake up when he was ready. On Tuesday I flew Sue, Jay and the boys back to Leicester as well as Sam and his dad who had agreed to stay there until they were sorted, and the sale completed. Upon returning home Sue found that Beth a friend of hers had lost her house in the storm due to a row of trees falling onto the roof and invited her to stay with them.

I spent the night at home packing a case of clean clothes and my laptop. The builders had finished patching it up and it looked as good as new it had even been given a spring clean. Heading for the garage, I saw my Tesla still with its charging cable in the side disconnecting it, I placed my bag in the boot and drove to the air base. It was with a heavy heart that I changed the steering wheel for the controls of the helicopter. Arriving back in Wales I found Dad and Scott worrying about insurance. They were saying it was an act of God and a clause in the paperwork allowed them to get out of paying. Instead, they offered a lump sum for the sale of the land or to keep the land for themselves.

Chapter Forty-Two
A New Plan

One day the following week, Harry found me sitting staring at Mum and Dad's shelter, Rex laying by my side. He had just arrived June having invited him for dinner. The house and debris had been cleared now all possession that were salvageable had been Collected and stored in Scott's shelter. Two skips stood in the garden ready to be collected both full.

"What's on your mind?" he said, sitting down beside me.

"Just thinking that if they hadn't of got out of the shelter and over to Scott, they would have been in that as it fell in. Maybe even sucked up as the storm passed over."

"That's true, but they weren't so don't worry."

"Any news on Adam?"

Not yet still showing good signs of improvement but still nothing drastic he will come round in his own time.

"Now what is really bothering you?" It's been weeks since you saw the shelter it can't have only just got to you. He had gotten to know me well over the last few weeks and could tell that something was bothering me.

"Don't know what you mean."

"Don't start that. I can see the cogs tuning in your brain, what are you planning?"

"The insurance won't pay. We can sell the land to them or keep the land. Either one doesn't fix the housing issue."

"So, what are you going to do?"

"Mum and Dad can come back to Leicester with me, but this was their dream retirement home. I don't want to take that away from them. Also, if I am to take up Patrick's offer, I would need a base here. Not Leicester."

"It looks like something you all need to discuss."

"I'm going to take Rex for a walk before dinner," I said, standing up. "Tell them I will be there soon."

I walked past the shelter and across the field baring the big H and opened the gate to the adjacent field. In the distance, I could see a for sale sign outside the neighbouring farm. It had been up for sale for ages, but it wasn't until now I gave it any thought. Failing to think of a better place to walk I headed towards the main house. As I approached, I could see the house had been badly damaged, the for-sale sign had been stuck back in the ground after being ripped out.

The land belonged to Mr Phillip heckles, who I found sitting outside his shelter in a foldable deck chair. "Can I help?" he said sternly as he saw me looking. He was a typical farmer-type build with a beard and weather-beaten face, he wore a green wax coat, mug-covered wellington boots and a wax flat cap.

"Sorry," I said, realising I was standing there staring. "I'm Rob, I'm staying with Scoot and June Dunlop over the other field."

"You're the guy with the helicopter," he said. "Here take a seat," he said, getting pulling out another chair from the shelter.

I looked at the sign it looked old and storm-damaged which told me the land had been on sale for some time.

"How long has the land been up for sale?" I asked as I took a seat and Rex flopped down beside me. He offered me a drink from his hip flask which I refused.

"Nigh on a year, and no takers yet of course the old house is gone now so nothing to sell but fields."

"How many fields have you got?" I asked.

"Sixteen a total of three hundred acres all told. Aye. Looks like I'm stuck with 'em now."

"Where does your land go?"

"The way you just came, that was two fields directly adjacent to Scott's field."

"Five more out back," he said five across past the house and that on yonder there.

"Quite a collection, and no one's interested."

"Not a one."

"Strange would have thought you would have been fighting them off."

"Not as strange as you may think, farming is the old now. Only old timers like me that bother and we're all giving it up."

"So, what will you do now?"

"Looks like I will have to move in with me sister. She's offered for years it means losing my independence sure but with no house to sell and farmland being undesirable. Well, I'm not in the position to be fussy now, am I?"

"Suppose not. Look thanks for your time. I will come back and see you another day if that's okay."

"Suit yourself, I can't promise I will be here mind."

Once I was far enough that Mr Heckles couldn't hear I fished the phone out my pocket and rang Jay.

"You alone?"

"Hold on." I could hear him walking out of the room telling Sue we would be back in a second.

"Now I am. What's happened?"

"Nothing. I need some advice but stay with me it might sound crazy."

"After the last few weeks crazy is normal."

"I want to build a housing estate."

"Well, that's just topped it, and where do you propose to do that."

"Right here, Dad and Scott can't claim insurance they can only sell or keep the land. That's four fields with the houses knocked down."

"I'm listening," he said, sounding interested now.

"But the fields adjacent are owned by a Mr Heckles, they have been up for sale for a year and with the house gone all he as to sell is land."

"How much does he have to sell?"

"Over three hundred acres, a total of sixteen fields and that's not including where his house is all put together, we could have close five hundred acres to play with."

"Okay," he said. "Keep it hushed for now I will get onto the council tomorrow and look at the likely hood of planning permission. If this works, he said you will be richer than you ever thought possible. But you will need capital."

"I know that. Why do you think I'm ringing you?"

"Have you spoken to the others about it?"

"No, it's only just come to me now after running into Mr Heckles."

"Okay go back and act natural." I put the phone down and made my way back to the shelter with a smile on my face I had a good feeling about this. It would solve everything.

"There you are," said Scott as I entered the garden. "Where did you go? Harry just said you went for a walk."

"I paid your neighbour Mr Heckles a visit."

"That misery guts, what did go see him for?"

"No reason." My smile getting bigger, I followed him into

the shelter and took my seat at the table. As Rex curled up in his bed.

It was later that night after everyone else had gone to bed that Harry came up to me as I was watching TV. "So, you going to tell me what caused that smirk on your face earlier. You're up to something and I want to know what."

"Just planning," I said, the smile returning.

"There it is again it's unnerving."

"Okay," I said, getting up and shutting the door, "But stay with me it's even more of a crazy idea than the helicopter, also you have to promise to keep it to yourself."

"Just tell me."

"I want to buy the land next door. And that combined with Scott's and Dad's, turn the whole area into a housing estate."

"You're serious, aren't you?" The shock was clearly visible on his face.

"Deadly, he as over three hundred acres running all the way up to Scott's border if we combine them all it would create nearly five hundred acres."

Jay is already looking into doing a feasibility study. "Its money I will need to find."

"This is a Rob Wolf plan written all over it, but I know Rob Wolf and if you need investors, I'm in."

The next morning, over breakfast and without going into detail, I told Dad and Scott not to accept the money but to wait asking them for time and trust. Surprisingly, Scott was the first to agree. And Dad was the one. Unsure.

Chapter Forty-Three
Everything Comes Together

Over the course of the next few days, Jay exchanged phone calls, as far as we could tell, the land didn't hold any restrictions on any database, he or his team could see. And as far as we could tell planning permission had never been submitted for the land. With no neighbours to complain us having bought them all out and owning the land there should be no one to object. We had arranged a meeting with the bank for the following Tuesday and Jay set about drumming up possible investors, Harry was already on board I also spoke to Sam, with them being on the hunt for a house he also offered up what he could.

It was late Friday morning, and I was sat at a desk in the games room also known as my room now. Mum and Dad have taken the spare. I was online trying and failing to read up on the housing market. My phone suddenly blurted into life. Picking it up and seeing it was Harry, I accepted the call. It was nothing new Harry ringing now often just for a chat. "And what can I do for you?" Not taking my eyes off the laptop.

"Adams awake," he said.

"I'll be right there." I hung up and grabbed my keys, I was still using the Land Rover although by now I had insisted I pay for its rental.

I found everyone in the living room, watching the soaps. "Come on, get up it's time to go Adam's awake."

"What!" Mum jumped off the sofa and was at my side in

seconds, closely followed by Dad and the others. The boys where back at school, but would walk home. And knew the entrance code so Scott and June joined us.

I was first in the car and starting up. Mum, Dad and Scott where in the back June in the passenger seat. now I was used to the size of the car and the fastest route to the hospital I set off at full speed. Hitting the road and narrow country lanes with full confidence. Once on the way, I rang Jay to tell him what had happened. He informed me him and Sue would be there by in a few hours.

We Still had the access passes. Although offering to give them back and being told to keep them. We had decided to stop using the staff canteen and stuck to visiting hours as much as possible. I scanned it at the barrier lifting them and finding a spot. All but one other patient from our endeavours' had been released now. Mr Peterson had been moved out of the ICU and off life support as with Adam it was a matter of time till he awoke. Only then that any brain damage could be assessed.

Knowing the way by now we headed straight forward seven and the room which had housed Adam all this time. As we entered the room, we saw Harry sitting beside him. Mum ran straight to his side and kissed him on the head and pulled him into a hug.

Thank God, you're all right, tears coming to her eyes Dad was close behind her more reserved, they had both been carrying such quilt over the whole incident and worried about any lasting conditions it may leave him with.

Jamie, has been and examined him and performed some basic reaction tests, and I must say that we haven't seen any issues and he responded well, we would like him to undergo another scan, just precautionary as the brain acts differently once conscious.

"Thank you," Dad said, shaking Harry's hand. "Who now stood at the end of the bed for everything you and your team have done."

"It's my pleasure. And the least any of us could do. Now you take care Adam and I will see you're checked on soon."

"Thank you, Doctor."

"It's Harry," he said, walking off and looking at his watch before pulling me aside.

"Thanks for sitting with him."

"It's not the first time, I come down sometimes to check on him; even in a coma he's better company than no one. In fact, I was sitting with him when he woke, I even rang you before telling the doctors got in here."

"Thanks, I appreciate it."

"My office at one, alone!" he whispered quickly before leaving.

I stood for a second wondering what I was needed for now. "And why alone?" Before concluding, I would find out at one. Turning around I walked over to Adam. I could see the fear shoot through his entire body as I got closer, in fact, he had been watching me since we entered, watching my every move as If he awaited an attack from a Ferocious animal.

"Have a good sleep?" I took a seat on the opposite side of the bed from Mum.

"Would you believe me if I said I was tired?" He still hadn't taken his eyes off me and answered as if unsure what to say. I tried to just act normal worried it may be some reaction or side effect of his injury, maybe he didn't recognise me, amnesia being a common side effect of head trauma, but he seemed to know everyone else.

"You couldn't get me a cup of tea could you," he asked, turning to Mum. "I'm parched. And water doesn't have any taste. Well, that fitted he never was one for water."

"Anything for you." She kissed his hand, walking to the door. "You want anything Rob?"

"No, I will be okay, thanks." Adam looked at Dad and gave him a silent sign to go as well. Scott and June also picked up on it and excused themselves saying they could use one as well. He waited till we were alone, till he looked back at me.

"I'm so sorry, I tried to protect them, he blurted out almost bringing himself to tears, so this was what it was all about he was scared of me and what I would say against him, but they left and then Dad was trapped in the house, Mum had followed even though I told her to go back in the shelter," he continued barely taking a breath. "I didn't mean."

"It's okay, I cut him off, you did the best you could, I couldn't have asked for more. And you did protect them you nearly got yourself killed protecting them."

"They told me what you did, bringing me here, he reached out and took my hand if it wasn't for you, I would have died. I love you."

"I love you too," I replied, giving him a hug. "That was the final straw that sent us both into a flood of tears as everyone walked back in."

"What's wrong?"

"Nothing," we said, pulling away from each other and wiping our eyes, just some brotherly love.

We sat and joked Mum, not leaving his side or letting go of him, as if scared that once she did it would all be over, and he would just go back to sleep. Looking at my watch it read Twelve-forty-five, I made an excuse to leave and headed to Harry's office, jade was back at the desk and waved me right through but I still knocked first. And waited for confirmation, before opening the door. Harry was sitting behind his desk as I expected but to my surprise Patrick was sat at the other side. "Take a seat?"

"I hope I'm not interrupting anything," I remarked as I took the seat next to Patrick.

"No, we have just finished discussing some business," said Patrick. "Harry said you were here, so I thought, I would speak to you personally."

"Well, it is always a pleasure, to see you, minister."

"Please call me, Patrick, first of all I'm glad to hear the update on your brother I bet you're all relived."

"Yes, massively, we can't thank the hospital enough."

"That's what we are here for, now are you still seriously considering my offer? If you changed your mind I understand. But I want to get this new base up and running as soon as possible and that means appointing a commander."

"Of course, I haven't changed my mind, but I'm not sure I will be suitable to command it."

"Nonsense." He picked up his briefcase and pulled out a folded piece of A4 paper, it had my name written on the front as he handed it over as he stood up. I unfolded it contained the information for the flight assessment.

"Harry here as the rest of the details, I really must be going. Good luck," he said. As he walked out the door.

"I sat reading the paper, with the time location and what I was required to bring with me on the day. While Harry saw Patrick to the lift."

"Well, who's the minister blue-eyed boy then?" He took a seat back behind his desk before pressing a button and asking Jade for fresh coffee.

"I'm afraid it may be me."

"Afraid?"

"I feel he thinks I'm some kind of superhuman I explained, and I don't want to let him down."

"Oh, you won't. I will make sure of it starting with this assessment." Harry filled me in on the details of how the test would work and I arranged to meet him at the hospital at eight a.m. Friday morning, he would be taking the day off and coming with me, after finishing the coffee. We both headed to the lift. And made our way downstairs.

"How are you getting on with the housing scheme?"

"Not a lot to tell at the moment, Jay hasn't found any obstacles yet and looks like we shouldn't have any objections."

"That's good. I hope you don't mind but I did mention it to Patrick in passing earlier. He said, not only does it sound like a good investment opportunity, but a government grant could also be obtained if a percentage of the houses were made affordable enough."

"I will mention it to Jay."

Sue and Jay had arrived by the time we got back to the room. Beth had stayed behind to see to the boys. Jay pulled me into the hallway. As I entered and Harry followed. I have a few people interested apparently Wales is in dire need of housing and anyone with the ability to produce them will really capitalise on the market.

"Harry here," as spoken to Patrick. "It not only sounds like he may be interested in investing but also giving some government funding to get it going."

"Really?"

"Yes," Harry replied. "Said its ideal and one of many long-term solutions to the current housing crisis. Where we could provide more suitable shelter as well. And would like to discuss with you some more."

"Give him this," Jay said, fishing out his card. "Tell him to ring me anytime."

"We should get going check on the boys," Scott said, coming out the room.

"Here take the car. I fished out the keys and handed them over. on formally hiring the car I had taken extra cover allowing multiple people to legally drive it." Scott included.

"What about you?"

"I will give them a ride back," Jay interrupted June as already invited us to dinner. "Later and to stay the night."

"That goes for you too," she said, pointing to Harry. In her no-nonsense voice. Almost demanding his attendance.

"My pleasure," replied Harry. "Wouldn't miss it for the world."

We went our separate ways, June and Scott back to the car park, me Jay and Harry into Adam's room. After a few more hours it was clear that Adam was getting tired and Toby had popped his head in saying they would get him ready for his scan soon. We decided we should let him get some rest knowing he was in good hands. And headed out. Jay drove, himself and Sue along with Mum and Dad. I opted to join Harry. I watched them out before heading to his office.

"Back so soon, Jade," said as I entered.

"I'm not staying, I'm just here to collect someone."

I'm glad you came along, it's done the professor so much good being able to get out and spend time with people. I've not seen him this happy since his farther died. It really took it out of him.

I almost fell through the door I was leaning on as it was

opened. I thought, I heard your voice he said walking out and shutting the door behind him. "What you two gossiping about?"

"Nothing," I said as Jade went with the much more honest, you.

"Oh, really. Well, you can tell me what she's been saying on the way. I'm starved."

Chapter Forty-Four
The Assessment

We pulled up outside. Everyone else having already beaten us here. We had decided to stop off at a service station, Harry not wanting to turn up empty handed. Brought two bottles of wine and three sets of flowers. One for each of them.

Everyone was in the shelter all except Jay and Rex, who we were told had gone for a wander to stretch their legs from all the driving. Harry having given June, Mum and Sue the flowers and having received a hug and kiss from all of them, handed the wine to Scott and joined me in my search for Jay. Who we soon found him wondering round the adjacent field.

"You do know your trespassing in Mr heckles land?"

"I suppose, I am," he said as we made our way towards the house. We stood at the end of the drive as I had done the first time. But this time there was no Mr heckles to be seen.

According to the property report and sales listing, the land consists of the field we just walked across. Two more that way and the others. Beyond the house. That's a lot of land without the other two properties.

"I know. I'm not going to lie I'm scared," I admitted.

"Not excited?"

"That as well. But it's a big job I just hope we can pull it off."

"It's been staring us in the face all along," said Jay. "But we were too busy trying to save two houses that can't be saved. To see the true potential. Just then my phone went."

"Where are you?" Demanded Mum's voice dinners nearly ready.

"Just on our way back, be there soon. We had better get going," I said sounds as if there waiting for us.

As Friday arrived, I got up early and suck out I didn't want any awkward questions. I made my way to the hospital and meet with Harry. Having parked and messaged him I was here we met in reception and headed for his jag.

"You didn't have to come; you will be bored while I'm assessed."

"I going to do some shopping and get some new clothes to replace those lost at the house."

He had country playing on the radio something we both enjoyed, it was a classic hour and Dolly Parton's working nine to five was playing.

It took nearly two hours to get to the base and once there we waited in reception there were four other people waiting to take the written assessment. As they were called though I waited to hear my name, but it didn't come. I was just about to ask the receptionist when my name was called from behind me turning round, I saw a man in a flight helmet and jacket holding a clipboard.

"Here," I said looking confused.

"I'm Ron Millan, I will be assessing your flying ability today."

We shook hands before Harry spoke. "We thought, the written assessment was first."

"Usually yes but looking back at your flying record it appears you took the equivalent back in 2022. During a refresher course. The written assessment being a standard test and not one specifically for the air ambulance. You've been signed off by the chief himself. And I'm told the health minister ordered this assessment specially. I'm to assess your ability to fly an air ambulance. Not a surprise considering your efforts a few weeks ago. Now if you would step this way."

"Good luck," Harry said as I left him in the reception me promising to ring once I was done.

I was taken into a changing room full of flight suits and helmets they were all organised on hooks in size order. I was told get changed to leave my stuff in a locker of which I had plenty to pick from. Picking up a medium. I was soon changed and ready and joining Ron to start the assessment.

Now there's three stages to the assessment one being the written which you already covered. Usually, you would go away while that was marked and report for assessment in the simulator. Which was designed to test your reaction speed securely, before your final practical assessment, we will start with the simulator, just to be on the safe side.

It had been years, since I had been in the simulator and it didn't come close to doing what it was designed for you simply couldn't get the feel of power behind the controls of an actual craft in a box, with a chair, on hydraulics. Upon entering the simulator, I took a seat and started up the initiation sequence. Acting as if this was a real craft and not a fake console with multiple screens. When Ron's voice came though the headphones.

Now you see a series of events unfold in front of you, you will be expected to fly through different weather conditions in an attempt to see how you adapt. I will be your AC operative and keep in contact when needed giving a clear and precise report. Of all conditions and actions, you feel you need to take. Remember

I am your eyes and ears once you're up there.

As the test started it was a summer day birds were in the sky and I was flying around hills and mountains checking the altitude I went higher. Alerting Ron to my altitude change as I did. A bird flew out in front of the craft. I knew this was made to trick me and test my reactions and ability to handle anything that could happen. This wasn't my first time in a simulator, so I was expecting all sorts of obstacles to arise. From there we went through raining, snowing and thunder with different wind speeds, in variable conditions which was easily corrected by the right control on the pedals. I was even tested on my ability to control it during a cross breeze. And perform an emergency landing due to engine failure. A pilot's worst nightmare.

The simulator took one hour to complete. After that I was given a break with the option of food. Sitting down with a sandwich and a coffee. I checked my phone and replied to a message from Harry asking how it was going and one from Patrick wishing me luck. I could only guess Harry had given him my number. Saving it officially It made him the most impressive and influential contact on my phone.

Ron also joined me at the table with a full fry-up and a cup of coffee so large it would have lasted all day. We spoke about my history with flying and how I had come to be a part of the crew the night of the storm, eventually a steward came and informed us that the craft was ready. We finished our food before I was led out to the flight pad and test craft. It was a helicopter with the same design and shape as the air ambulance but did have any logos or equipment inside but did feature dual controls. Before getting in I checked it over following all the security procedures. This was an assessment after all. This can and did take up to forty minutes as a full examination is advised when piloting a new craft. I found three points of minor severity one of which was unknown to the base and impressively noted down for the crew to fix later all the others purposely placed as part of the assessment. Getting in the cockpit Ron at the side of me he explained what we would be doing during this stage of the assessment.

We were to attend to a staged emergency, of a man with suspected spinal fusion and were required to transport him safely and securely back to the hospital, in this case, it would be back to base. Looking up the squawk number and coordinates in my flight pack. I started up the helicopter and contacted control informing them I was ready to take off, stating the squawk code, name and reason for taking of this being a medical assessment flight.

Once up I was a quick trip over fields the test was designed to see how you handled different heights and I was soon going higher to avoid the summit of a mount Snowdown. Once over and past the hills. I headed for the patient who was in an alcove with a small space to land but still bigger than the playing field I used on the first rescue, as I approached, I circled and hovered to access the landing ground before firmly and securely bringing her down to solid ground, after landing the patient was loaded on board followed by two people imposing as doctors. After getting confirmation that the patent and staff where all secularly on board and fastened in. I was soon back in the air rising high enough out of the alcove and slowly spinning the craft around, before pulling forward and once again heading over the mountains and back to base. The whole time Ron would tick boxes on his clipboard or write something down. Not once having to reach for the joint controls on which he could take over if needed. Once down he looked at his watch and wrote the land time down allowing him to judge my response time.

Shutting off and stepping out, I was taken back to the locker room where I took off my flight suit. Afterwards, I was told that all the data would be analysed, and results forwarded this being an assessment due to judge my ability to go on to further training. And not as to my right to be a part of the air ambulance that would take a lot more time and a few more assessments. Before I was subjected to a more stringent and brutal assessment. But I was reassured I had done very well indeed.

"I had just got my phone out to text Harry when I saw him already waiting in reception for me. Hope I haven't kept you long?"

"No, not at all. Only been back here ten minutes." Thanking Ron, we headed to the car. "Well, how did it go?"

"As well as can be expected. Was very straight forward a simple passenger pickup?"

"Well, in that case, I think that deserves lunch on me. I happen to have spotted a rather interesting-looking restaurant not far from here. I'm dying to try."

Chapter Forty-Five
The Plan Comes Together

Having come back from the assessment. I wasn't surprised to have been getting questions from everyone as to where I had gone. Luckily, Harry was ahead of me and while purchasing some stuff for himself had brought me some nice straight-cut jeans a smart-looking black and white t-shirt and casual-looking jacket. That mixed with lunch, we passed the whole thing off as a shopping trip, which successfully fooled them all. Things weren't improved Sunday when I announced I had an important meeting in Leicester and would be needing to spend a few days there. I hoped to return Tuesday evening but could be Wednesday morning.

Having decided to take a few days leave to visit a cousin who lived in Leicester. Harry tagged along and left toby in charge of the hospital for the weekend. Julie was now used to him spending nights and the occasional day away from the office but to spend the sum total of two maybe three days came as a shock to her. But true to his word he was outside picking me up first thing Monday morning, leaving Scott and Dad full use of the rental.

Having informed Carl and Sean of my plans as well as departure time it came as no shock to find the helicopter on the helipad ready and waiting and the fight pack all prepared. Harry now having been in it once before and had full confidence in my flying ability. Was perfectly at ease and enjoying the view.

Sean was out of the office and opening the door as soon as I landed. "Welcome back mate." He pulled me into a hug. "You know you missed our annual flying day I had to go out alone. But don't worry I gave yours a run as well."

"Thanks, I will make it up next month and we will go out together."

"Who's your friend?" Sean hadn't met Harry before and wasn't aware I was bringing anyone with me either.

"Sorry, this is Professor Harry Silks. Director of medicine for North Wales. Harry this is my friend Sean. Chief air warden of Leicester Airfield."

"Nice to meet you," they said in unison, shaking hands.

"So, what's the chief of medicine for North Wales travelling to Leicester with the likes of Rob for?"

After checking in the aircraft. I went out to the parking lot where I found my Tesla exactly where I left it. Sean knowing how much I loved the car having come with me to buy it, had took the liberty of putting a cover over it and connecting a charger to top it up ready.

"Ready and waiting, for you, sir." I disconnected the charger before we both pulled at one corner of the cover. And folded it like you would a tent until it was small enough to fit in its bag.

"Wow," exclaimed Harry as the light hit the perfectly polished paintwork. Lighting up the silver flecks in the paint. The large alloy's two-tone in colour glistening. All are counteracted by the cream leather seats accompanied with matching Tesla logo neck rests.

"Take it, you approve?"

"It almost puts my jag to shame," he said, opening the passenger door and looking in.

"I will be in contact, I promised. Sean, I expect in the next few days I will be flying back. I put mine and Harry's bag in the boot along with the car cover, before getting in and starting up. It felt weird but right being back behind the wheel of my beloved Tesla. The Land Rover was okay now I had got used to it. But it would never beat this."

It wasn't long till I was back pulling into my street and finally into the garage of what was seeming less to be my home than June's shelter. Getting out I realised the quad bike was still at Jays, I grabbed the bags out the boot and headed for the door. Placing my finger on the scanner and opening up into the hallway. Although not large it was a decent size with a white gloss tiled floor a black rug and a console table on which stood more mail. Sue had been nipping in now and then to check the place over and collect my mail. Bending down to collect the few letters that lay on the floor I added them to the stack and carried them though the open plan living room into the kitchen.

The room was dark with the blinds shut. So, I asked Alexa to open the blinds as I messaged Jay and told him to meet me at the house.

"I can see why you're reluctant to move," Harry said following me into the kitchen. "This place is stunning."

"Thanks, it's one of Jay's developments, it used to be the show home, I'm hoping we can create something similar in Wales."

After making myself and Harry a coffee, I sat down at the breakfast bar Harry had already taken a seat at and started to read through the post most of it junk mail and going straight in the bin, I was halfway through reading a letter about the increase of council tax when the doorbell rang and the screen showed Jay at the door, were in the kitchen, I said while buzzing him in. Having finished reading I dropping the letter and went to make him a coffee.

"Wasn't expecting to see you here, Harry," he said, shaking his hands. "What brings you to Leicester?"

"Going to catch up with a distant cousin to try and rekindle some of my family if possible."

"You always have us," I reminded him. While handing a mug over to Jay.

"What did Sue say?"

"She doesn't know I'm here; I told her last night I have a lot of work to do and may be home late. She knows something up just doesn't know what."

"Well let's keep it that way," I said, heading to the living room.

We spent the afternoon drafting a business plan and crunching numbers most of which Jay had already done having gotten his administration staff to work on it for the last few days. between the three of us we had managed to get backing of nearly one million from investors, Patrick had contacted Jay, the day after he returned home from Wales, not only had he wanted to invest but as suggested by Harry offered a significant grant from the government to make affordable housing on at least one hundred acres of the land. By six we had formed the plan and had a stable financial structure to show the bank. Jay having decided there was little more we could do now and Sue having rang three times asking where he was excused himself and went home.

Having looked in the fridge for food it occurred to me that there wasn't anything having not been here for over a month now. So, with Harry in tow we went shopping, where we ran into Sam and his dad, who I agreeing to pick up later for a gym session, which Harry also wanted to join. We settled on something quick and healthy, so after stocking up on a few essentials we headed back and made a chicken noodle stir fry. Which Harry claimed was better than any Chinese he had ever had.

I went upstairs and pulled my gym bag, still in the bedroom I packed some fresh clothes and grabbed a spare bag for Harry chucking some clothes and spare gym shoes in for him as well.

Sam was already outside as we pulled up a for-sale sign outside the house and his dad waved us off from the doorway.

"How's it going with the sale?"

"Okay, a few people are interested so far, one looks promising."

"When have you got to go back?"

"Not sure, will only be here a few days, would have come up tomorrow but wanted to be here ready for the bank."

"Are you nervous?"

Bricking it, no pun intended. "I don't even know where to start when it comes to something like this."

"That's why you have, Jay."

We pulled up outside the gym and pulled the bags out the back. I handed one to Harry as we walking into reception Hailey was at the desk.

"I would like to sign in a quest, if I can," I said as I approached. She handed Harry the quest book as she buzzed Sam through to the changing rooms, giving a little wave and blushing as she did.

After filling out the quest book and adding my membership number. We were also buzzed though. Where we joined Sam, who was halfway through changing.

"You still talking then," I said after standing her up. I said as I stopped in front of the lockers.

"I didn't stand her up I rang from Wales to apologise." She insisted we re-arranged for this Friday instead.

"Have you told her you moving?"

"No, see how things go first. She's a big fan of yours by the way."

"Well, he might not be here much longer either," Harry said, instantly realising he let it slip.

"What does that mean?"

"He means I may have a new job as a pilot for the air ambulance," I said, shutting the locker and removing the key.

"Really?"

"Yes," Patrick asked me. "I took the assessment the other day."

"Patrick?"

"Sorry, the health minister."

"The health minister offered you a job," he said, shitting his door and removing the key as well closely followed by Harry.

"Yes," I said as we entered the gym it was quiet with it being late. "But it's a secret for now."

"But where will you move to?" he asked as we went to the treadmills. Harry looked as lost as we did.

"Wales, Swansea Hospital will be my base hospital."

Having got Harry all set up and telling him to just do what he wanted and stop when he's ready I took the middle treadmill between them both.

"So, you will be a pilot for them full-time?"

Commander inserted Harry who was doing better than expected having had access to the hospital's free gym membership and frequenting it occasionally.

"What does that mean?"

"It means, I will be the head man."

"We did the usual workout with the addition of some weights. Although it had only been a few weeks since I was last here it showed. Harry had managed to keep up only tapping out the last half hour." Heading for the changing rooms and promising to meet us in the café.

The next morning, I rolled out of bed my arms and legs hurting from yesterday's exertion, I shuffled to the shower and turned it on hoping the hot water would relax the muscles. And wake me up I needed to be my best today. I had forgotten Harry was here and he nearly gave me a heart attack when I saw him sitting at the breakfast bar on his laptop, toast and coffee at his side of him, I hope you don't mind I didn't want to wake you.

"Don't be daft I told you to make yourself at home."

Chucking some toast in the toaster and a pod in the coffee machine. I joined him at the table. Ever the workaholic he was logged into work email and responding to the most important while binning the ones of little importance. It was nine a.m. when Jay arrived, I was still in the kitchen eating breakfast, and Harry having turned the laptop off was now watching the news. Buzzing him in, I couldn't help but notice that he was carrying his best suit. "You're supposed to wear it not carry it."

And you're supposed to be dressed ready not lounging in a tracksuit." Besides I had to sneak it out of the house like I said, "Sue knows there is something up if she saw me wearing it. Well, it would confirm it so thought it best to get changed here. What's your excuse?"

"I think he's got you," announced Harry from the sofa.

Having no reasonable excuse, I simply told Jay he could use my room and I would get changed after. After a quick change, I met Jay back in the kitchen and we had a drink while we talked though the plan once again just before we left.

I drove and we parked on the top floor of the multi-story, where we said goodbye to Harry who had arranged to meet his cousin in a local café. We were almost at the entrance when we saw Sue and Beth walking down the high street. Quickly we slipped down a side passage and stood flat against the wall. Jay was supposed to be at work, and I was supposed to be in Wales finding us both dressed in our best suits heading to the bank now would mean a lot of explaining and we didn't have time. We held our breath as they walked past.

"She must be wrong he's still in Wales and won't be back till Adam's okay."

"Well, that's what she said. She let him and his mate Sam into the gym late last night, said he even signed in a quest, tall man smartly dressed with thick black hair. I no Hailey wouldn't make it up."

"Sounds like Harry. But he wouldn't be here in Leicester."

"Sounds like I've been caught," I said to Jay. "Who was giving me a death stare?"

"Certainly does, she will be on the phone with your mum next who knows you're here."

We waited till they were a fair distance in front before darting out and making a run for the entrance.

Once inside, we checked they were across the road heading to the car park. Looks like we got away with it.

We turned round to see a clerk looking at us. "Can I be of assistance," he asked clearly wondering if he should be calling security.

"We have an appointment, under JRC (Jay Roberts Construction)."

"If you would follow me." He headed to a stand with a computer. "I thought, it sounded better under the company name."

After logging in he found the details and told us to take a seat.

We sat on the armchairs while we waited. Hoping Sue or Beth didn't decide to pass by again. "This is it," Jay said, "if this goes through the next stage is approval of planning permission."

"Mr Jay Roberts." We stood up. "I'm Jake Henry, the business adviser I will be overseeing your loan application."

"This is Mr Wolf my business partner in this venture."

"Have we met before," he asked. "You look familiar?"

"I don't think so."

"Well, if you would follow me into the office."

The office was right at the end of the corridor. It was a small white square with a desk three chairs and a computer.

So, I can see from your application, that it's a loan to do with property development. And a hefty amount as well, you must have a lot of land.

"Around five hundred acres," said Jay. "We had agreed to let Jay do the talking as much as possible."

"That is a lot, where is this land?"

"North Wales."

Just then, it clicked looking over at me. "Of course Mr Wolf you were on the news, you're the local hero that the papers printed the story about."

"Afraid so," I replied.

"Well done," he said, shaking my hand again. "Good work. Anyway, back to this application is all the land in your possession."

"Only two hundred acres the other three is up for sale at a market price of half a million."

"And what funds do you have available?"

"We have investments of over one million. And an application for a government affordability grant awaiting approval. If planning permission is approved."

"And what stage is the planning permission at."

"Still on the drawing board, a summery is in the plan, but a research and feasibility study shows no objection on the land."

"Are you willing to use personal investment to start the project allowing the bank's requirements to be meet?"

"Yes."

"Right can I see the business plan for this venture?"

Harry handed over the envelope that had only been a week in the making with the office and finalised with me last night.

"All looks okay to me. Your company is familiar with big projects like this I see."

"Yes, but always as the contractor."

"Yes. I see, I can't give you a definite answer today," he said. "As I'm sure you are aware projects of this magnitude needs to be assessed more closely. And backed by the government if you were to secure a grant as significant as the one you're proposing."

"The backing is on the back page; it's backed by Jeffery Clay."

"The housing minister?"

"Yes."

"Well, in that case I don't see a problem with this and expect that with the experience, the company involved and backed by the governing body as security to the bank. It will now be down to approval of planning permission."

"The bank will be in touch within the next forty-eight hours. I wish you luck."

We shook hands and made our exit.

"When did you get it backed by the government? That wasn't on the plan last night."

"I thought, it would be a little surprise for you." Patrick waved it under his nose yesterday and couriered it over, first thing this morning, "I don't think we will have any problem now."

"So, now what?"

"Well, in forty-eight hours if it's approved, we sign the agreement and with the approval of planning permission the money becomes ours."

"And investors?"

"Money's already as good as in the bank but we can't use it till we have official baking from the bank loan to cover us against losses that way we aren't held responsible if the investment fails."

"What investment is that!"

"We didn't need to look to know who it was." She was sitting in the armchairs in front of us, the clerk from before at his desk behind them with a smirk on his face. Clearly having been involved in us getting caught like two naughty schoolboys.

"Come on, I'm waiting, because you're supposed to be at work and you're supposed to be in Wales but yet I find you dressed up hiding from me in an alleyway on the way to the bank."

"Not here," said Jay. "Let's go find somewhere to get a drink and we will tell you the whole story."

Chapter Forty-Six
Coming Clean

Sue had insisted seen as we had dressed up, we had better be going somewhere nice for lunch and made it clear that we would be paying. Deciding on an up-market café further down the high street. We headed there Sue almost running she was walking so fast. Matters were made worse when she spotted Harry walking alone towards us. "And you, what are you doing here?"

Harry looked upset and not his usual self. "What happened?"

She didn't show. "I couldn't wait any longer I feel a fool for even trying."

"It's her loss. Mate come on, come with us, I could use a friendly face," I said, pointing towards Sue. "Which only made things worse but hey she was Jay's problem tonight not mine he would be the one sleeping in the spare room not me."

Having been seated at a table for five. And given menus. We were left alone to peruse the menu me and Jay took particularly long making sure to read every description and using the menu to block Sue's stare. Eventually having to consider that a menu doesn't take that long to read both settled for the honey roast ham and crunchy salad baguette with a bucket of gourmet seasoned fries, Sue had until now had been consoling Harry. But yet the fire in her eyes told us she was only seconds away from exploding. Beth had remained silent. It wasn't till the lunch orders where in that Sue started again. Well come on then I'm waiting.

We explained the whole project to Sue who as expected was angry that we had made such a decision without her consent. It took so long between her interruptions that the food had arrived halfway though.

"It's one thing building the estates, but funding them how do you propose to pay for all this?"

"A mixture of personal investment, external investors, government affordability grant, and the bank."

"Are you mad? If this fails, we could lose everything. How much do you intend to borrow? And who the hell do you think will invest in an idea this stupid."

"There's me for a start," said Harry, halfway through taking a bite of his burger.

"You dragged him into this as well, and how much is the bank supposed to fork out?"

"Five million."

"What! You have gone mad; I can't believe you got Dad to go along with this. It completely unlike him."

We looked at each other.

"He doesn't know, either does he?" she said, sinking into her chair. "What's about Scott and June?" Another look to each other seemed to confirm all of that.

"Look he knows I'm planning something just not what I said, let's face it, he can't claim from insurance and they are faced with a choice, either sell the land to them for one hundred thousand or keep it. You know as well as I do that it's not enough to start again this way, we buy the land at market value and with planning permission that goes up. And they take a ten per cent cut of the profit of any house sold on that land."

"Alternatively," Jay said, "they invest the land in exchange for a fifty per cent cut of the profits from any of the houses sold on their land. We will even give them a one hundred-thousand-pound advance. The same as they would receive from the insurance."

"You have really thought about this, haven't you?"

"Yes," we both said.

"Please just trust us we know what we're doing, it a longer way round but it's a plan that benefits all."

"What do you think, Beth?" Sue asked.

"I don't see what the problem is. It's clearly been thought through and worked out."

"Go with it," she said clearly happy that her opinion had been called upon, it didn't look like anyone lost. Apart from the insurance company that will probably do the same thing once it's been obtained. Might as well make the money yourself.

"Okay," Sue said. "But you need to tell Dad what's happening."

"When we have the banks approval," Jay said. "If we don't, he sells the land and moves back here, leaving the Dunlop's to do the same. And Mr Philips to wait for another buyer."

"How much are you set to make out of this," Beth asked.

"Who knows but with a 50/50 share on three hundred acres safe to say a few million each that's before our cut on the other houses."

"I'm warming to this idea already," Sue said.

"That night me and Harry were invited to dinner round Sue's. The boys where back at school and had told all their friends about the trip. They even asked if I could bring take them to school in it. So, all their friends could see. Of course, I couldn't so the next day, I took the boys to school in the Tesla.

I had spoken to Sue the night after the boys had gone to bed before detailing my latest plan which involved Sue arranging to see the school principal. Having dropped them all off I appeared to leave promising to pick them up later before moving the car and sneaking back though the door to reception, when the boys weren't looking. Mrs Pauline rose was in her early thirties and looked way too young to run a school. She was tall and thin with black hair. With distinguished good looks and good check bones. She could have been a model in a previous career.

"What a pleasure," she said, shaking my hand. "I've heard so much about you Mr Wolf and not only from the press. What can I do for you?"

"Well," the boys asked. "Yesterday if I could drop them off today in the helicopter so their friends could see it," I said as I took a seat. "I know it's a ridiculous suggestion, and not one I'm proposing. But it did get me thinking about whether it would be possible to arrange some kind of event with the school to show them the craft and maybe do some education on aircrafts and first aid."

"Interesting, I see where you're coming from and I know other schools have put on similar events. But I would have to run it through the school board and get approval. It would take considerable planning, but it would be good for morale and the kids could learn from it. If you would leave your number, I will bring it up in the board meeting next week and get back to you." I wrote my number down and stood up. "Thanks for seeing me at short notice," I said.

"Not at all, any time."

That done I collected the car and drove back to Sue's, I had promised her we would go get lunch like we used to, she had insisted Harry join us and not be left out, after collecting them we drove to Bradgate park, a nature park most famous for hosting Old john tower at the top of the hill in the shape of a beer tankard.

Half way down the walk was a café, we would always go as kids on a Sunday afternoon it was something we had been meaning to do for a while now but never actually doing it, so today was the day. An attempt to make up for yesterday an idea she had warmed to quite well now.

"Sorry about yesterday," she said as we sat at the café. "I didn't mean to be so hard on you. Harry had left us saying he wanted a closer look at the castle."

"It's okay, it's a big thing we should have told you earlier we just wanted to make sure it was possible first."

"What do you think Dad will say?"

"I don't know, I'm sure he won't like the idea to many risks for him to find but he will come round, I hope."

"I don't know what we would do without you, you always seem to find the answers to our problems, but I can't help but feel there's something else you're not telling me."

"What do you mean?"

"Well, there's a reason you should never play poker and that's because you wear your heart on your sleeve and can't lie to save your life. And although I don't think you lied to me there's something you're holding back."

"Is it about the houses?"

"No, it's not about the houses. It's my job."

"What about it? I thought the pub was closed leaving you unemployed."

"It has, I'm on about what could possibly be my new job."

"In another pub?"

"No."

"Restaurant?"

"No."

"Then what?"

"Pilot for the air ambulance." I watched as her face fell in a mix of shock and delight.

"You serious? You want to make a living doing it that's amazing Rob why would you hide that?"

"Because it's not confirmed yet that's why I haven't said anything. I took the assessment last week and I'm waiting for the results. Its all-Patrick's idea."

"So, what's the problem I'm sure you passed the assessment."

"It means moving to Wales they want to make me commander for North Wales region."

"Then move."

"Where to?"

"Your building enough houses keep one. Or buy more land with the profits and build a bigger one. I can't see any of us being short of cash if it all works."

"It's between us, is said not even Jay knows about it. Only me, Patrick and Harry."

Just then the waitress appeared to take our order. I ordered a cream tea for three. I could just see Harry in the distance having his photo taken at the steps to the entrance of the tankard. You would never have known he was chief of medicine for North Wales looking at him. He was acting like a big kid and enjoying every minute of his break. We sat just chatting for a while till Harry came back. He was all read faced and if you didn't know it was him you wouldn't have recognised him; he had switched with some convincing out of his suit and into some casual jeans and smart t shirt. His thick black hair not combed back and styled but ran free and untamed. By stripping back his clothing we had unearthed the inner Harry. Where the pressures of the hospital and his professional life didn't exist.

He fell into his seat next to Sue. Clearly out of breath from running down the hill. Sorry guys but couldn't not get a picture of that it's amazing. The waitress arrived with the cake stand and tea tray. Sue poured and handed one round with a side plate for the cakes and sandwiches. Before offering a toast. "To your new job?"

"She knows?"

"Yes, I just told her."

"Well, in that case, it's my pleasure to inform you that I while checking my emails earlier, I had a message from Patrick. You passed the first assessment and you're to await further instructions for training."

Chapter Forty-Seven
The Contracts

I had hosted dinner last night, Sue having cooked for us the night before, Harry had helped and proved be quite a competent sous chef. But after having ran round after the boys all evening and a mid-day hike. Me and Harry had decided on a lie in. Surprisingly, I was up before him today and preparing his favourite breakfast the full English, he had soon stumbled into the kitchen once the smell off bacon and eggs frying had roused him from his bed. I had already laid out orange juice and coffee on the breakfast bar. I must say that bed is so comfortable. I don't think I've slept like that in months.

"Well, it will do you good." I handed him a plate. It contained two rashers of bacon, two sausages, one fried egg, button mushrooms and backed beans. I put toast on side plates. I had just sat down when the doorbell went. Looking into the screen I could see Jay and Sue standing at the door. I buzzed them in and stabbed my fork into a sausage.

"Something smells good."

"More in the fridge if you want some help yourself pans still on the hob."

"Don't mind if I do," said Jay, heading to the fridge and gabbing the bacon.

"You just had breakfast."

"Cereal. That's not breakfast."

"Yes, it is."

"Well, you won't anything then," I said, knowing full well she couldn't resist a bacon sandwich.

"Oh. Fine just one bacon butty."

"Knew it," Jay said, chuckling sausages followed by bacon in the pan.

"What can we do for you anyway," I asked. "I take it you didn't just come to raid my fridge?"

"No, we want to speak to you about how were going to break this to the others. I've told Jay about your new job opportunity and he agrees it's about time we were honest with them."

"He does, or you told him he does?" Harry said, causing me to laugh and choke on a baked bean.

"You're worse than children? When do you intend to tell them about your new job, they will be so proud of you?"

"I think we should break the news of the development first," said Jay. Clearly feeling more confident with support and a hot pan in his hand. "That way if they take it badly, we can soften the blow, bread?"

"In the bottom cupboard."

"I agree with Jay," said Harry. "Training could take weeks or months to sort yet. We should know about the housing later today and that directly affects them."

"Exactly," Jay said, slicing two sausage and bacon sandwiches before handing one to Sue.

"I get the impression, I'm out numbered."

"Then be quite and eat your breakfast," Jay said while taking a bite of his own.

We got the call later that morning the bank had approved the loan. We arranged to sign, the papers later that afternoon and Jay phoned his property solicitor asking him to formally put an offer on the heckles land to draw up the papers for buying it.

As we walked in were meet by Jake who escorted us though to his office instantly. This time Sue had come with us now feeling invested in this project and wanted to take an active role. It took an hour to sign everything, having to sign various different documents, but eventually we walked out with a loan of five million. Already contracts had been sent out to investors giving us free use of the money Harry had been the first to sign, Mr Philips estate agent had been contacted in regards of buying the land at full asking price. And immediately accepted. And a meeting was arranged for the following day between me, Jay, Mr Philips and both solicitors.

Which left the rest of the day to wonder what would happen. We decided to put off telling the others till tomorrow. Neither of us felt in a rush to find out what Dad would say we could guess. Besides which Harry wanted to go shopping for more casual clothes. And Sue wanted to bring the kids along who had been desperate to see Adam but were already at school it was agreed that they would have a sick day tomorrow. Even josh Beth would keep him home claiming food poisoning along with Tyler and Declan. It now being common knowledge that Beth was staying with Sue after her house was destroyed.

Deciding we needed to celebrate but needing somewhere the boys could go we settled on Quacks. The name of which interested Harry enough to make it certain he was coming. Jay and Sue picked the boys up and met us at the restaurant. Once in they were straight to the play area. Harry had ordered Champaign. And had fallen in love with the restaurant and the all you can eat buffet, if only jade and toby could see him now, I just hoped he would step back more now and not let professor silks take over once he was back to work, and allow himself to be Harry.

The next morning, we set off early. Me and Harry in the Tesla. Jay, Sue, Tyler and Declan together. Kyle Jays' property solicitor would follow up in his own vehicle. We had taken the decision to drive, because one the helicopter although faster was expensive to keep refuelling. Also, it allowed us more freedom over who could come and go where and when, not to mention freeing up the rental for Scott and June.

I had rung Mum to inform her I was coming back but failed to say anything about any of the others. We stopped at a service station midway to regroup before taking the on the other half of the journey. It also gave us time to formalise the plan of action we would take and formally meet Kyle who until now had only been known by Jay and Sue. We agreed to just let me and Jay do the talking followed by Kyle. Harry although promising to come up later didn't want to be there so I agreed to drop him off at his car. Allowing him to head back to the office and check on things. He had promised to not start back fully till Monday and had kept his casual clothing as means of insuring, he stuck to it. He also wanted to shock jade and toby with his wild new look.

As we pulled up one after another, and we saw them once again sitting on the log seats. All except June who had just come out the shower after coming in from a night shift. "What are you doing here," Mum said, giving Sue and the boys a hug as Scott walked up to me.

"You got your pride and joy back then." Pointing to the car as he spoke.

"I sure did, she's a bit slower than the helicopter but twice as comfortable."

"I thought, I heard voices," June said, emerging from the shelter. "I assumed it was you, kissing me on the cheek as a greeting."

"Who's the guys with Jay?"

"We will get that in a moment, suddenly feeling nervous. I need to speak to you all about something."

"Is everything okay?"

"I hope it will be. depends on what you all think."

"Well, how about we talk in the kitchen? Come on I will make some coffee."

Once we had all settled in the kitchen leaving the boys to play with Rex outside, me and Jay got their attention.

"Okay," I said. "Remember how I asked for time and trust in regard to what to do with your land and the insurers. Well with the help of Jay here I hope we have come to a solution that suites all of us."

"I had nothing to do with it," blurted out Sue, looking at Dad in particular.

"I have feeling in not going to like this."

"No, Dad you're probably not to start with so please just hear us out before, you say no." I looked at Jay signalling him to take over after all we were business partners now.

"Last week Rob rang with a business opportunity. It involves the land from you both and the land of your neighbour, Mr Heckles. As you know his land is up for sale all three hundred acres of it."

"Yes, for anyone rich enough to buy it," said Scott. "I told him he won't sell it one million he wanted for it."

"Well, with the damage from the storm destroying the house and outbuildings that figure halved, and now all his land is up for sale at half a million or was until yesterday when we put in an offer to buy it."

"You what?" Dad said. "Don't we have enough land going to waste without buying more. Mum put her hand on his shoulder hear him out first remember. Well, what's he going to do with three hundred acres of land he grumbled?"

"Build a housing estate, hopefully combining your land creating an estate roughly the size of five hundred acres."

"With what money," Dad said. "We should have just sold up," he said to Mum.

"We spent the last week drumming up investments of over one million enough to purchase land and get plans drawn up. We have also been given a business loan of five million for construction. That combined with our personal investment and government grant. We should have close nine million to bring this project in and secure a hefty profit for us all."

"So where does that leave us?" asked Scott.

"Well. The terms of your insurance you can either take the money offered. Or keep the land for yourself. If you keep the land, you can do one of three things either have no part and try to rebuild yourself. Alternatively, you sell to us at a fair market price for land with building potential. If you do this you will also receive a further ten per cent of all profits generated by the sale of houses on your land. The last is you put the land in as an investment and sell us the right to build on it and any profit generated from houses sold on your land goes 50/50 between us and yourself."

"How much are we looking at for building rights?"

"About one hundred thousand."

"You're serious, aren't you?" said Dad, staring at us in utter disbelief.

"Yes, this way we all come out with more money than we could have dreamed of the sale estimate of an estate this size is about one billion with half going on costs and investors."

As we looked, they were all just staring at each other in

disbelief. I know it's a lot to take in, so this is Kyle Jay's property solicitor. He can walk you through the process and answer any questions you may have we will leave you to think it over.

"We stepped outside and took in the air well that went well?"

"I think they are in too shocked to answer," Jay replied.

"I hope they agree."

We sat outside for an hour before Kyle appeared, I left them to think it over; it looks like they might go for it. But it's time we got a move on and saw Mr heckles.

As we walked into the entrance to Mr Heckles drive, he was pacing the area.

"Hello, Mr heckles, its Rob Wolf I was here the other day."

"Yes, yes," he said. "I remember, you will have to excuse me I'm waiting for the estate agent can you believe it someone actually put an offer in half a million."

"I know, it was me."

He stopped pacing and looked directly at me. "You?"

"Well, not only me. This is Jay Roberts of JRC. He's my business partner."

Just then a blue Peugeot pulled into the drive.

"Sorry, I'm late, took the wrong turn. You must be Kyle Rows," she said, heading straight to Kyle and shaking hands. "I'm Lily Jones from Gerald and Cole estate agents."

Twenty minutes later, after the paperwork was signed and sealed in Kyle's briefcase a copy in lily's as well we left and headed back to the shelter. Leaving Mr Phillips to celebrate in peace.

Stopping before we entered the shelter, I looked at Jay. "You ready?"

"We have three hundred," he said. "Let's get the other two."

We walked in the kitchen where it looked like no one had

moved.

"Everything all right?" I was afraid to ask.

"Yes," said Scott. "I think we reached a decision taking June's hand we would like to invest the land, a smile creeping across his face I know we won't see any profits for a while, but it will be worth it."

"I will have the papers made up and sent over," said Kyle, shaking hands. "Welcome aboard."

Looking over at Mum and Dad, Sue nudged him.

"Oh, go on then, we will invest as well."

"You sure? You don't have to."

"Well, I trusted you so far just don't let me down now."

Chapter Forty-Eight
To New Beginnings – *Sue/Rob*

It was the start of July and the sun was beating down shinning like a beacon off the polished exterior of the helicopter. It now stood proudly on the playing field of St Jones community college. It was the last day of term and as a treat Pauline the head teacher had cancelled all lessons in favour of what was now called emergency service's day. She had spoken to the board and personally made all the arrangements, necessary not only for me to fulfil the promise. I had made to bring the helicopter along with a crew of volunteer medical staff from the unit to the school in an aim to try and educate them on the workings of and good deeds done by the air ambulance. But it now being emergency services day Pauline had arranged for all the emergency services to also be present. In attendance were a police car, manned by community support officers, a fire engine, with off duty fireman and an ambulance. Also manned by some off duty paramedics, all in a joint effort to educate and show appreciation for all of our front-line workers, I had to give it to her, Pauline had really taken it to a new level, even arranging basic first aid classes and talks from people serving in the emergency services. One of which was Harry. He was her head speaker and most influential talk of the day.

Sally had also been recruited by Harry to do a talk on nursing along with June. Both would also hold a first aid class for cuts and burns. Sally had become good friends with June after that night and the two could often be found heading off together for lunch and a quiet coffee.

The school had been opened up to students and parents, the kids had dressed up as their favourite emergency worker. Of course, Scott, had come up the boys as well, and all were present at the school. Them having come over in a convoy from Wales this morning, June, Scott, Jake and Jacob had come in one car. Harry, Adam and Sally in another. Mum and Dad had come up with me a few days ago. Wanting to spend some time with Sue and the boys.

I was stood by the helicopter. When Sue and Mum. Came up I had just taken my place, after leaving it with the crew to go and watch June and Sally's talk. On which they couldn't help but call me up as their star appearance.

"Having fun?"

"Yes, I am, everyone wants to go for a ride and not just the kids."

"Well, with you in that uniform, who wouldn't?"

"I had borrowed a flight suit from the air base during my training last week having passed the assessment with ease. Patrick had been fast in enrolling me onto a training course and into my final exam. He was getting worried about setting up the second branch before the end of the general election with right as he had failed. But with the conservative leader losing support on the campaign by announcing plans to privatise the NHS, labour walked right back in and he was reinstated."

"Have you heard from Patrick, yet?" She had asked this every day for a week.

"Not yet, hopefully soon." I had taken my final exam last week and was waiting for the results to come back. Over the last six months, I had spent the whole time flying or driving backwards and forwards between Wales and Leicester for training. We had found a rental with five bedrooms, and the property was shared between Mum, Dad, June, Scott, Jake, Jacob and Adam. Who was now back at the care home, fully recovered, although we were still waiting for him to outgrow the buzz cut? He had sported to try, and hide where his head had been shaved. When training, I used the sofa bed in the conservatory. And often found Harry there on a camping bed as well. Jade had now got used to him being absent, and Toby, finding he enjoyed taking more responsibility, had allowed Harry to step back more and be himself.

"We will see you later," Sue said. "I better go back and get ready for tonight. Are you sure you will have time to help?"

"Yes, it won't take long to get back."

"Well, don't forget your bringing the boys back with you, Josh and Beth as well."

"They had already reminded me four times, in fear that I would forget. After some special arrangements with the school and parental release forms being signed, wavering any responsibility to the school. Tyler, Declan and Josh would all leave with me as I marked the end of the event by taking off as the school watched."

Fifteen minutes before the event ended, my air crew was delivered for me: two small pilots and a doctor. Behind them were Pauline and Harry. Harry had taken a shine to Pauline as soon has he had arrived. Both now had rumours going around that they were now an item. "These belong to you," she said, pushing the boys forward. Beth was still in the crowd; she was supposedly joining us to keep an eye on the kids, but I expected. I had more to do with wanting to go up herself.

"I just want to thank you both said Pauline to me and Harry;

it done the school a power of good. This event really helped to bring everyone together, and if weren't for you coming to me, I wouldn't have even thought about it."

"You did an amazing job; it wasn't my idea to bring in so many other emergency services. You should be proud."

"Who is ready for a ride in the helicopter?" Beth said as she walked over.

"Ever been up in one?" Pauline asked.

"No."

"Don't worry, the boys know what to do; they will show you," replied Harry.

"Right, you all get in and settled?"

I took down the collapsible banner and packed the complimentary pens and booklets away as Declan and Tyler showed Beth how to work the safety strap. After today the ambulance would undergo a makeover, an idea Sean had had before about adding seats and making into a carrier craft, which it was used as more now, it would be better that rely on then safety straps.

"See you later, Uncle Harry," the boys shouted as I shut the doors. We had adopted Harry and made him an honorary Uncle to the boys. He had also become good friends with Adam, often meeting up when they could.

Pauline radioed though to reception, who put an alert through the speakers that the ambulance was due to depart and to assemble in the playground. Teachers and emergency workers formed a barrier around the ambulance, making sure people, especially kids, kept a safe distance. It didn't take long until I was on to AC and lifting off the ground. Once high enough, I spun to add dramatic effect and, at full speed, flew right over the school.

By the time I arrived back at Sue's with Beth and the boys,

she was in full party mode and had already set the table, and Jay was outside in the garden setting up the barbecue. We had extended an invite to Patrick, but being a minister in government took up so much of your personal life it was impossible to arrange anything, so we left the invite open if he could make it.

I spent the next two hours making burgers, kebabs and chicken skews ready to be cooked later. I was still in the kitchen marinating some Cajun chicken when everyone arrived. Harry was the first to find me. Having returned from the school, his excuse was that he had to help clean up, more like couldn't get away from Pauline.

"Is Patrick here yet?"

"No, I'm not sure he can make it."

"He said, he was when I spoke to him earlier."

Maybe he's just been delayed. "Did you find the place, okay?" This was the first time he had driven in Leicester.

"Wasn't too hard, but man, the traffic up here is something else."

"Yeah, remind me to show you the back route."

I washed my hands and went to say hello to everyone. Adam was being squashed to death by Sue a habit she had formed every time she saw him.

While June and Scott was given a tour of the house by Mum.

The boys had all retreated to the garden to play football, and Sally was talking to Dad.

Just then, the doorbell went again, and Sue finally let go of Adam to answer.

"Hey, bro, how are you feeling?"

"Fed up, mainly of people asking me that it's been six months."

"Sorry, I will stop."

I felt a hand come on my shoulder and spun round to see Patrick behind me. In his hand, he held a folded navy uniform, a cap that had gold lining and bore the logo of the air ambulance, and a certificate sealed in a solid gold frame.

"These are for you, Commander," he said, handing them over and putting the cap on my head.

"Commander! You mean, I passed."

"Yes. As of next month, you will be the commander in charge of the air rescue for the Northwest of Wales, reporting directly to Swansea Hospital. I'm sorry, I didn't tell you earlier, but I couldn't resist doing it in person."

"You told him," Harry said, walking up to us. He had changed out of his suit now and looked much more relaxed in his casual jeans.

"Did you know?"

"Only since this morning, well done, you earned it."

Mum having finished the tour, re-entered the living room. What going on? I handed her the certificate from the top of the pile; it took her a few seconds before she realised you did it. "I knew you would." She gave me a hug and ran off search of Dad.

"Congratulations," Scott said. "We're in good hands now."

I went in search of Jay, who was still outside. "What's up, partner?"

Looking up, he noticed the hat and uniform I was carrying.

"I take it you passed then; I knew you would, and I have more news. I was waiting to catch you alone, but now seems as good a time as any, the kids being the only ones around and too busy playing to pay us any attention."

"I heard back from the council today; they approved the planning permission."

"We are in business."

"We are."

"Who knows?"

"No one yet, I wanted you to be the first."

"Well, I think we should go break the news to our investors, don't you?"

We walked back into the house, where Mum was pouring the champagne into flutes, and handing them around to everyone in the room. "It deserved a toast," she said, handing me a glass.

"I would like to say a few words if I can," said Jay. Have taken a glass and used a spoon from the buffet table to bang on the side of the glass.

"First of all, I want to thank you all for coming. Before we start this party, I have some, exciting news that me and my partner here would like to share with you, especially as most of you have an invested interest. Earlier today, I received a letter from the council approving the planning permission for eight thousand houses to be built across five hundred acres of land in North Wales."

The room erupted into applause and cheers as he spoke. "And with Rob being recently qualified, I think that's cause for a double celebration." "So," he said, raising his glass to new beginnings for us all.

"New beginnings," everyone echoed.